Praise for Peter Leonard

"Peter Leonard has a good ear for voices, a good eye for detail, and a talent for bringing together elements that can't do anything but explode."
– Thomas Perry, *New York Times*-bestselling author

"Fast, sly, and full of twists."
– Carl Hiaasen, *New York Times*-bestselling author, on *Trust Me*

"Memorable characters and dialogue – come to think of it not unlike what Leonard's father, Elmore Leonard, creates."
– *Seattle Times*

""Peter Leonard should be on your must-read list if he is not there already."
– *Bookreporter*

"Leonard gets better and better."
– *Uncut*

"If you haven't read Leonard before – and you must – this is a great place to start."
– *The Guardian*, on *Voices of the Dead*

"This is 'don't miss' crime fiction at its very best."
– *Blogcritics*, on *All He Saw Was the Girl*

Eyes Closed Tight

EYES CLOSED TIGHT

Peter Leonard

The Story Plant
Stamford, Connecticut

The Story Plant
Studio Digital CT, LLC
P.O. Box 4331
Stamford, CT 06907

Print ISBN-13: 978-1-61188-114-1
E-book ISBN: 978-1-61188-115-8

Visit our website at www.TheStoryPlant.com

First Story Plant Printing: March 2014
Printed in the United States of America
0 9 8 7 6 5 4 3 2 1

For John Brennan

ACKNOWLEDGMENTS

I want to thank my agent, Jeff Posternak at Wylie New York, Lou Aronica, my enthusiastic publisher, copy editor Nora Tamada, who did a bang-up job, and Tim Mayer, my former business partner, for his astute editorial observations and suggestions.

ONE

O'Clair got up, put on a pair of shorts and a T-shirt, glanced at Virginia's cute face and naked shoulder sticking out from under the covers, and went outside. It was seven twenty-five, big orange sun coming up over the ocean, clear sky; looked like another perfect day. O'Clair had moved to Florida from Detroit three months earlier, bought an eighteen-unit motel on the beach called Pirate's Cove; it had a friendly pirate on the sign surrounded by neon lights.

The motel was at the corner of Briny Avenue and SE Fifth Street in Pompano Beach. Four-story condo to the north and public beach access immediately south, and next to that, a massive empty lot that a developer was going to build a twenty-five-story apartment building on.

The idea of living through two years of heavy construction had O'Clair concerned, but what could he do about it?

He'd brought a paper grocery bag with him and walked around the pool, picking up empties, a dozen or so lite beer cans left by a group of kids from Boston University who'd been staying at the motel the past three days. There were nine of them, three girls and six guys. They'd caravanned down from snowy Massachusetts a week after Christmas.

He fished a few more beer cans out of the pool with the skimmer, picked up cigarette butts that had been stamped out on the concrete patio, and threw them in the bag with the empties. O'Clair straightened the lounge chairs in even rows, adjusted the back rests so they were all at the same angle, and noticed one of the chairs was missing. He scanned the pool area, didn't see it, glanced over the short brick wall that separated the motel from the beach and there it was, twenty yards from where he was standing.

O'Clair kicked off his sandals, opened the gate and walked down three steps to the beach. As he got closer, he could see a girl asleep, stretched out on the lounge chair, one leg straight, the other slightly bent at the knee, arms at her sides. She was a knockout, long blonde hair, thin and stacked, wearing a white T-shirt and denim capris, early twenties. He didn't recognize her, but figured she was with the group from Boston. She looked so peaceful he didn't want to wake her. "You should go to your room," O'Clair said, looking down at her.

The girl didn't respond. He touched her shoulder, shook her gently. Either she was a heavy sleeper or something was wrong. He touched her neck, felt for a pulse, there wasn't one. Her skin was cold, body starting to stiffen, definitely in the early stages of rigor. He looked at the sand around the lounge chair, surprised it was smooth, no footprints. Glanced toward the water at the joggers and walkers moving by. O'Clair went back up to the patio, wiped the sand off his feet, and slipped his sandals on.

Virginia was standing behind the registration counter, yawning, eyes not quite open all the way, holding a mug of coffee.

"What do you want for breakfast?"

"There's a dead girl on the beach." O'Clair said, picking up the phone and dialing 911.

Virginia's face went from a half smile, thinking he was kidding, to deadpan, seeing he wasn't. "What happened?"

*

The cruiser was white with gold and green stripes that ran along the side, light bar flashing. O'Clair watched it pull up in front, taking up three parking spaces. Two young-looking cops in tan uniforms got out and squared the caps on their heads. O'Clair went outside, met them and introduced himself.

"You the one found the body?" Officer Diaz, the dark-skinned cop said.

O'Clair nodded.

"You know her?" Diaz pulled the brim lower over his eyes to block the morning sun, the top of a crisp white T-shirt visible under the uniform.

"At first I thought she was with the group from BU. Now I don't think so."

"What's BU?" the big, pale one, Officer Bush said, showing his weightlifter's arms, uniform shirt bulging over his gut.

"Boston University. Nine kids staying with us, units seventeen and eighteen." O'Clair didn't know the sleeping arrangements and didn't care. They were paying $720 a night for two rooms, staying for five days.

An EMS van pulled up and parked facing the police cruiser. Two paramedics got out, opened the rear door, slid the gurney out, and O'Clair led them through the breezeway, past the pool, to the beach. The paramedics set the gurney next to the lounge chair, examined the girl and pronounced her dead.

Officer Bush said, "What time did you find her?"

"Around twenty to eight."

"How can you be sure?"

"I looked at my watch," O'Clair said, like it was a big mystery.

Diaz grinned, showing straight white teeth, reminding

O'Clair of Erik Estrada, his tan polyester uniform glinting in the morning sun. "Did you touch the body?"

"Her neck, felt for a pulse." O'Clair saw Virginia wander down, standing at the seawall with her cup of coffee, watching them. Officer Bush went back to the cruiser and got stakes and tape, then set up a perimeter around the dead girl, protecting the crime scene. The paramedics picked up the gurney and left, leaving the body for the evidence tech.

Diaz took a spiral-bound notebook out of his shirt pocket, wrote something and looked up at O'Clair. "Ever see her before? Maybe lying in the sun, walking the beach?"

"I don't think so," O'Clair said. "Someone like that I would remember."

Diaz said, "You see anyone else?"

"College kids out by the pool." He almost said drinking beer, but caught himself, he doubted they were twenty-one and didn't want to get them in trouble.

"What time was that?"

"Around eleven o'clock."

"Then what happened?"

"I went to bed."

Diaz said, "Anything else you remember? Any noises?"

"No."

The evidence tech arrived carrying a tool box, set it on the sand a few feet from the lounge chair, opened it, took out a camera, and shot the crime scene from various angles. Diaz searched the surrounding area for evidence and Bush questioned the morning joggers and walkers wandering up toward the scene. O'Clair watched from the patio, leaning against the seawall. Virginia had gone back to the office.

A guy in a tan, lightweight suit walked by O'Clair and went down the steps to the beach. He had to be with homicide. The evidence tech, wearing white rubber gloves, was swabbing the dead girl's fingernails. He glanced at the guy in the suit.

"What do you got?"

"Fatal."

"I figured that unless you were doing her nails."

"Not much here," the evidence tech said, "couple hairs, maybe a latent, and something you're not going to believe." He whispered something to the suit that O'Clair couldn't hear.

"Jesus, I've seen a lot, but I haven't seen that." The homicide investigator shook his head. "Where's the blood?"

"That's what I want to know."

"How'd she die?"

"You want a guess? That's about all I can give you right now. She was asphyxiated, been gone about four hours."

"Who found her?"

The evidence tech turned and pointed at O'Clair above them on the patio. The detective came up the steps and stood facing him.

"I'm Holland, Pompano Beach Homicide." He had a goatee and a crooked nose, early thirties. "What's your name, sir?"

"O'Clair."

"I understand you found her."

"That's right."

"You down here for a vacation, or what?"

"I own the place, bought it three months ago."

"Where you from, Cleveland, Buffalo, someplace like that?"

"Detroit," O'Clair said.

"Even worse," Holland said, breaking into a grin. "Just kidding. I got nothing against the Motor City."

"Well, that's a relief," O'Clair said.

Holland wore his shield on his belt and a holstered Glock on his right hip.

"You married?"

"Living with a girl named Virginia, helps me run the place."

"The hot number in the office?"

O'Clair fixed a hard stare on him.

"How'd you arrange that?"

"I must have some hidden talents."

"You must," Holland said. "Tell me what you saw this morning."

"Same thing you did—dead girl on a lounge chair," O'Clair said. "Know who she is?"

"No ID. No idea. Have to check with missing persons. Was the chair left on the beach?"

"It shouldn't have been. The lounge chairs are supposed to be kept in the pool enclosure. It's one of our rules here at Pirate's Cove."

"Your guests break the rules very often?"

"Oh, you know how it is. Get in the Jacuzzi with a beer, without taking a shower, and you've broken two right there." O'Clair paused, playing it straight. "The rules are from the previous owner, guy named Moran. I keep them posted 'cause I think they're funny. Someone sat down and wrote them in all seriousness."

"What do you think happened? This girl was walking by and got tired, saw your place, went up, got a lounge chair, brought it to the beach, lay down, and died in her sleep?"

"I'd ask the medical examiner."

The evidence tech was taking off the rubber gloves, closing the top of the tool box.

Holland said, "What else did you see?"

"You're asking the wrong question," O'Clair said. "It's not what I saw, it's what I didn't see."

"Okay. What didn't you see?"

"There were no footprints in the sand. Like she was beamed there."

"So the wind erased them," Holland said.

"You really believe that?"

"It's the only plausible explanation I can think of."

"What else didn't you see?"

"No obvious cause of death. No evidence of a struggle. In fact, no evidence at all." O'Clair looked at Holland, caught something in his expression.

"You sound like you know the trade," Holland said. "What'd you do before you became an innkeeper?"

"Worked homicide in Detroit."

Holland grinned. "I had a feeling. Then you must've seen her eyes were missing, right? Bulbs removed, empty sockets."

"But no blood," O'Clair said. "So it was done somewhere else. Find the primary crime scene, you'll find the evidence."

"You weren't going to say anything?"

"It's not my case," O'Clair said. "I figured somebody was going to notice sooner or later, it wasn't you or the evidence tech it would've been the ME."

"Why do you think the girl ended up here?"

"I have no idea. Why don't you roll her over, maybe you'll find something."

Occasionally there was a crucial piece of evidence under the body, a lead. It could be a round that would be tested for ballistics comparison against other homicides. It could be money or drugs, suggesting a possible motive, or it could be a cell phone that would lead to the possible killer or killers.

But there was nothing under the dead girl. No ID. No cell phone. Her body was bagged and the remains taken to the Broward County Medical Examiner's Office. They took O'Clair's lounge chair too.

"It's evidence," Holland said. "You'll get it back eventually."

O'Clair doubted it. He knew what happened to evidence.

Bush and Diaz went upstairs, woke the BU students, and brought them down to the pool, nine kids looking hung over, yawning. Eight twenty in the morning was the middle of the night for them. O'Clair had noticed they usually didn't get up till after noon. Holland questioned them one by one, showed photos of the dead girl, took statements, and sent them back to their rooms. No one knew or had ever seen the girl before. No one had seen anything suspicious or heard anything during the night.

The MacGuidwins from Mt. Pearl, Newfoundland in unit two, who had complained about the students making too much noise, were questioned next by Holland. O'Clair watched the fair-skinned, red-haired couple shaking their heads.

As it got hotter, Holland commandeered unit seven for his makeshift interrogation room and brought the other renters in two-by-two for questioning. There were the Burnses, Susan and Randy, from Troy, Michigan; the Mitchells, Joe and Jean, from San Antonio, Texas; the Belmonts, John and Shannon, from Chicago, Illinois; and the Mayers, Steve and Julie, from Syracuse, New York. Steve Mayer woke up with four-alarm heartburn at three-thirty a.m., got up, took a Nexium, walked out by the pool and remembered seeing the lounge chair on the beach, but didn't think anything of it. None of the other renters saw or heard anything.

O'Clair walked Holland out to his car at eleven twenty, glad to finally get rid of him.

"Miss the life?" Holland said.

"Are you kidding?"

"Some things about it I'll bet." He handed O'Clair a card. "Call me if you think of something."

*

She drove back from her date with Skip in Miami. What kind of fifty-year-old man calls himself Skip? God he was boring, too, talking about injection-molded parts his former company made.

"Like what?"

He'd put his champagne flute down, eyes lit up and said, "Escutcheon plates, center console assemblies, and sail panels."

She was sorry she'd asked.

"We had twenty-five presses ranging in size from fifty-five tons to fifteen hundred."

"Wow."

"Wow is right. We cranked out thousands of parts a day."

She thought Skip might soil himself he was so excited. The pros: she'd only been with him an hour or so and had made twelve hundred dollars. The cons: he was boring and he had bad breath.

*

Now she was on Interstate 95, almost to Pompano, took the Atlantic Boulevard exit and decided to stop at Publix to pick up a bottle of wine and some groceries. She pulled in and had her pick of spaces in the almost empty lot, went in and bought a few things. When she came out there was a man on crutches moving slowly, trying to carry a plastic grocery bag in his right hand holding onto the crutch. She caught up to him and said, "Looks like you can use some help."

"If you could grab the bag."

"Where's your car?"

"Right here," he said, stopping behind a silver Buick.

She took the grocery bag from him. "What happened to your foot?"

"Ruptured Achilles."

"Oh that must hurt." Now she recognized him. He was a client. They'd met at the Ritz-Carlton in Lauderdale. She couldn't think of his name, and wondered if she should say something.

He pressed a button on the key fob he was holding and the trunk popped open. She reached in and put the bag in the trunk, then felt a wet cloth pressed on her face, it smelled sweet. She tried to fight but didn't have the strength. She started to fade and felt him lift her off the ground.

TWO

Frank had flown from Detroit to Fort Lauderdale right after Christmas. He wanted to see the houses and get the lay of the land. He'd put deposits on three, renting each for the month of January. Then he sat on the beach behind the Pirate's Cove under an umbrella, watching the activity around the pool with binoculars, guests swimming and sitting in the sun.

O'Clair appeared occasionally, looking different. He'd traded his cheap suits in for shorts and T-shirts. Frank got a kick out of seeing the ex-homicide detective doing menial work, cleaning the pool and straightening the lounge chairs, jobs that seemed more suited to his IQ.

Frank enjoyed watching the good-looking, dark-haired girl who worked there. He would see her come out of the office to talk to O'Clair, or appear with a tool box in her hand apparently on her way to fix something. And there was the maid with her sultry good looks. She would arrive in the morning at 8:30, wearing a bright-colored island dress and a straw hat. Something about her excited him.

That night Frank had gone online and found Glamor Girls Escorts, South Florida's premier escort service. He studied the faces of the girls in the gallery, liked one named Ashley, clicked on her, and there were eight more photos of her. The usual stuff: dressed up, undressed, and everything in between. He filled out an online application in his real name with his business and credit card information, e-mail address, and phone number. One of the questions: Had he ever been arrested? Although Frank had, he said no.

His application was accepted and he made a date with Ashley. The escort service booked a suite at the Ritz-Carlton in Fort Lauderdale. All he had to do was arrive at the prearranged time and Ashley would be waiting for what was sure to be a memorable evening.

*

Frank rang the bell and the door opened. She looked better in person, blonde hair up, wearing a cocktail dress.

He stepped in and she closed the door and offered her hand. "I'm Ashley."

"Nice to meet you. I'm Frank."

"That's not the name they told me."

"It's my nickname."

The floor was marble. She led him into an elegant eight-hundred-square-foot living room with off-white chairs and couch on an Oriental rug and a wall of glass that looked out at the ocean. He sat on the couch and she sat next to him, close but not too close. There was a bottle of Krug champagne that had already been opened in an ice bucket on the coffee table, next to it was a half-full flute with lipstick on the rim and an empty one.

"I started without you. I hope you don't mind. Would you like some?"

Frank nodded. She picked up the empty flute, grabbed the neck of the bottle, pulled it out of the bucket, filled the flute halfway and handed it to him. She put the bottle back in the bucket, picked up her glass, clinked his, and said, "To us."

Frank sipped the champagne and sat back. "You've got good taste."

"I think it's a great way to get things going." Ashley smiled, showing perfect teeth and red lips, leaning forward, long, tan legs coming out of the black cocktail dress. "So what do you do?"

"I can see this was a mistake. My wife died a few months ago. I thought I was ready, but I'm not." He put the flute on the coffee table and stood up.

"If I did something to offend you, I apologize."

"It's not you, it's me. You're a very pretty girl." He started moving toward the door.

"If you change your mind, please ask for me again."

*

It was dark when Frank went out and got his car. He told the valet he was waiting for someone, parked the Lacrosse on the side of the driveway, and waited. Fifteen minutes later Ashley walked out of the hotel and handed her ticket to the valet. She had changed into jeans and a blouse, a big purse slung over one shoulder.

He followed her Mercedes sedan to the Harbor Cove condos in Pompano right on the Intracoastal. She parked in a space that said: Reserved for 3C. He watched her enter the building, waited, and saw a light go on in a third-floor condo. He went to the building entrance and checked the directory. G. McMillen was in 3C. He wondered what the "G" stood for. It had cost him twenty-five hundred to find out where she lived, but it was worth every penny.

*

Frank was waiting in the condo parking lot the next evening at five forty-five when G. McMillen, aka Ashley, appeared, coming out of the building, carrying the shoulder bag. He followed her south on I-95, bumper-to-bumper traffic, trying to stay close without making it obvious. An hour later she got off the highway and drove to the W Hotel in South Beach. It looked like she had another client and he had no idea how long she would be. What if she spent the night? He parked on the street with a view of the hotel entrance. At eight o'clock he got out of the car, walked down Collins Avenue to a restaurant, picked up a Cuban sandwich and a Coke to go, and went back to the car and ate.

A little after nine she walked out of the hotel. Frank held binoculars, zooming and holding on her face. He saw the Mercedes pull up, saw her get in, and saw it come toward him along the circular drive. He followed her back to Pompano, thinking he might have an opportunity at the condo when she parked her car. Instead of going straight back she stopped at the Publix on Atlantic Boulevard.

Frank parked next to her, put on the walking boot, and poured chloroform on a handkerchief. He had bought it from an online dental supply company, eight ounces for $63.23. It smelled sweet, which surprised him. He got out, popped the trunk, and took out the crutches and a plastic Publix bag that held a six pack of Coke. He made his way to the store entrance, looked through the big window, and saw Ashley at a register paying for a few things. He was moving toward the car when she came up behind him, and the rest was history.

*

Frank backed into the garage, put the door down, and opened the trunk. She was still unconscious. He lifted her out, carried her to the work bench, and tied her wrists and ankles together. He clamped the rebar in the jaws of the vise, and cut an eight-inch piece with the hacksaw and brushed the shavings onto the garage floor.

She was trying to open her eyes, lids fluttering, head sag-
ging to the left, trying to fight the anesthetic. It took a few
minutes and when she was fully awake she said, "Frank, I'm
flattered you wanted to see me again."

He wasn't expecting that.

"I liked you. I was hoping you'd call."

He had kidnapped her and tied her up and she was grinning and coming onto him. "What's your name?"

"Ashley."

"Your real name."

She told him.

"I like that. You're the girl next door, aren't you?"

"That's me."

"Not really, you're a prostitute."

"I'm an escort. If I wasn't, we wouldn't have met."

This whore was trying to con him, trying to save herself.
How dumb did she think he was? He took out his phone,
snapped a couple photographs, and took the X-Acto knife
out of his pocket.

THREE

"Hear that?"

Virginia walked past him with a screwdriver in her hand. It was the dryer making a strange thumping noise.

O'Clair said, "What is it?"

"Needs a new belt."

"How do you know that?"

"Are you serious?"

Why was he surprised? She'd fixed the disposal in unit ten and installed a new faucet in fourteen. O'Clair followed her into the utility room, watched her pull the dryer out from the wall and turn it sideways.

"Need some help?" He pictured her as a sexy repair girl wearing a tool belt and high heels.

"No thanks," she said, like he was getting in the way. Virginia took off the service panel, squatted and wedged a six-inch piece of two-by-four under the drum and cut the cracked belt off with scissors. Held the belt up and said, "See?"

No, he didn't see and he didn't say anything. When he'd met Virginia four months earlier she'd had purple hair, a stud in her tongue, and another one under her lower lip. She wore crazy outfits, black fingerless gloves, and a spiked dog collar—emo all the way. Once they got to Florida she changed her tune, stopped coloring her hair and wearing the goofy fucking clothes, and what do you know? She was a knockout.

O'Clair wondered what she'd seen in him from the beginning. He was forty-five and she was twenty-six and attractive. He'd never admit it but he was insecure about Virginia, worried she was going to wake up one morning, look at him and say, "What am I doing with a beast like you?"

But she stayed. Like he was her special project, trying to make him a little hipper and more interesting. She introduced him to new music, groups he'd never hear of: the National, Wilco, Arcade Fire, and Band of Horses. Introduced him to hip, new clothes, buying Tommy Bahama shirts, Revo shades, and platinum Fubu shorts. O'Clair had tried the new clothes on, looked at himself in the mirror and thought he looked like a clown, but wore the stuff for her, feeling self-conscious the first couple times he'd gone out in public, but he was used to it by now. He watched her install the new dryer belt and said, "Seriously, where'd you learn all this?"

"My dad."

O'Clair couldn't believe it. He'd grown up in a house with a tool drawer that had a screwdriver, pliers, a hammer, and a bunch of mismatched screws and nails. O'Clair's father was a liquor salesman who sold Teacher's scotch to the wholesaler, the state of Michigan. His father couldn't do anything handy and O'Clair wasn't much better. When he'd moved into his house in Ferndale he used the existing wall hooks to hang the few framed prints he'd acquired, none centered on the wall or the same height. Friends would come over and ask why O'Clair decided to put the pictures where he did. One girl he'd dated asked if it was influenced by *feng shui*. O'Clair said, "No, it was influenced by not giving a shit."

*

He was cleaning the pool the next morning when Holland called.

"Girl's name is Gloria McMillen. Cause of death was determined to be asphyxiation. Manner of death was ruled to be homicide. The killer had skill. Her eyes were surgically removed with some kind of scalpel."

"Find out if it was an X-Acto knife," O'Clair said.

"Why do you say that?"

"Was she sexually assaulted?"

"With a metal rod," Holland said. "Why would he do that?"

"Maybe he doesn't like women. Maybe he wasn't breast fed or his mother wasn't nice to him."

"How do you know it's a him?"

"You have to be strong to carry a one-hundred-twenty-pound girl from the street to the beach. It's got to be seventy yards."

"How do you know so much about this?"

"I had a case like it a few years ago, although the cause of death was way different."

"You think the murders are related?"

"I'm not saying that." O'Clair paused, but he was thinking it. "Guy named Alvin Monroe killed two prostitutes, shot them once in the head, cut their eyeballs out with an X-Acto blade, and raped them with a metal rod. Alvin was convicted of first degree murder and given consecutive life sentences without the possibility of parole."

"A copycat," Holland said.

Holland was watching too many cop shows. "Details of the murders were never disclosed in the newspapers."

"Maybe somebody came to trial, heard the evidence in the courtroom."

"Anything's possible," O'Clair said. "Why wait six years

to come after me? Let me think about it, talk to my former partner." O'Clair paused. "Tell me more about the girl."

"Gloria's mother called two days ago, said her daughter was missing, e-mailed a photo, came and identified the body. Gloria McMillen was twenty. She was attending classes at Broward College and worked as a cashier at Publix."

"Gloria have a boyfriend?"

"Her high school sweetheart, a kid named Joey Van Antwerp," Holland said. "But they broke up six months ago."

"Why?"

"The mother doesn't know."

"I hope he's on your list. Any evidence? Any other suspects?"

"Nothing yet. Not much to go on. Unless we get lucky."

"You've got to work the case," O'Clair said. "Make your own luck. How long you been doing this?"

"Eighteen months."

"How many homicides you worked primary?"

"Six, not counting this one." Holland sounded like he was apologizing. "How about you?"

"Fifteen hundred or so."

"I'm going to Gloria's place, look around. Want to come?"

O'Clair did feel a sense of responsibility. Maybe Holland was right—someone was trying to tell him something.

Holland picked him up twenty minutes later. O'Clair got in the car and said, "What's the crime like down here?"

Holland glanced at him. "You talking homicide?"

"Yeah. How many murders did you have in Pompano last year?"

"Eight, and that's high for a town with a population of just over a hundred thousand. Way above the national average." Holland took a right on NE Fifth Street.

"What kind of situations?"

"Everything you can think of. Two were domestic, husbands killed their wives. Both arrested and prosecuted." Holland paused. "One, a teen from Iowa arrived in town by bus, gave birth, and threw the kid down a trash chute. The girl confessed and posted a photo of herself on Facebook with a caption that said: *People you will see in hell.*"

O'Clair had investigated his share of dead babies: beaten to death by the mother's boyfriend or the mother herself 'cause the baby was crying too much. It was something you never got used to.

"Had another one," Holland said, "guy named Ricardo Arzate, killed his friend at a birthday party, shot him twice and disappeared. You see a Puerto Rican with a tat of the Virgin Mary on his right pec, give me a call."

"Good luck," O'Clair said. "You know how many Puerto Ricans have the Blessed Virgin tattooed on their chests?"

Holland pulled into the parking lot of the Harbor Cove condominiums less than a mile from his motel. They got out and took the elevator up to the third floor, then walked down the hall to 3C. Holland had a key, unlocked the door and they went in. It was a two-bedroom condo on the Intracoastal, beautifully furnished. "How's someone who works at a grocery store afford a place like this? Did her parents buy it for her?"

"The mother said Gloria saved up."

"I'd find out who's financing it and how much she put down."

They went in the bedroom that had a queen-size bed. O'Clair checked the big, organized dressing room, shoes on one side, lined up on floor-to-ceiling shelves, thirty-six pairs. Her clothes were on the other side. He wasn't an expert, but everything looked expensive. O'Clair went in the adjoining bathroom. The counter was cluttered with makeup containers, smudges of color on the white Formica countertop, towels on the tile floor, shampoo, conditioner, bath oils, and candles lining the flat side of the tub.

The second bedroom was used as an office. O'Clair sat behind the sleek desk in a high-backed swivel office chair, going through the drawers, taking out things of interest: Gloria McMillen's checkbook, pay stubs, phone bills, bank statements, lining them up on the desktop next to her Mac-Book.

Holland came in the room and stood next to him. "What do you have?"

"What do you want to know? She put forty grand down on the condo, had a fifteen-year mortgage, paying twenty-two hundred a month. She drove a Mercedes E-Class. Her lease with Mercedes-Benz Credit was seven hundred thirty-eight a month, and she had seventy-five grand in a savings account."

"How would she have that kind of money making ten dollars an hour as a cashier at Publix?"

"She didn't. Looks like she quit that job six months ago, but didn't tell her mother. Gloria's been getting a weekly check from XYZ Company. Different amounts, but adds up to almost one hundred and thirty thousand since July."

Holland said, "Is there an address?"

"A post office box in Coral Gables."

Holland rubbed his jaw. "What's XYZ do, they're paying a twenty-year-old girl two hundred and sixty grand a year?"

"It's a shell company for an escort service." O'Clair handed him a stack of eight and a half by eleven pages Gloria must've printed from the escort web site.

Holland started reading.

"Everything you want to know about Glamor Girls," O'Clair said. "It's all there: rates, reservations, customer rewards, FAQs. Spend fifty thousand a year and you're a platinum member."

"What's that get you?"

"Complimentary limo service, discounts at hotels."

"How much do they charge?"

"Depends where you're at," O'Clair said. "You've got the rate sheet."

Holland shuffled through a couple pages, found what he was looking for. "In Boca it's eight hundred to a thousand an hour, two hour minimum."

"How about Pompano?"

"Doesn't say, but Lauderdale is only seven hundred to nine hundred," Holland said. "What a deal, huh? They take Visa, MasterCard, American Express, and Discover. Listen to this: *'Someone once said, "The best things in life are free." Our classy ladies would love to hang out with you for nothing, but the reality is, hair, nails, makeup, and designer outfits are expensive.'"*

O'Clair booted up the MacBook, brought up Safari, typed in the web site, and the Glamor Girls home page appeared. Rows of color shots of hot-looking girls wearing high heels, posing in bikinis and lingerie. Girls with names like Francesca and Desiree, Isabella and Darcey, Alix, Chandler, and Bayley. O'Clair had never met girls with any of those names. He scrolled down and saw Gloria McMillen in a casual pose, sultry expression. She was leaning against an ornate bannister, one leg straight, the other bent, heel hooked on the metalwork. The name under the photograph was Ashley. "So they don't know she's dead."

"They suspect something's wrong. Come in and listen to her messages," Holland said, walking out of the room.

O'Clair followed him into the kitchen. There was a Panasonic answering machine on the brown granite counter over a built-in wine cooler.

"She was killed around four a.m.," Holland said. "These came in later that morning. I think you're right, the escort people don't know she's dead or they'd get rid of her picture, wouldn't they?" Holland pressed the message button.

"Glor, it's Pam, tried your cell, no answer. A gentleman named Rick is asking for you this evening, call for the particulars. Oh, and how was your date?"

"Pause it," O'Clair said. "What time did that call come in?"

"Yesterday. Ten thirty in the morning."

"Sounds like she was with someone the night she was killed. Which may or may not be the perp. But it's a place to start."

Holland pressed the button again. "It's your mother, where are you? Are we still having lunch? I'll meet you at the restaurant."

"Glor, it's Pam. Remember Barry from last week? He wants to know if you're available tomorrow evening at seven. You're becoming very popular. What're you doing to these poor guys?"

"It's your mother. Where were you? We were supposed to meet for lunch."

"Call me by four or I'll have to cancel your date. This isn't like you."

"Pam, the girl on the answering machine," O'Clair said, "you've got her number, right? You should be able to get an address."

FOUR

O'Clair walked in the office, leaned against the counter.

Virginia said, "Would you like a room?"

"Only if you come with it." He went around on her side, put his arms around her, and kissed her. "What's happening?"

"The BU students checked out; couldn't wait to go."

O'Clair would miss seeing the young girls in bathing suits and the guys working their asses off to get their attention. The guys doing back flips off the board and cannon balls, trying to drain the pool, flexing and doing handstands, arm wrestling. It was really entertaining.

"And the MacGuidwins have decided to cut their stay short. Mrs. said she saw a centipede on the chesterfield, which surprised her in such a dekey establishment."

The MacGuidwins had been a pain in the ass since they checked in. The water wasn't cold enough. The water wasn't hot enough. The bathroom smelled of mildew. 'The college boys were going through the two-fours, eh?'

"I'm surprised there wasn't a mass exodus. Murder has a way of making people uncomfortable."

"A guy named Foley checked in, I put him in eight. He wants to go deep sea fishing. I told him to go down to Hillsborough, talk to the charter captains."

"Where's he from?"

"Pittsburgh." Virginia paused. "You've got something on your mind, I can see it. How'd it go today?"

"The dead girl worked for an escort service."

"How was it being a cop again?"

"It took me back."

"How about Holland?"

"Good guy but not very experienced."

"The look on your face says you liked it."

"I'm helping out is all. Is that a problem?"

"No, I think it's great," Virginia said. "This is the happiest I've seen you since you left Detroit."

"What're you saying? I'm difficult to live with?"

"I don't think you're cut out to run a motel, deal with people," Virginia said and smiled. "Not to mention your contempt for humanity."

"You may be on to something," O'Clair said.

"So what's next?"

"All we have is a phone number, a web site, and a post office box. We need an address. The ideal thing would be to have a female cop apply for a job at the escort service, go undercover."

"Is that a pun?"

O'Clair gave her an impatient look.

"So why don't they?"

"Holland said they don't have anyone on the payroll that could pull it off."

"Is that another pun? You're on a roll."

"You're having a good time," O'Clair said, "aren't you?"

"I may have a solution to your problem."

"Send you in to fix the dryer?"

"You're close," Virginia said. "Send me in looking for a job. I'll apply online."

"No way."

"I thought you liked my looks."

"That's got nothing to do with it. It's too dangerous."

"I'll e-mail an application. Find out where the place is and tell you. What's dangerous about that?"

"You need photos of yourself."

"Yeah? What's the problem? I'll pose, you shoot." She pulled her hair back, gave him a seductive smile. "We can do it early, take advantage of the soft morning light. What do you think?"

"I don't know. I'm too hungry to think. What're we having for dinner?"

*

Virginia grilled hog snapper and served it over black beans and rice. They ate on TV tables and watched *Dancing with the Stars*, one of Virginia's favorite shows. She told O'Clair she was going to teach him the *Paso Doble*, a Latin dance he'd never heard of. He didn't really like the show, but watched it 'cause Virginia loved it. This was new for O'Clair, wanting to make someone else happy, wanting to spend time with a girl, looking forward to it. They had fun together. He could kid around with her, say anything and she wouldn't take offense. Most girls, in his experience, you had to be careful what you said. He was thinking about his ex-wife, Joan, the Armenian dental hygienist. Joan might've said something like: 'I didn't sleep very well last night,' and O'Clair would say: 'Yeah, you look a little tired.' Joan would say: 'Oh, you think I look tired?' taking offense. Virginia, on the other hand, was low-key and easy going, liked to fix things and liked people, attributes that came in handy running a motel.

*

They got up early the next morning, O'Clair, with the sun behind him, shooting Virginia on the steps that led to the beach, Virginia with her hands on her hips in a black bikini, smiling, friendly and approachable, then looking sexy, a wisp of hair across her forehead covering part of her left eye, a seductive expression.

Oak said, "Jesus. This one's the winner."

When they finished, Virginia went online and read the escort service requirements. You had to be between eighteen and twenty-seven. She was twenty-six and a half. You had to give your height and weight. She was five six, 117. Hair and eye color: brown and blue, and her measurements, which were 34-23-34.

'You've got the best body I've ever seen,' Oak had said the first time he saw her naked. 'And I started looking at *Playboy* when I was fifteen.'

Virginia filled out the application and attached half a dozen digital shots O'Clair had taken. "They're asking for a short bio, education, accomplishments. Think I should tell them I fix appliances?"

"That'll impress them," O'Clair said, looking up from the newspaper.

"Says they expect me to be on call six days a week, twelve hours a day, sitting around a condo in Miami till somebody asks for me. How far do you want me to go?"

"Find out where they're located and get them to hire you. I'll seal off a five block area."

"Where'd you get that?"

"It's what cops say in movies. 'I'm going to seal off a five block area,' like you just press a button."

"Well, I think it sounds exciting. It'll be like I'm acting."

Virginia e-mailed her information and got a response an hour later. "They want to know if I'm available for a personal interview."

"When?"

"Tomorrow morning at ten, 419 Dixie Highway."

*

Virginia parked in the lot and looked at herself in the rearview mirror. She was wearing a white sleeveless blouse, gold hoop earrings and red lipstick that matched her fingernails and toenails, black capris and white knockoff Prada sandals. She got out of the car, not sure if she was being watched, went in the four-story office building and took the elevator up to the third floor. She walked down the hall, found the suite, and tried the handle. The door was locked. There was a little box with a button on it built into the wall next to the door. She pressed it and a man's voice said, "May I help you?"

"It's Virginia. I'm here for the ten o'clock appointment."

The door buzzed and she opened it and was met by a dark-haired guy, mid-thirties, who looked like an aging frat boy in khakis and a golf shirt.

"Hi, I'm Brad, come on in have a seat," he said, arm outstretched, palm open, indicating a black leather couch opposite a cheap desk that had a digital camera on it. He closed the door, locked it, and sat behind the desk. "If it's all right I'd like to record the interview."

"No problem," Virginia said.

Brad picked up the camera, pointed the lens at her and made a couple adjustments. "What's your name?"

"Virginia Delaney."

"How old are you, Virginia?"

"Twenty-six."

"Did you bring your ID?"

Virginia reached into her bag, brought out her wallet, unzipped it, took out her driver's license, and held it up.

"Can I see it?"

Virginia got up and handed the license to him. He glanced at it and said, "You're from Michigan, huh? Where's Ferndale?"

"It's a suburb of Detroit." Virginia took a couple steps back and sat on the couch.

"How long have you been down here?"

"Three months."

"How'd you hear about us?"

"I went online."

"You know what we do?"

"Provide twenty-four-hour outcall escort services," Virginia said, trying to make it sound conversational. "For upscale gentlemen and couples in select Florida cities."

Brad grinned. "I see you did your homework. Have you ever been an escort?"

"Never."

"A call girl, hooker, prostitute, or whatever you want to call it?"

"No."

"A stripper?"

"Nope."

"Do you have a boyfriend?"

"Not right now."

"Why do you want to be an escort?"

"The money. Fifty grand a month."

"That's what the top girls earn."

She gave him a seductive smile. "I'm going to be one of the top girls."

"You have a college degree?"

"Two years at Oakland Community."

"Speak any foreign languages?"

"A little French."

"Say something."

"*Je voudrais le gateau.*"

"All right, stand up for me."

She did.

"Now turn around."

She spun in a circle and came back facing him.

"Now I need you to take off your clothes."

"That was never mentioned, never part of the deal." Virginia was nervous now. What was this pervert going to do?

"Look, you're applying for a job where you can earn as much as a corporate CEO. We've got to make sure you're qualified. It's completely up to you. If you'd rather not, I understand. Let me say though, there are plenty of attractive young ladies that would give anything to be in your position. Should I turn off the camera or do you want to continue?"

Virginia knew what O'Clair would've said, but she didn't mind as long as it didn't go any further than taking her clothes off. "Okay."

She unbuttoned the blouse and took it off, unhooked the bra from behind but palmed the cups, doing a slow reveal, lowering one side then the other.

Brad's jaw dropped. "My god, are those real?" He picked up the camera and started recording.

"One hundred percent home grown."

"Let's see the rest."

Virginia stepped out of the sandals, undid the clasp on the capris and slid them over her hips and down her legs and stepped out of them wearing a black thong.

"Turn around for me."

Virginia moved slowly in a circle, giving Brad a good look at the butt that Oak said was the best he'd ever seen in his life.

"Now take that off," Brad said, voice rising an octave.

"I think you get the idea," Virginia said.

"I want to make sure you're neat and trim down there. A landing strip or a Hitler are okay, but we don't want to have to do any defoliating."

"You don't, take my word for it." Virginia started getting dressed. When she finished she said, "What's the next step?"

"I'll show the video to my associates, see what they think."

"What do you think?"

"You've got a great look. That's what it's all about. But it isn't up to me. Someone will contact you either way."

Virginia moved to the door, trying to hide how anxious she was to get out of there. She turned, smiled at Brad and said, "Thanks."

"If for some reason it doesn't work out, I'd like to see you," Brad said.

Virginia wondered where this dork got his confidence. She walked out and closed the door. Took the elevator down and walked across the parking lot to her car. Oak and Holland were in Oak's Seville. They didn't wave or acknowledge her, but seeing them there made her feel better.

She got in the Honda and drove back to Pompano. Jady, the housekeeper, was behind the counter when she went in the office. "Anything happen while we were gone?"

"A man come by lookin' for Mr. Oak."

"A policeman?"

"No, ma'am."

"Call me Virginia."

"Yes, ma'am."

"He say what he wanted?"

"No, ma'am."

"How'd you like working the desk?"

"Doesn't seem like work, getting paid to stand around and there's rooms need cleanin'. I can't ax you to pay me for not doin' anything, now can I?"

"You helped us out and we're going to pay you."

Jady was a twenty-three-year-old Honduran with high cheekbones, dark chocolate skin, and when she smiled, which she did a lot, she showed big white teeth. Jady cleaned all day and was still smiling when she went home to a trailer park in Lantana to make dinner for her husband and two kids.

Jady told Virginia she left the Bahamas so she wouldn't have to clean rooms at one of the big hotels, came to the US, got a visa, and ended up getting a job cleaning rooms. She and Oak trusted Jady and paid her fifteen dollars an hour, appreciably more than the going rate for maids.

O'Clair and Holland came in as Jady was leaving.

"Well," O'Clair said. "How'd it go?"

"Good, I think. They're going to let me know."

Holland said, "Tell us what happened?"

She did, leaving out the part about taking off her clothes. O'Clair would've driven back to Coral Gables and thrown him out the window.

*

Virginia got an e-mail from the escort service a few hours later. It said, *CONGRATULATIONS, VIRGINIA!!!* in the subject bar. Below, in letter format, it said:

Dear Virginia,

I can't invite you to join our elite family of models just yet, but you've made it through the first round. We're very excited about you. We think you have the potential to become one of our top models, earning up to $50,000 every month. Please call to set up your second interview at: 305-568-8866. We're all very anxious to meet you.

Sincerely,
Jan Arquilla
Director of Operations

"Second interview? I thought you were in." O'Clair sounded agitated.

"Me too. But what difference does it make? I talked to the director of operations. I'm supposed to go to Bayside, this shopping mall on Biscayne Boulevard in Miami, leave my car at valet, and somebody will pick me up. I'm supposed to call when I get there. You'll be there too. You'll follow me." She could tell O'Clair didn't like it; she could see it on his face, hear it in his voice. He wasn't good at hiding his feelings.

"I'm Irish," he'd once told her. "My ancestors were potato farmers. What did they know about hiding their feelings?"

"You don't want me to go, do you?"

"You get in a car with somebody, I can't protect you."

"I'll be there too," Holland said. "I can get back up, if you think we need it."

"I'll be all right," Virginia said. "I think this is on the level. They're being cautious, they've got a lot at stake."

"You sound like you want to do it," O'Clair said, eyes on Virginia.

"If I can help solve Gloria McMillen's murder, I'm all for it."

Holland glanced at O'Clair. "Then we're all in agreement, huh?"

FIVE

The next morning, nine thirty, they followed Virginia on Interstate 95 to the Bayside Mall in Holland's souped-up, high-performance Volkswagen GTI. Holland was undercover in jeans, sandals, a blue Nine Inch Nails T-shirt, sunglasses, and a NASCAR cap. He looked so different, O'Clair couldn't believe it.

The mall was cool, built on different levels right on Biscayne Bay. Holland pulled over to the curb and O'Clair watched her park at valet, get out, and make a call on her cell. Then she was moving. Virginia walked out to Port Boulevard, a black Mercedes stopped and she got in and it sped off.

Holland blew past the valet stand, went right on Port Boulevard, weaving through traffic. They lost the Benz but then O'Clair saw it up ahead, 550 SEL with blacked-out windows. When the Benz turned left onto Biscayne Boulevard, they were two cars behind it. O'Clair felt big in the tapered Recaro passenger seat, his shoulders extending beyond the seat back like it was designed for jockeys and bantamweights, not 230-pound men. O'Clair had to hand it to Holland, he was a good driver and the car was a little rocket.

They followed the Benz to Coral Gables and then through a neighborhood of big houses on big lots and watched it turn into a gated estate at 5890 SW 117th Street.

O'Clair noticed cameras on the wall near the entrance, and a six-foot-high white stucco wall topped with red tile that went around the perimeter of the property.

*

Virginia was in the back seat of the Mercedes, leaning against black leather, left arm on the armrest. She glanced at the driver, a big man with a ponytail. He'd introduced himself as Chano, speaking with a heavy accent and smelling of bad cologne. She could see him looking at her in the rearview mirror. Eyes on her, a hint of a grin on his face.

"You been there before?"

"No."

"You like it."

"Where're we going?"

"Very soon you see."

"Where're you from?"

"Coo-ba."

"I hear it's nice, huh?"

"Very beautiful," Chano said, smiling in the mirror. "Sometime you should go."

"I will. Have you worked for Mrs. Arquilla very long?"

"Two year."

"How many girls does she have?"

"Twenty, thirty, forty."

"Are they all beautiful?"

"Not more than you," Chano said, grinning. "No, I am serious."

"Thank you."

Chano turned left into a residential area, made a couple more turns, and pulled up at the entrance of a gated estate. The gates opened. He drove in and parked on the circular drive in front of a massive mission-style villa with white stucco walls and red tile roofs. Chano got out and opened her door.

"What do you think?"

"Wow."

Chano smiled.

*

Virginia was escorted to a big glassed-in Florida room with rattan furniture, mahogany frames, and green floral cushions. Through the floor-to-ceiling windows she could see a swimming pool with a rock outcropping and waterfall surrounded by a slate patio and sculpted gardens.

Jan Arquilla had an almond-shaped face that made her look slightly Asian. She was mid-forties, petite, well-dressed, dark hair pulled back, sitting across a glass coffee table from Virginia.

"I have to tell you I'm impressed. You have a great look and a great body. Our clients will like you, there's no doubt about that, but you know what's more important than anything? Confidence. If you're confident, the client thinks he's getting his money's worth. Tell me about yourself. Who is Virginia Delaney?"

"I grew up in Garden City, a blue collar suburb of Detroit. Went to Garden City high and Oakland Community College. I have an older sister, Karen, currently living in St. Tropez."

Jan's eyes lit up. "What does she do?"

"She's a former model."

"How about you? Ever do any modeling?"

"It never interested me. I used to go to Karen's shoots and it was really boring, standing around waiting for the photographer to get the lighting right."

Jan Arquilla smiled. "I know what you mean. I was a

swimsuit model in my younger days." She paused. "What about your parents?"

"My dad was a manufacturer's rep; he called on Chrysler. He was killed in a car accident when I was thirteen. My mother freaked out and never recovered. She found God and joined one of those fake non-denominational churches. My sister and I called it *COTMUS. The Church of Totally Made Up Shit.*"

"Were you religious growing up?"

"I was brought up Catholic, but except for weddings and funerals I haven't been to church in years."

"You went to college for a couple years, why'd you quit?"

"I couldn't afford it."

"How'd you support yourself?"

"I worked in a retail store that sold fetishy fashion, kinky kitsch, if you know what that is. Leather corsets, spanking benches, penis whips. I'm giving you a broad range."

"How classy," Jan Arquilla said. "You don't look like the type. Tell me why you want to be an escort."

"'Cause I can make a fortune."

"There's a misconception about escorts. They're not all uneducated, drug addict losers from broken homes. Most of our ladies are college educated, beautiful, funny, and well-rounded." Jan paused. "Work hard and follow the rules and you'll do very well."

"What do you charge, and what percent do I get?"

"The rates vary depending on the per capita income of the city. We split fifty-fifty."

"That doesn't seem fair."

"To whom, you or the agency?"

"Me."

Jan Arquilla frowned. "Here's how it works: we have the reputation, we've cultivated the brand. We promote you on our web site. We handle all the bookings, billing, screening, transportation, and security. All you have to do is show up, entertain the client, and move on to the next one." She was getting a little worked up, and paused now to compose herself. "No money exchanges hands. You're forbidden to give your contact information to a client. He wants a date with you, he calls us. Is that understood?"

Virginia nodded.

"Our top models are making fifty thousand dollars a month. I think someone like you can get there very quickly. Do you have a boyfriend?"

"I left him in Detroit."

"Good. What about a job."

"I work part time at a motel in Pompano."

"Not anymore. This is your job. Your only job. You'll be on call Tuesday through Saturday from seven p.m. until seven a.m."

"Who are the clients?"

"Businessmen, politicians, judges, attorneys, airline pilots, men with means, and occasionally couples."

"Anyone ever have a problem?"

"What do you mean?"

"With perverts or psychos."

"We screen everyone we do business with. That includes a background check, police record. It's thorough, but even so, occasionally we get a bad apple. Most of our clients come to us because they're lonely. They're looking for someone to confide in, someone to talk to, someone to cuddle with. They want to feel like someone loves them even if it's just for a short time. You're going to need a name. Being an escort is fulfilling a customer's fantasy. You're taking on a new identity, a new personality. Unleashing this new self that's inside you. You have to be sexy, sensuous, mysterious."

"How about Ally?" Virginia said, thinking about a girl she went to high school with and always liked the name.

"That's good. Names that end in a vowel seem to work best. They're sexier, more exotic." She paused. "Your job is to make the client feel like he's the most important man in the world. You're going to like some of these guys, but you don't, you never allow yourself to get involved, fall in love." Her eyes held on Virginia. "I think that about covers it." Jan Arquilla stood up now. "Actually, there is one more thing. I wonder about a test drive. It can help. If someone asks what you're like in bed we have firsthand knowledge."

"I don't know." Virginia was nervous now. She got up. "When?"

"No time like the present."

"With who?"

"My ex."

Like it had been choreographed, a tall, tan, silver-haired man wearing golf clothes walked into the room, grinning.

"Kenny, say hello to Virginia Delaney. Virginia this is my former husband, and current business partner."

He had to be close to sixty, thin used-car-salesman mustache and hair slicked back. He gave her the creeps.

"I was just telling Virginia about the test drive."

The ex grinned. "Honey, there's no substitute for finding out how a chassis handles sharp curves, winding roads, and straightaways."

Virginia thought he was kidding with that dumb metaphor, but he wasn't. "I hear what you're saying. Let me think about it."

"Don't think too long," Kenny Arquilla said and walked out of the room.

"Don't be fooled by his age. You'll like him. All the girls do."

"You don't mind?"

"God, no. We've been divorced for ten years."

She'd been married to him and now she was his pimp.

"Training begins tomorrow morning at nine sharp."

*

Jady was behind the counter, dusting when they walked in the office.

"How'd it go?" Virginia said.

"Dead girl's mother come for Mr. Oak. She outside by the pool. And a man come by also."

"What'd he want?"

"You, Mr. Oak."

"A police officer?"

"No, sir."

"What'd he say?"

"Ask when you be back."

"What'd he look like?"

"Man have a full head of hair, dark but also gray. Not as big as you, but not small. About your age," Jady said.

"So an old man," Virginia said.

Jady flashed a quick, toothy grin. "No, Mr. Oak not old."

"All right, thanks."

Jady went off to clean, Virginia to change, and O'Clair walked outside to see Mrs. McMillen.

"Call me Audrey," she said after introductions.

Audrey McMillen was sitting at one of the outdoor tables under the raised umbrella, smoking. There were half a dozen brown-tipped butts in the ashtray.

"How does a young, hardworking girl end up dead?" she said, voice breaking, and pain on her face. She felt the loss, carried it like a weight.

"I don't know."

"It doesn't make sense and the police won't tell me anything."

"The case is wide open. They don't know anything yet."

Audrey was blonde and pretty, mid-forties, wearing a white designer T-shirt, red shorts, and black sunglasses. The daughter had gotten her mother's looks and more.

"Where did you find her?" Audrey McMillen stubbed her cigarette out in the ashtray.

"On the beach."

"Will you show me?"

O'Clair led her past the pool, through the gate, and down the steps. "I found Gloria here," he said pointing to the spot. "In a lounge chair. I thought she was sleeping."

Mrs. McMillen started to cry now and O'Clair moved next to her, waiting for a sign that she wanted to be comforted, but it didn't come. She opened her purse, took out a Kleenex, and wiped her eyes.

"What about Mr. McMillen?"

"We're divorced. He lives in Norfolk, Virginia."

"How long's it been?"

"Fifteen years."

"Did he see much of Gloria?"

"Not at all. Nothing whatsoever." Audrey paused. "Richard's got problems."

"What's he do?"

"He's a manufacturer's rep, sells gaskets."

"You tell him what happened?"

"I left a message on his machine. Haven't heard back, which is typical."

O'Clair was going to ask about Gloria's boyfriend, but what was the point? The boyfriend didn't strangle her and take out her eyes. "I'll ask Detective Holland to call you as soon as he has something."

O'Clair walked Audrey McMillen to her car, thinking about his next move, thinking like a homicide cop again.

SIX

"You're a real fashionista I see," Holland said, looking across the interior at O'Clair in a tan wash 'n' wear suit he'd bought in 1995 when he was ten pounds lighter. "Where do you get a suit like that?"

"Sears," O'Clair said. "It's the only one I kept, gave everything else to the Goodwill."

"It's a classic."

"You can throw it in the washer and dryer," O'Clair said, messing with him. "Or take it outside, hose it down, and watch it spring back to life."

They drove to Jan Arquilla's residence in Coconut Grove, arriving at 9:00 a.m. Holland flashed his badge at the heavyset security guard who had come through the gate.

"Detectives Holland and O'Clair to see Mrs. Arquilla."

"She didn't say nothing to me." He was a tan meathead in a Hawaiian shirt, spoke with a Spanish accent. "She expecting you?"

"No," Holland said.

"You got a search warrant?"

"Stop fucking around and get Mrs. Arquilla on the phone," O'Clair said. "Tell her two homicide detectives are here investigating a murder."

The security guard squatted next to the car on Holland's side, looked across the interior at O'Clair. "You're the tough one, huh?"

"I'm the diplomatic one," O'Clair said. "So that tells you where you stand. I'm the best hope you've got of staying out of jail."

"For what?"

"Obstructing a murder investigation, or maybe it's an immigration violation. You look like an illegal alien. We better cuff you, hand you over to Homeland Security."

"What're you talking about? I was born here."

"We don't know that," O'Clair said. "You got your birth certificate with you?"

The security guard lost the attitude, stood up and made a call on his cell phone, spoke Spanish, listened, and put the phone back in his shirt pocket. "OK, you pull up there." He pointed to the circular drive. "Someone be out to get you."

Holland glanced at him. "I'm impressed, but can you back it up?"

"I hope I don't have to," O'Clair said.

They parked and got out. "Look at this place," Holland said, wide-eyed, admiring the villa. "What's something like this cost?"

"More than you make in your career," a good-looking, dark-haired woman said, coming out of the house. "I'm Jan Arquilla, what can I do for you?"

"We need to ask you some questions. I'm Detective Holland," he said, showing his ID. "This is Detective O'Clair."

"Pompano, huh? You're a little out of your jurisdiction, aren't you?"

O'Clair said, "You want to talk out here, or should we go in, get comfortable?"

"You're right, I'm being rude. Please come in."

They followed her inside, down a black-and-white tile hallway to a porch with floor-to-ceiling windows, dark rattan furniture, and a view of the pool and gardens.

"Something to drink, iced tea, a soft drink, coffee?"

O'Clair shook his head, and then Holland did too.

"Nice place you have here," Holland said.

"Okay, what can I do for you?"

"Gloria McMillen was murdered two nights ago."

"What does that have to do with me?"

"Gloria worked for you," O'Clair said. "And we know you booked a date for her that night. We've got cell phone tower records and the tape from her answering machine."

Jan Arquilla crossed her legs, met his gaze. "I don't know what you're talking about."

"You don't, huh?" O'Clair unfolded a printout from the escort web site, held it up and handed it to her. Gloria McMillen, also known as Ashley, second photo in the first row, one of twelve shots on the page.

"What's this?"

"We know you've taken her picture off the site 'cause you haven't heard from her in a few days. Let me tell you something: whoever killed Gloria—and we're reasonably sure it was a client—will probably come back for more. All your escorts are in danger. Who was Gloria's date the night of January fourth? We know you screen all your clients, do background checks. What's his name?"

Jan Arquilla was good, she didn't squirm or flinch, just sat there calm as could be. "Even if I was in the business, I wouldn't compromise the identity of a client. If we shared sensitive information with the police we wouldn't be in business for long."

Holland said, "What do you know about XYZ Company?"

"Never heard of it."

"That's interesting," O'Clair said. "We've got your phone records and guess what? You get on average a hundred calls a week from XYZ in Coral Gables."

"This girl Gloria, how was she killed?"

"Asphyxiated," O'Clair said. He wasn't going to mention the missing eyeballs.

"How do you know it's murder? Maybe she just stopped breathing."

"Gloria had also been sexually assaulted with a metal rod," O'Clair said. "Think she did that to herself?"

Jan Arquilla took her eyes off him for the first time, glanced across the room, and came back. "I'm trying to cooperate and you're trying to intimidate me. Should I call my lawyer?"

"We're not really interested in you or your business, are we?" O'Clair said.

"All we want to do, Mrs. Arquilla," Holland said, "is get a murderer off the streets."

"But if you want to be difficult," O'Clair said, "I was thinking the IRS would be interested in your operation. God, they love things like this. XYZ, a shell company laundering money at an offshore bank in the Bahamas or wherever. That's just a guess, but I'll bet it's not far off."

Now it was Holland's turn. "Mrs. Arquilla, ever spend time in county lockup? The food's awful and you wear an outfit worn by who knows how many before you. No makeup. No trips to the beauty parlor. No getting your nails done. Be a real change for you, I bet."

"All right, I think you've made your point. If I give you a name that'll be the end of this, is that what you're saying?" She looked at O'Clair and O'Clair looked at Holland.

"Mrs. Arquilla, I don't know that that's a guarantee," Holland said. "But it's a step in the right direction."

She gave Holland a dirty look. "You said you want a name. I'll give you the name of my attorney, who's going to be here before I say another word."

"I wouldn't do that," O'Clair said. "I think we're close. I

think we can work this out among ourselves." Now O'Clair nodded at Holland.

"Absolutely. Tell us who the guy is, we'll get out of your hair," Holland said. "How's that sound, Mrs. Arquilla?"

"Give me a minute," she said, getting up and walking out of the room.

Holland grinned at O'Clair. "Good work. You see her face when you said IRS? Looked like she was going to be sick. People'd rather have a murderer after them than those assholes. Think she's going to give us the right name?"

Jan Arquilla came back in the room. "It's his name and contact information," she said, all business, handing a piece of note paper to O'Clair. "He's fifty-six and married, lives at Old Port Cove in North Palm Beach. The night with Gloria was his first and only time."

O'Clair said, "When she didn't check in the next day, what'd you think?"

"She'd had enough," Jan Arquilla said. "It happens. Some girls are cut out for it and some aren't."

O'Clair said, "You owed her some money, didn't you?"

"We put a check in the mail."

"You know that girl you interviewed yesterday, Virginia Delaney? She decided not to take the job after all."

"That's too bad, she could've made a lot of money."

*

They took 95 to PGA Boulevard in heavy traffic, seniors driving too slow and everyone else driving too fast. It took a little over an hour, Holland making small talk most of the way.

"You going to marry her?"

"Who?"

"Who do you think? The hottie you're living with. You're a lucky guy."

"We'll see," O'Clair said.

"Don't let her get away. That one's a keeper."

"I'll see what I can do," O'Clair said, wondering why Holland was concerned about his relationship with Virginia all of a sudden, making sure O'Clair's intentions were honorable.

"How old is she?"

"Twenty-six."

"What, about five five, one fifteen?"

O'Clair said, "What's your sudden interest in my girlfriend?"

"Just curious. Don't worry, I'm married."

"You think I'm worried?"

They passed a golf course on the right.

Holland said, "Ever play PGA National? Five championship golf courses. They had the Honda Classic there last year."

"I don't play golf."

"Why?"

"It takes too long."

"Guy your size, you could hit it a ton."

"No thanks."

"Play any sports?"

"Football. I played linebacker at Michigan State 1987 for George Perles. We went nine-two-and-one. Won the Big Ten and beat USC twenty to seventeen in the Rose Bowl."

"No shit. I'm impressed," Holland said, grinning. "No wonder you got the cheerleader."

They took a right on A1A and a left into Old Port Cove, a giant condo complex that bordered Lake Worth to the east. They pulled up to the security hut and a stocky guy about O'Clair's age came out and approached the Malibu.

"Can I help you?"

Holland pulled out his ID, opened it, and showed it to

the guard. "Holland, Pompano Homicide. Here to talk to a suspect. And this here's Detective O'Clair from Detroit." He paused. "You sure look familiar. You're not Ray Kubas' nephew by any chance, are you?"

The guard nodded. "You knew Ray, huh?"

"Who didn't?"

"Isn't that the truth?"

"So you were a cop, huh?" Holland said, sounding like there was a little country boy in his voice.

"Gene Rowan. Twenty-two years with Florida Highway Patrol up in Cross City."

"Pleasure to meet you, trooper. Dixie County, oh yeah, I've passed through there a time or two. John T. still in charge?"

"Does a bear shit in the woods?" The guard paused. "This suspect got a name?"

"Howard Chilson, but everyone calls him Skip."

"He expecting you?"

"No, and we'd like to keep it that way," Holland said.

The guard said, "What's he accused of?"

"Possible suspect in a homicide."

"Mr. Chilson's in L7. Head for Lake Point Towers." He pointed at a high rise in the distance. "Park on the north side and walk toward the pool. It's a condo with its own entrance."

Holland knocked on the door. O'Clair glanced down the walkway at two teenagers in bikinis, going to the pool. The door opened, a heavy woman with short blonde hair, mid-fifties, eyed them with suspicion.

"Can I help you?"

Her blonde hair was parted down the middle and dark along the part.

"We're looking for Howard Chilson," Holland said, flashing his shield. "Pompano Beach Homicide. I'm Detective Holland. This is Detective O'Clair."

"What's this about?"

"A homicide investigation. We need to ask Mr. Chilson some questions."

"Skip's not here. He's on the boat."

O'Clair said, "Where's that?"

"Right over there," Mrs. Chilson said, pointing. "The marina." She gave them the slip number.

*

It took them a couple minutes to find it, a fifty-one-foot Hatteras called *Keel-Joy*. O'Clair guessed it was better than *Wet Dream* and *Seaduction*, names he'd seen on boats in the Detroit River.

"Wait here, I'll go see if I can find him," Holland said, climbing down a short ladder onto the deck. O'Clair looked around. There were some big boats. A few had to be over a hundred feet long. Tiger Woods' yacht, he'd read, docked at this marina. Holland came back on deck, waved O'Clair aboard.

Chilson, a balding guy in tennis whites and deck shoes was sitting in an overstuffed chair when they walked in the salon.

"Mr. Chilson, this is my colleague, Detective O'Clair."

Chilson didn't get up or attempt to shake hands and O'Clair didn't either. It wasn't a social occasion.

"What's this about?" Chilson said, anger in his voice.

"A homicide."

"What's that have to do with me?"

"The escort you were out with three nights ago was murdered."

"And you think I had something to do with it?" He

rubbed his jaw with an open hand. "This is all I need." He shook his head.

"Tell us about your date," O'Clair said.

Chilson rubbed the bridge of his nose with his thumb and index finger. "Jesus Christ. First time I've ever done anything like this and look what happens."

O'Clair said, "What did?"

"Nothing."

"You paid for a high-price call girl and nothing happened?" O'Clair paused. "We want to know where you went, what you did."

"I think I should call my lawyer," Chilson said.

"You didn't do anything, you've got nothing to worry about," O'Clair said. "Help us, we'll help you."

"My wife's going to—" He didn't finish, looked at the floor, and then fixed his attention on O'Clair. "We met at the W in South Beach, Ashley was already in the suite when I arrived at six."

"Who arranged for the room?"

"They did, and tacked on twenty percent. The suite alone was fourteen hundred."

O'Clair said, "How much was the girl?"

"Twelve hundred an hour, minimum two hours."

Holland said, "What'd you do?"

"We played pinochle," Howard "Skip" Chilson said. "What are you, a priest? What do you think we did? Jesus." Temper flaring, turning mean in a split second.

"You don't want to be polite, we can take you in, have this conversation," Holland said.

Chilson gave him a hard look. "I went to the room, we introduced ourselves. I popped open a bottle of champagne, we sat on the terrace, looking out at the ocean."

O'Clair said, "What'd you talk about?"

"All kinds of things. She asked me what I did for a living and actually sounded interested."

Holland said, "What'd you tell her?"

"I owned a manufacturing company, made injection molded parts for GM. Escutcheon plates, sail panels, grommet plugs, and boots. I sold the company a few years ago."

Holland said, "What else?"

"She asked about my wife."

Holland said, "How long you been married?"

"Thirty-five years."

O'Clair said, "Things getting a little stale, huh?"

Howard Chilson ignored him. "I told her about the Hatteras, told her I'd take her to Bimini sometime. We talked about tennis. She said she wanted to learn how to play; I said I'd give her lessons."

Holland said, "So you hit it off, huh?"

"Twelve hundred an hour makes it easy. We went inside, she gave me a back rub. It's a good way to break the ice, get things going without feeling awkward. We ended up in bed together, what a surprise, huh?"

O'Clair said, "Then what happened?"

"What, your parents never told you the facts of life?"

"I mean after," O'Clair said. "What'd you do?"

"Took a shower and left."

Holland said, "What time was it?"

"Ten to nine." Chilson scratched his head.

O'Clair said, "You leave together?"

"No, I went first. I told her I wanted to see her again and asked for her phone number and she said I had to call the escort company."

Holland said, "That pissed you off, didn't it?"

"Not particularly."

"You waited for her, didn't you? Followed her home," Holland said.

"No, I came straight back here."

O'Clair said, "What time did you get home?"

"A little after ten," Chilson said. "You don't believe me, ask my wife."

"Where'd you tell her you were?"

"Having dinner with friends in Miami. What'd you tell her you came to see me about?"

"We're investigating a homicide," O'Clair said.

"Am I under arrest?"

Holland glanced at him, and O'Clair shook his head. "Not yet, but we want you to come down to Pompano and take a polygraph."

SEVEN

Frank watched the maid sitting on the bench, waiting for the bus on Atlantic Boulevard. He watched till she got on and followed it west, out past the turnpike. The bus stopped and the maid got out and walked half a mile to a mobile home park called Whispering Palms, built on flat, dusty acreage.

He could take her right now, and decided to wait till morning. Something didn't feel right. He'd been watching her for a couple days. She arrived at the motel at eight thirty and left promptly at five to catch the bus at five twenty-five. He knew her name was Jady Martinez. She was a twenty-three-year-old Honduran married to a laborer. They had two young kids. He'd followed her from the trailer park to a Publix on Saturday a week earlier, driving the husband's pickup truck. He followed her, pushing a shopping cart, watched her buy a couple whole chickens, onions, jalapeños, tomatoes, and garlic. He pictured chicken baked in a spicy red sauce, served over rice, washed down with cold beer, and started to get hungry.

Frank followed her to a mall off 95, watched her buy clothes for her kids at a Target. Then he followed her back to the trailer park. After seeing Jady Martinez several times, her looks had really grown on him. She was attractive. Thin black hair that hung to her shoulders, dark eyes, olive skin, and a nice, trim figure.

At the motel she changed into a uniform, a khaki-colored smock and a red bandana covering her hair. When the work day was over she changed back into street clothes. Today she wore a red print skirt and a yellow blouse. She made up her face with heavy lavender eye shadow and bright red lipstick. Frank imagined the musky smell of sweat on her body mixing with cheap perfume.

At seven forty the next morning he was parked on the side of the road about two hundred yards from the trailer park. No traffic. He opened the trunk, unscrewed the jack, jacked up the right rear side of the car, took out the spare and leaned it against the rear bumper, then took out a Dominican Montecristo and lit it with a plastic lighter, puffing hard against a slight breeze to get it going.

At seven forty-six he saw someone walk out of the trailer park, too far away to identify, although he would have bet it was Jady Martinez. That was confirmed a few minutes later. He could tell by the way she walked it was the maid. She was wearing an orange skirt and a white blouse, sunglasses and sandals, a straw bag over her shoulder.

He was fitting the spare in the trunk as she approached, glanced at her, and said, "Morning."

She stopped, seemed confused, gave him a puzzled look. He spun and wrapped his arms around her, picked her up, threw her in the trunk and slammed the lid closed. She had dropped her bag. He tossed it on the backseat and drove to the house he'd rented in Pompano, pulled in the garage and closed the door. The maid had been quiet for a while but now was shouting in Spanish.

*

It was the same man who had come to the motel, asking for Mr. Oak. There was something strange about him, something that made her nervous. Now Jady was so afraid she felt sick in her stomach. She never bothered anyone. She was a domestic, cleaned rooms all day and went home to her family.

Jady moved her hands across the smooth carpet lining the trunk and felt something metal, a tire-changing wrench. She turned on her back and held it in two hands. What did the man want with her? What was he going to do?

Only thirty minutes earlier Jady was thinking how lucky they were. She had a good job, and now Eduardo did also. The children were in school. They owned a 2004 Palm Harbor mobile home and lived in a nice place with many friends. She could feel the car slowing down, stopping. She heard the trunk pop open, saw the man standing behind the car, looking at her, metal shelves behind him. It looked like a garage. He reached in to grab her and she swung the wrench, the end glancing off the man's shoulder. He stepped back and held his arms up for protection. Jady swung the wrench at him again but he was out of range. She scrambled out of the trunk and he was on her, pulled the wrench out of her hands, punched her in the face. She went down on the cement floor, dazed, dizzy. He tied her wrists and ankles together with something and dragged her in the house.

EIGHT

Since the students had gone, cleaning the pool wasn't as much work. There were no beer cans or cigarette butts to pick up and none of the other guests were doing cannon balls, so the water level stayed constant. O'Clair skimmed a few bugs and palm fronds out of the water. It was eight o'clock and he could already feel the sun, hot and bright rising over the ocean. He straightened the lounge chairs and noticed one was missing, glanced at the beach and saw it where he'd found Gloria McMillen.

O'Clair had a bad feeling. He laid the skimmer down and walked to the gate, opened it, and went down the steps to the beach. The back of the lounge chair was tilted up and he could see someone through the vinyl slats, and then he was looking down at Jady in repose, legs straight, hands crossed on her stomach, ligature marks on her wrists, left cheek bruised, skin cool but no signs of rigor. So she'd only been dead a few hours. The sand around the lounge chair was smooth. The only footprints were his. O'Clair lifted her eyelids, looking into empty sockets, her eyes were gone just like Gloria McMillen and the two hookers in Detroit.

Jady's aunt had called last night, said her niece had left for work and never came home. O'Clair told her Jady never showed up. Now he knew why. He walked north thirty paces, looking for evidence, something, anything, glanced back at Jady. He moved toward the water, small waves breaking on shore, joggers running on the hard, wet sand. From this angle she looked like someone who'd fallen asleep on the beach. He went south and then west to the public access. That's how the killer had brought her down to the beach just as he had Gloria McMillen.

He moved back around to his property, stood behind the lounge chair and saw a footprint in the sand next to the stairs, the tread pattern of an athletic shoe. O'Clair took out his cell phone and called Holland. It rang for a while and went to voice mail. "Get over here. We've got another fatal."

"Don't tell me," Holland answered, sounding like he'd just woken up.

"Same MO. Get your team together." O'Clair put the phone in his shorts' pocket and walked up the steps to the patio. He saw Virginia coming toward him, moving past the pool, carrying two mugs of coffee. She handed one to O'Clair.

"What's going on?"

"You better sit down."

"Who's that?" Virginia said, looking at the lounge chair.

"He killed Jady."

"Oh my God."

Virginia steadied her mug on top of the deck rail, moved to O'Clair, and put her arms around him.

"She's got two little kids. Who'd do this?"

Someone was sending him a message—that was pretty clear now.

Virginia started down the steps to the beach. O'Clair grabbed her arm.

"It's a crime scene. You can't go down there." He sipped the coffee, hearing sirens in the distance, and then he heard tires screeching and car doors closing and the clap of boots on concrete, two uniforms, Diaz and Bush leading the

charge, EMS techs wheeling a gurney behind the patrol-
men, the evidence tech coming next. Holland bringing up
the rear, said, "Know who it is?"

"Jady Martinez," O'Clair said. "Our maid." He watched
Diaz and Bush secure the crime scene. The EMS techs pronounced Jady dead at eight twenty-three and left.

Holland leaned over the railing and said, "What do you
think the time of death was?"

"Four, four thirty, give or take," the evidence tech said.
"It's a guess."

Holland said, "Who gets killed at four in the morning?
She should've been home sleeping."

The evidence tech was shooting photographs, different
angles of the crime scene.

Holland said, "Why you think this character's dropping
bodies off on your beach?" He tapped a Marlboro out of the
pack and lit up.

"He's trying to get my attention," O'Clair said. "How you
think he's doing?"

Holland took a drag and blew out smoke. "You know
what happened?"

"She didn't come to work yesterday. Her aunt called last
night, asking was Jady working late. She'd left that morning
at the regular time. No one's seen her since."

"Someone did." Holland fieldstripped the cigarette and
put the butt in his sport coat pocket. "We've got an escort
and a maid, you think there's a connection?"

O'Clair was convinced it had something to do with him.
One body might be a coincidence, but not two. He decided
not to say anything about it to Holland. He needed time to
think.

"How well did you know her, the maid?"

"She showed up on time, worked her tail off and always

had a smile on her face. Clean up after people, see if you can do that."

"She was probably smoking something."

"Maybe she was just a happy person," O'Clair said. "Hard as that might be for you to believe. Jady's aunt said a friend, lives at the trailer park, saw a car on the road that morning; man changing a tire."

"Let's go talk to him," Holland said.

*

Frank watched the action, parked on the beach road. It was like TV, only better 'cause he was one of the characters, the bad guy, the antagonist. He got out of the car and walked down Briny Avenue to the public beach access, where he had carried the maid's body the night before. He stood with the gawkers near the life guard shack, watching the cops investigate the crime scene. They were looking for evidence but they weren't going to find anything. He watched O'Clair up on the patio talking to Holland. He had to believe O'Clair was getting concerned, wondering what was going on, these dead girls appearing in front of his motel, their eyes missing, just like a case O'Clair had investigated in Detroit in 2006.

*

He thought about the maid, her dark eyes watching him come in the bedroom. He had tied her spread-eagle to the bedposts. She was frantic, terrified, probably thought he was going to rape her. It didn't affect him. He didn't care, felt nothing. She'd been laying there for nineteen hours and now it was time. He put on a pair of rubber surgical gloves and stood, looking down at her.

She said, "Please, I have children."

"Don't worry. It's going to be okay." He took his phone out, framed her face and said, "Smile." He put the phone in his pocket, ripped a strip of duct tape off the role, put a strip over her mouth and pressed another piece over her nostrils. She panicked, pulling at the ropes, eyes wild, twisting and jerking her body, staring at him, eyes pleading. It was interesting to see what a person would do to stay alive.

When the maid stopped moving, he cut out her eyes with an X-Acto blade, severed the optic nerve and the retinal blood vessels. He untied the ropes, removed the duct tape and carried Jady Martinez to the garage and laid her in the trunk lined with Visqueen. It was nine minutes after four.

*

The man's name was Hector Bos. Like Jady, he was Honduran. A "Hondo" Holland had said on the way over, sounding like they were an inferior breed. O'Clair felt claustrophobic, three of them standing in the tiny kitchen of the man's mobile home. Bos, tan and wiry and missing a front tooth, was leaning against the stove, O'Clair and Holland were a few feet away leaning against a Formica counter. It was hot in the little room that smelled of sweat and garlic.

Holland said, "Where was the man changing the tire?"

Hector Bos pointed out the trailer window toward the road. "About halfway to the stop sign."

"What kind of car?" O'Clair tried to balance his big can on the stool.

"Silver Buick," Hector Bos said with a Spanish accent, "Lacrosse, I *thin.*"

Holland said, "Did you see the license tag?"

"No, the trunk was open."

O'Clair said, "Any idea what year?"

"The new one."

Holland said, "Did you see the man?"

"Just a quick look," Hector Bos said. "He was on the other side, squatting next to the jack, wearing sunglasses and a cap."

"You see Jady Martinez near the car?" O'Clair said.

"Not near the car. I see her walk out the park."

O'Clair said, "Anything else you remember?"

"I *thin* the man was smoking a cigar. He was smoking something."

Holland said, "Can you show us where it was?"

*

They followed the pickup, stopping behind it on the side of the road.

"This is it," Hector Bos said, getting out of his truck. "Man was changing the tire right here."

O'Clair could see tire tracks in the gravel and the square indentation made by the jack stand.

"Still need me, want me to stay?"

"No, you can go," Holland said, "and thanks."

"No problem. I hope you catch this guy," Hector Bos said, getting back into his truck that said *Broward Electrical* on the side, and under the name: *Prices that won't shock you.*

O'Clair watched Hector Bos make a U-turn heading back to the trailer park. He walked along the gravel shoulder, looking in the ditch at empty fast food wrappers. He stepped over the ditch into a dusty field that had once grown lettuce and was now mostly weeds. He walked deeper into the field and then changed course, moving parallel to the car. O'Clair went ten feet and saw a dark brown cigar nub about two inches long, the paper band still attached.

Holland saw him and said, "Got something?"

O'Clair glanced at Holland smoking a cigarette. "Could be." He crouched, stabbed the cigar with his pen tip and looked at it. The band said *Montecristo.*

"Think it's his?"

"How do I know?" O'Clair said. "If it is, maybe we get a saliva sample and if we're lucky his DNA's in the system." He went back to the car. Holland gave him a plastic evidence bag for the cigar.

"I was thinking, we should check the car rental places, see who rented a Buick Lacrosse in the past week or so, and get a list of Lacrosse owners in South Florida." It was getting hot. Holland took a folded bandana out of his pocket and wiped his forehead.

"You think he used his own car, or rented one? That'd be really dumb either way, wouldn't it? No, I think this boy stole it. I'd get a list of stolen Lacrosses in the area."

*

As it turned out the cigar butt didn't yield any positive results. No latents, which was a long shot anyway, and no DNA match from CODIS. Both Budget and Avis e-mailed Holland a list of customers who had rented Buicks at Fort Lauderdale and West Palm Beach airports over the past three weeks. There were sixty-six names, but sixty-two could be eliminated because the cars had been returned a few days before Jady had been abducted. The four remaining suspects were men in their mid-seventies and therefore removed from further consideration.

Holland was still compiling a list of Buick Lacrosse owners from the Florida Department of Motor Vehicles. He was also checking Lacrosses that had been stolen in South Florida.

*

In the meantime Howard Chilson had come to Holland's office for a polygraph, and the examiner determined that

Mr. Chilson's statement was truthful. O'Clair knew he wasn't their man. So now seventy-two hours after Gloria McMillen's murder, and thirty-six hours after Jady Martinez's they had very little—no suspects, no circumstance, and no probable cause. The case was wide open. His investigator's instinct told him again that these homicides were somehow related to Alvin Monroe, who he'd arrested for a double in 2006, Alvin serving consecutive life sentences without the possibility of parole. O'Clair believed there was something in Alvin's file that would help them find the Pompano killer.

NINE

Virginia didn't like it and O'Clair didn't either, but didn't think he had a choice. Two girls were murdered on his beach and he felt a responsibility to help solve the crimes.

"I don't want you to go."

"I think you should come with me. You can visit your mother."

"Who's going to run the place?"

Good question. They'd have to shut down. O'Clair had talked to Holland, who had agreed to keep an eye on Virginia. Holland had assured him he'd have Broward deputies checking on her during the day, and Holland would be there at night, sleeping on the couch.

Virginia said, "How long are you going to be gone?"

"Three days, four at the most," O'Clair said. "You can fix the disposal in unit six, and the air-conditioner in twelve is broken. I'll be back before you know it."

"I hope you don't find me on a lounge chair on the beach."

"Lock your door, and I'm going to give you this." He handed her a Glock 21. "Anyone comes in here at night, isn't Holland or one of the guests, point and shoot. You've got fifteen rounds, and remember the trigger and safety have to be depressed at the same time." O'Clair took the gun back and demonstrated the technique.

"Oh, okay. Somebody comes to kill me, shouldn't be a

problem remembering that. Look, I don't want to shoot someone. I don't even like to kill bugs."

"Try it." He handed her the gun and watched her get it on the second try. "And keep practicing. I want you to be able to do it without thinking about it."

Virginia tried it several more times and got it right every time.

"It's going to be all right," O'Clair said. "Holland or one of his men will be here every night till I come back, and sheriff's deputies will be patrolling regularly. If I thought you were in danger, you think I'd go?"

Virginia meant more to him than anyone in the world.

*

Virginia had been afraid at night since the Iraqi hit men had woken her up, looking for her sister, and beat the hell out of her. She didn't have to worry about the Iraqis anymore. O'Clair had seen to that, shot them both in a Chicago department store. And when he returned to Detroit, Virginia had moved in with him and they were still going strong.

She was definitely uneasy knowing there was a killer hanging around, leaving bodies in front of the motel, but felt better knowing Holland would be staying there at night.

Virginia booked O'Clair a Delta flight online, got him an aisle seat and printed his boarding pass. He packed the few warm clothes he hadn't gotten rid of or given away, including his blue overcoat that took up a third of the suitcase. It was seventeen degrees in the Motor City, going down to six degrees that night and they'd just gotten eight inches of snow. Going to Detroit wouldn't have been in his top hundred things to do if he didn't have to. When O'Clair moved to Florida, he wondered if he'd ever go back.

They got in bed early, watched TV, O'Clair thinking

about aspects of the Alvin Monroe case, picturing Alvin in the courtroom, wide-eyed, enjoying the notoriety the trial had brought him. Never seemed to grasp the consequences of what he'd done, or what was going to happen to him—that he was about to be convicted and sent away for the rest of his life. Alvin continued to smile at the jurors and the judge and grin at the prosecutor.

Virginia turned off the TV and slid over and kissed him. She liked to sleep in the nude and he had to admit it came in handy at times like this. She got on top of him and they made love slowly in the dark, and after, she slept with her soft body pressed against him.

*

O'Clair woke up early, looking at Virginia sleeping next to him, still not used to the idea that this good-looking girl was living with him. He'd say, "You should be with somebody younger, likes to do what you do."

She'd say, "I don't want somebody younger. I want you."

Their age difference was okay now, but Virginia would be forty-two when he was sixty, and it would only get worse from there. O'Clair decided to quit being a pussy and enjoy it. He got up, put on a pair of shorts and a T-shirt and went outside, walked past the pool, staring into the sun rising over the ocean, relieved not to see a lounge chair on the beach.

*

Homicide had moved from 1300 Beaubian downtown to Grand River and Lesure on the West Side, a brown brick three-story building that looked like a small manufacturing company. O'Clair parked in the visitors' lot and got out, shoes disappearing in the snow, felt the wind come through the overcoat, and buttoned it up to his neck. He looked up at the white, opaque sky and wished he was back in Pompano.

In the lobby, O'Clair gave his name to the black desk sergeant, forties, who looked vaguely familiar.

"What can I do for you?"

"I'm here to see DeAndre Jones," O'Clair said. DeAndre was a young, inexperienced investigator when they became partners in 2004.

"The Lieu, huh?"

It sounded strange to hear that, to think DeAndre was now the lieutenant in charge of homicide. O'Clair used to make fun of the bow ties he wore, telling DeAndre he was trying to look like Louis Farrakhan. Asking, did he join the Nation of Islam? Pissing DeAndre off 'cause he'd been brought up a God-fearing Baptist.

The desk sergeant said, "You a PO?"

"I was." What gave him away? Was it the beat-up overcoat, or the wear and tear on his face?

"What are you now?"

"Retired."

"You're lucky."

It didn't have anything to do with luck. You put in your time you could retire, collect a pension. DeAndre came through the door that said *No Admittance*, wearing a light blue dress shirt and a striped designer tie—he'd always been stylish, a Smith & Wesson .40 in a black holster on his hip, DeAndre flashing that megawatt smile. Now O'Clair got it, he was the new breed, the smart, good-looking inner city cop.

"Make way for the Lieu," O'Clair said. "So you're the top dog, huh?"

"You believe that? Department recognizes talent after all." DeAndre grinned. "Look at you, Oak, looking good. I always heard retirement gave a man some years back and I can see it's true. Come in, let me show you around."

DeAndre took him into a big space divided by walls lined with cubicles. It seemed bigger than it was because the ceiling went up two stories. With a PC at every workstation, homicide looked a lot more orderly and professional. "I miss the charm of 1300," O'Clair said.

"Oh, that what you call it? Yeah, right," DeAndre said, getting it, grinning. "Sergeant O'Clair has not lost his sense of humor, I see."

DeAndre took him around, introduced him to the young investigators, the black dudes in their three-piece suits and natural sense of style, better dressed than the white guys. It had always been that way.

O'Clair recognized Charles McKoy, his partner from 1998 to 2004, a lean six-footer wearing a Borsalino with a feather on the side and a black cashmere overcoat. "I thought you retired."

"They were shorthanded," Charles said. "Asked me to help out, now going on two years. What're you doing here?"

"Checking up on homicide investigators."

Charles grinned. "You miss it, huh? I heard you was an innkeeper now, bought a motel in Florida. Was going to bring Squad Three down for spring break." He paused. "So what you doing up here, miss the weather, come to Detroit in January?"

O'Clair was thinking of their last case together. A twenty-year-old Latino male, Domingo Rosario had been stabbed in the back four times. A witness saw him running down Twenty-Third Street in Mexican Town. Domingo fell on the sidewalk and died. Carol Black was the homicide investigator at the scene. Charles and O'Clair were assigned the case the next morning. Carol had said, "Based on how

Domingo was dressed and the fact he was wearing eye makeup, I thought he might be gay."

Charles had said, "Might be gay. See the motherfucker's web site? He's stretched out on a bed naked, says, *Bend Me Over*." Charles had smiled. "I'd say he's gay as the day is long."

DeAndre had the only office in homicide. It was on the second floor. O'Clair went up, walked in and closed the door.

"OK," DeAndre said. "Tell me what's going on."

O'Clair started with Gloria McMillen and moved onto Jady Martinez, giving details of the homicides and backgrounds on the girls.

"And you think this has something to do with Alvin Monroe?"

"Two women murdered, had their eyes cut out, bodies placed on the beach right behind the motel."

"Cause of death isn't even close," DeAndre said. "Alvin, as you may recall, used a revolver, shot each one in the head first."

"Maybe it's a friend of Alvin's or someone who roomed with him," O'Clair said. "Got released. Alvin's paying him to continue his work."

"Paying him with what? Alvin doesn't have any money."

"He still at Ionia?"

"Going to be there the next two hundred and four years."

"Or maybe Alvin's the wrong guy," O'Clair said.

"You serious? The evidence was there. We had probable cause and a shitload of circumstance. Everything pointed to him as I recall."

"I know," O'Clair said. "I remember telling you I'd never seen so much evidence. It seemed too perfect." Alvin had taken a polygraph and passed, not that O'Clair had much faith in the test. Looking back, maybe he'd passed 'cause he was innocent. "What do you remember about the case?"

"I remember Peggy King, the way we found her, naked, shot in the head, body starting to decomp. I remember the heat and the smell. That stench that gets on you, your hair, your clothes. I smelled that smell for a couple days."

O'Clair said, "And so many flies, it was like something out of the *Ten Commandments*. I thought Moses was going to appear." He paused. "I want to go through the file, see if maybe we missed something, or overlooked something."

DeAndre handed O'Clair a pile of accordion folders. "Here you go. Been through 'em a hundred times. I don't know what you're going to find."

O'Clair took everything to a conference room on the first floor, folded his overcoat across the back of a chair, and sat down. He opened the first folder and slid out the files. Each one labeled; Investigator's Report, Scene Photos, Victim, Statements, Morgue Photos, Evidence, Witnesses, Intel, Cell Phone. He took out the investigator's report and started to read his crime scene summary in clean Catholic-grade-school cursive that Sister Mary Andrews would've been proud of.

Complainant #2 Peggy Miller-King

Height: 5' 6", Weight: 147, Hair: Brown, Eye Color: Unknown,

DOB: 6-7-75, SSN: 367-54-0229, Age: 36, Sex: F

Police were dispatched to 3670 Bethune on a fatal shooting. At the scene and securing were several members of the central district. On the scene and in charge from Homicide section were Sergeant O'Clair, badge #416 and Ofc. Jones badge #996

Scene:

The scene takes place inside the deceased Peggy Miller-King's apartment. The apartment building sits on the north side of Bethune just west of Churchill. This is a residential neighborhood in the city of Detroit. The body of the deceased is faceup, arms bent slightly at the elbows, bare breasts pancaked on her chest. Body resting on the open floor in a pool of coagulated blood. Head north, feet south, mouth open, eyes closed. Her clothes were lying around the room: skirt in the foyer, blouse in the hallway leading to the bed-room, sandals next to the couch. Single gunshot wound through-and-through. Bullet entered the forehead and exited out through the parietal lobe, blowing out a portion of brain and skull. Spatter is consistent with single shot to the head. The shooting was fatal. Manner of death was ruled to be homicide. The deceased was pronounced dead at 5:45 p.m., August 7, 2006. The shooter used a pillow to muffle the gunshot. The pillow was next to the body, and was scorched with gun-powder residue. There was a spent .38 casing on the floor. Peggy Miller-King was conveyed to the Wayne County Medical Examiner's Office. Sergeant O'Clair will testify to his observations.

Work requested:

Photographs and a search for evidence of firearms, trace evidence prints, and blood evi-dence.

O'Clair studied the crime scene photos, the gritty reality popping in his head like flash bulbs. The photos taken by the medical examiner showed the little red entrance wound in Peggy's forehead in one color print, and the back of her head blown apart in another. A third photo showed close-ups of ligature marks on her wrists.

They had examined Peggy's clothes, scrapings from her fingernails for DNA or blood typing. The last photograph showed her eyes had been removed. The left socket was empty. The right one had a piece of razor blade that had broken off.

Evidence:

He looked at the submitted evidence: Spent casing, .38 Spl + p, head stamped "R – P" semi-jacketed hollow point cartridge. Spent slug, frag found in the living room wall. Pubic hairs thought to be those of an African American were found on the deceased's chest and back.

Laboratory Analysis:

A microscopic comparison was conducted on the spent casing, .38. It was compared to the casing found at Cyntree Johnson's crime scene, and was determined that both casings were fired from the same weapon and are caliber compatible to fired projectiles on lab sheet F07-0463E. All evidence was sent to Property Section pending recovery of a suspected weapon. There was a note on the bottom of the page that said: *Spent casing was fired from an SW revolver. Why did shooter remove and discard a spent casing at crime scene?*

*

O'Clair remembered questioning Peggy's neighbor, Lovette Jacobs. He took her Q&A out of the Statement File.

> Q: Did you hear anything unusual this afternoon or evening?
> A: I was in the shower, heard what I believe was fireworks next door.

Q: Fireworks, huh? That common? You hear fireworks on a regular basis?
A: No. (She gave him a blank look.)

Q: Did you knock on your neighbor's door and investigate?
A: It stop.

Q: Were you friends with the deceased?
A: Who?

Q: Your neighbor, Peggy.
A: I seen her around.

Q: Ever hang out with her?
A: No.

Q: What do you do for a living?
A: I's currently unemployed.

Q: What was your last job?
A: Manicurist. Shontee's Nail Affair.

Q: When's the last time you saw Peggy?
A: S'morning. Said she was goin' down to the Westin, what she went down to and returned.

Q: So you saw her this afternoon?
A: Uh-huh.

Q: What time was that?
A: 'Round 5:30.

Q: Do you remember seeing anyone else on your floor that afternoon or evening?
A: Is only two of us. (There were two vacant apartments.)

Q: No one, you're sure?
A: 'Cept for Pinball.

Q: Who's Pinball?
A: He the plumber.

Q: What's his real name?
A: Alvin something. Monroe, I think.

Q: Know where Alvin Monroe lives?
A: (Lovette Jacobs shook her head.)

TEN

Detroit 2006.

O'Clair had looked up Alvin's address through the Department of Motor Vehicles, a house on Edison Avenue in the historic Boston-Edison neighborhood. It was an impressive three-story colonial. O'Clair and DeAndre drove over from 1300 and parked in front. Here's how O'Clair remembered the scene:

He knocked on the front door, it opened and a white guy, mid-thirties with dark hair and a big nose was standing there. O'Clair flashed his shield and introduced them. Henry Cooper stood in the opening, staring at them.

"Is Alvin here?"

"Alvin who?"

"Alvin Monroe, goes by Pinball."

"Why would he be here?"

"He doesn't live here?"

"Are you kidding?"

"But you know him."

"He's one of my tenants. I own a building on Cass." Cooper was calm, looking O'Clair in the eye. "What'd he do?"

O'Clair said, "Why would he have your address on his driver's license?"

"Maybe he's trying to impress someone."

DeAndre said, "What's he do?"

"He's a plumber," Cooper said, looking at O'Clair. "I give him a place to live, he fixes the plumbing problems in my buildings."

It was August. O'Clair wiped sweat off his forehead with a hanky. "Why's he called Pinball?"

"You'll have to ask him. Maybe he's crazy, off the wall, or maybe he likes playing it. You know how it works. Sometimes it's literal, sometimes it means something else. Someone gave him the name either to be funny or ironical."

O'Clair said, "How many buildings do you own?"

"Two," Henry Cooper said. "The one on Cass and another on Bethune. Both residential apartments."

DeAndre said, "Mr. Cooper, do you know a woman named Cyntree Johnson, lived at the Bonaparte Apartments?"

"Doesn't ring a bell, but I don't pay attention to who my tenants are. I leave that to the manager."

"She was found murdered in her apartment a week ago," O'Clair said.

"I do remember that."

Now it was DeAndre's turn.

"How about Peggy Miller-King, Mr. Cooper?"

"Another tragedy," Cooper said, no expression. "I read about it in the paper."

O'Clair said, "Why do you think someone's killing your tenants?"

"Maybe they haven't been paying their rent." Cooper grinned, glancing first at O'Clair and then DeAndre. "No, I'm sorry, that wasn't appropriate under the circumstances."

*

"What you make of Cooper?" DeAndre said when they were in the car driving back to homicide.

"I didn't care for the man. Something odd about him."

"Think he knows anything?"

"Why would he be involved?"

"I don't know, but he is one strange dude."

"I'm more interested in Alvin. He did eighteen months in Jackson for aggravated assault, beat up a prostitute named Lakisha Brewer. Pinball liked to get rough with the ladies." O'Clair paused. "The girl that testified against Alvin—not the victim, but another hooker named Cyntree Johnson—said she saw the whole thing, and based on the strength of her testimony Alvin Monroe had been convicted."

"Looking for motive? Don't have to look far."

O'Clair had met Peggy Miller-King after Cynny'd been murdered. Word on the street, they were friends. He picked her up walking down Woodward Avenue near Grand Boulevard, Peggy in a white blouse and one of her trademark short plaid skirts—Leggy Peggy—O'Clair thinking, *With legs like that, she should drop the hemline to her shoe tops.* O'Clair pulled the car over to the curb, got out and introduced himself, said he wanted to talk to her.

"About what?"

"Get in, you'll find out."

"Am I under arrest?"

"No, but it can be arranged."

They went to a Starbucks, guys checking out Peggy in the short skirt with her big legs as they got their drinks—black coffee for him, Frappuccino for her—and sat at a table. Black dudes looking at her, probably thinking: *baby got back. Big legs, big booty.*

O'Clair said, "You always dress like this?"

"No, I usually wear a blazer. I'm the only Detroit streetwalker who buys their clothes at Ann Taylor. Is that why you're here, do you want to talk about women's fashions?"

Peg didn't look so good up close. She had black eyeliner

circling bloodshot eyes, dilated pupils. Her nose was bruised and running and she wiped it with the back of her hand and wiped the hand on her skirt under the table. Peggy was a mess. "What happened to your nose?"

"A john broke it."

"Why didn't you call the police?"

"And say what, I had a client get out of hand?" Peggy sipped her cold coffee, hands on the bottle like she was trying to cool off.

"Why not?"

"What planet are you living on?"

"Was he a regular?"

"I'd been with him a couple times before."

"You don't know his name, do you?"

"Frank."

"Frank what?"

"He didn't say."

"What'd he look like?"

"White, five eleven, thirty-something, dark hair."

"What set him off?"

"I wouldn't pose."

"What do you mean?"

"He wanted to take pictures and I didn't want him to. So he hit me a few times and left. I couldn't work for a couple weeks. I looked like I'd been in a prizefight." Peggy wiped her runny nose again this time with a napkin.

"Where'd this happen?"

"The Viking Motel on Grand River."

"Can you remember the date?"

"It was a few weeks ago."

O'Clair took out a black-and-white crime scene photo of Cynny Johnson, shot once in the forehead with a large caliber weapon, lying in a pool of blood. "Know who did this?"

Peggy stared at the photograph, eyes glued to it, and

shook her head. O'Clair showed her a photo of Alvin Monroe and she made a face.

"You don't like him, I can see that."

"He's the plumber that takes care of our building. Comes around, has his own key. He came to my apartment one night, wanted a freebie. I told him to take a hike."

"You think Alvin killed Cynny?"

"No idea."

"Ever see Alvin with a gun?"

"Not that I recall."

"When did you get hooked on crack?"

"Two years ago. This young guy I worked with at Deloitte & Touche invited me to a concert at the Magic Stick, a crazy group from New York, the Yeah Yeah Yeahs. I was trying to broaden my horizons. How do you think I did?"

O'Clair sipped his coffee. "You were an accountant?"

"Uh-huh. Companies hired us to audit their books, make sure they were Sarbanes-Oxley compliant."

"What's that?"

"It's also known as the Public Company Accounting Reform and Investor Protection Act. It was established after the Enron scandal to prevent corporate fraud. It's named after the two guys who sponsored it. Paul Sarbanes, a senator from Maryland, and Michael Oxley, a US Representative from Ohio."

O'Clair was sorry he'd asked. The thought of it was so boring his brain hurt. "No wonder you wanted to get out, have a few drinks."

"Jeff, the young guy who worked for me, took out a pipe before the concert and asked if I wanted to get high. He said, 'Try it, you'll like it.' That was the understatement of the century. It was all downhill from there."

"Where's your husband?"

"We're divorced. He married the girl he should've married in the first place. Mousey little thing named Helen who does what she's told. They're perfect for each other."

"What about your job?"

"Stay up all night freebasing, your accounting skills start to diminish. Once I got into smoking crack I lasted about three weeks at Deloitte & Touche. I got a couple warnings and said, fuck it."

"Why didn't you go to rehab?"

"I didn't want to."

"You prefer this life, huh? Banging street trash so you can get your fix."

"I must 'cause I've been at it going on two and a half years." Peggy sipped the Frappuccino. "When I'm strung out, dope sick, I'd fuck a dog with anthrax to cop."

"You miss accounting?"

"I do at times, I liked it. But I like getting high a lot more."

O'Clair felt sorry for her. "Get any more surprise visits, call me."

Next time O'Clair saw Peggy she was dead.

He pulled out the Q&A interview he had with Peggy's husband, Dick King. He remembered driving out to the King residence on Bradway in Bloomfield Village. Alvin Monroe was high up on the list of suspects, but when a wife is murdered the husband is always number one.

Dick King was a GM executive in charge of marketing for the Chevy Lumina, whatever that was. Little guy, about five eight, 150 pounds. O'Clair couldn't picture Dick and Peggy together. She would've crushed him with those massive thighs. King led him into a formal living room that looked like it had been decorated by a woman. They sat in chairs upholstered in green floral.

*

Q: When's the last time you saw Peggy?
A: Mid-May. She came to the house to pick up some of her things I had boxed and put in the basement. She looked like death and smelled awful.

Q: Do you know where she lives?
A: An apartment, a dump behind Henry Ford Hospital, Bethune at Churchill.

Q: Did you go see her?
A: I tried to help her, tried to get her to go to rehab. She laughed at me.

Q: When was that?
A: 2004. Peggy had been gone about a month.

Q: How long were you married?
A: Fourteen years. One day everything was fine, the next day she was addicted to crack. The first time she disappeared, Peggy said she was going to the gas station and came home three days later.

Q: What did you do?
A: Called the police.

Q: What did you say when she came home?
A: The obvious. Where have you been? Why didn't you call me? I've been worried to death.

Q: She tell you anything?
A: She looked at me and said, 'I'm going to bed.' (King paused.) A week later we were at my niece's birthday party. We ran out of ice cream. Peggy volunteered to go and never came back to the party. I tried her cell, she didn't answer. Came home a week later in the same outfit she was wearing at the party. I asked where the ice cream was. She didn't get it. I asked where she'd

been. She couldn't remember, and it got worse from
there. I got the Merrill Lynch statement and saw ATM
cash withdrawals totaling $20,000. We had a joint cash
management account. I said ,'What did you spend all
that money on?' She looked at me with glassy, bloodshot eyes, and didn't seem to know what I was talking
about.

Q: When did you file for divorce?
A: About a month later. I hired a private detective to
follow her for a few days. She spent most of her time in
one crack house or another.

Q: Do you think it's odd Peggy died before the divorce
was final?
A: Now we're getting to the real reason you're here.
OK. Do I think it's odd? I think the whole thing's odd. I
think it's odd Peggy started smoking crack cocaine, got
fired from her job, and left me. What're you alluding
to? You think I had her killed so I wouldn't have to split
the assets with her? I didn't care about the money. I'd
written her off and moved on.

Q: Do you own an X-Acto knife, Mr. King?

*

As it turned out he did, but O'Clair was convinced Dick
King had nothing to do with the death of his ex-wife. He
closed the file and opened the folder that said, *Cyntree Johnson*, the first murdered prostitute. Cynny was five six, 170
pounds—heavy for a hooker. There were three mug shots
of her going back ten years—different looks and hair styles.
She lived in the same apartment building as Peggy. He
scanned the investigator's report, list of evidence, laboratory analysis, witnesses.

The first photo, taken by the medical examiner, showed
Cynny's face in close-up, a little hole in the center of her

forehead, severe trauma to the back of her head like someone put an explosive device inside her skull. Cyntree's hands
had been bound together in front. There were ligature
marks on her wrists, the marks consistent with Peggy and
the two girls in Florida.

O'Clair closed that file and opened one that said, *Antoine
Burnett* on the side. Antoine had found Cyntree Johnson's
body and called the police. Antoine was the manager of the
Bonaparte Apartment building. He was also a preacher at
the Sweet Kingdom Church of God. O'Clair had questioned
him briefly at the crime scene, and then stopped by his
church in the basement of an old office building on West
Grand Boulevard—for Sunday services.

O'Clair had grown up watching Oral Roberts on TV.
Oral would place his hand on the head of a stuttering boy
and cure him. "Heal in the name of the Lord," or something
like that, and the stuttering boy started talking with the
assurance of a newscaster.

Preacher Burnett didn't heal people. He told his congregation of sixty God-fearing souls to: 'Go into all the
world and preach the gospel to every creature. He who
believes and is baptized will be saved, but he who does not
believe will be condemned. And these signs follow those
who believe: In my name they will cast out demons; they
will speak with new tongues; they will take up serpents, and
if they drink anything deadly it will by no means hurt them;
they will lay hands on the sick and they will recover.' Mark
16:15–19.

"And do you know why? Because Jesus said so."

Preacher Burnett would ask questions and the answer
was always: 'Because Jesus said so.' Antoine was short and
bald, with a gap-toothed smile and a lot of charisma.

After the service, O'Clair walked up to the pulpit as the
congregation was making its way to the back of the room.

"Hey, Antoine, who do you see when you look in the mirror?"

"I see a man of God. I see a man for others."

"You see any dead prostitutes?"

"I feel the loss of these women of the street. 'Israelites are warned not to let their daughters get into prostitution lest they be punished by death.' Leviticus 19:29. I counseled those ladies. I tried to help them. I believe, had I been successful, two daughters of Jesus would be alive today. I say this with a heavy heart."

Antoine was laying it on thick, looking like he was carrying the weight of the world on those stocky shoulders.

O'Clair said, "Own a firearm preacher?"

Antoine's face was fixed like granite. "Are you making light of this, Detective?"

"Ever been convicted of a crime?" O'Clair had dug deep on Antoine, found out about his previous life. "Still go by Wiggy?" His street name when he was a member of the Chambers Brothers' organization, selling heroin in the projects.

"The Lord knocked me down, shone a light from heaven and said, 'Antoine, Antoine, why persecutist thou me?'"

"It didn't have anything to do with the fact that you were incarcerated for thirty months?"

"People change. That, Detective, is all I'll say on the matter. If you'll excuse me I have a baptism."

Antoine's day job was managing the Bonaparte Apartment building. The preacher lived in a first-floor apartment with his wife, Rosie, an RN at Henry Ford Hospital. Rosie had provided an alibi for Antoine, saying he'd been with her when the two prostitutes were killed. O'Clair had considered Antoine Burnett a suspect. Antoine knew the two ladies, knew their habits, their routines, lived in close proximity. What O'Clair was missing was a motive and a weapon.

He closed the file.

On a piece of note paper, O'Clair wrote:

Who had access?
Antoine Burnett.
Alvin Monroe.
Henry Cooper.

Who had motive?
Dick King.

ELEVEN

Detroit 2006.

O'Clair knocked on the apartment door, heavy wood showing the cracks and gouges of age, DeAndre next to him in a white shirt, striped bow tie, and a gray summer-weight Brooks Brothers suit. It was hot, steamy on August 18.

Alvin Monroe opened the door and O'Clair flashed his shield, identified himself, gave his rank and DeAndre's.

"What's this about?" Alvin said, standing in the open door, filling the space with his skinny frame. Alvin was a nervous little guy, the size of a lightweight, five seven, one thirty-five, a light-skinned black guy with a sparse mustache and wet, oily hair combed back, wearing a denim shirt with the sleeves cut off, showing tat-covered arms.

O'Clair showed him a shot of Peggy taken from the Deloitte & Touche Annual Report, Peggy with short hair, wearing a blazer, taken two years earlier. He could hear a TV on in the apartment.

"That one of the hookers was killed?"

"How do you know she was a hooker?"

"I seen her on the street selling her pussy."

"Ever buy her services?"

"Don't pay for it," Alvin said. "Don't have to."

DeAndre said, "You're a ladies' man, huh, Alvin?"

"Got it going on or you don't," Alvin said. "What can I say?"

DeAndre said, "Why don't you invite us in, we'll talk."

"What you think we doin'?"

"Got something to hide?" O'Clair took a half step over the threshold.

"Want to come in? Come the fuck in."

O'Clair said, "What do you prefer, Alvin or Pinball?"

"Whatever, man," Alvin said, sounding Hispanic now.

O'Clair thought of Cheech and Chong, Alvin sounding like them but without the mellow weed buzz. "Alvin, where'd you get the accent at?"

"What accent? Man, this how I talk."

"You know Cyntree Johnson and Peggy Miller-King?"

"I fix their plumbing, clean their pipes."

O'Clair thought it sounded like the punchline to a dirty joke.

Alvin swung the door open. There was a white Styrofoam container on a TV table positioned next to a plaid couch that had seen better days. *Jeopardy* was on an old nineteen-inch Sony across the room. The meal on the TV table smelled like pad thai.

"You did two and a half years for aggravated assault, I understand," O'Clair said, "beat up a hooker named Lakisha Brewer."

"That's right," Alvin said. "Did my time, paid for my crime."

"You got out and the witness that testified against you, Cyntree Johnson, was murdered. Think that's strange?"

"No, I think hooking's a high-risk profession." Alvin sat on the couch, picked up his fork, and started to eat.

"You're on record as saying you were going to get her," O'Clair said.

"Heat of the moment," Alvin said. "Had thirty months to cool off."

DeAndre said, "Mind if we look around?"

"Got a warrant?"

DeAndre shook his head.

"Then I guess you better go," Alvin said, rolling his fork through Asian noodles, trying to see the TV, but DeAndre was in the way. "You mind?"

They sat in the Plymouth on Cass, half a block from Alvin's building. One thing O'Clair knew, Alvin was a partier, went out drinking several nights a week.

"If he's our man," DeAndre said, "he doesn't fit the profile. See, Alvin's forty-four, has a regular job. Most serial killers are white motherfuckers in their twenties and thirties."

"So he's an exception to the rule," O'Clair said.

"Eighty-five percent are Caucasian. That's a lot of fucked-up white dudes." DeAndre glanced at him from behind the wheel. "What do you know about Alvin's past? Most serial killers come from dysfunctional families, been abused, did too many drugs or drank too much."

"Alvin never knew his father," O'Clair said. "His mother made him sleep in the basement so he wouldn't molest his younger sister."

"There you go," DeAndre said. "The pre-crime stressor. The thing that turned the man into a crazed killer."

"Come on," O'Clair said. "I slept in the basement too; I'm not going around killing people."

"How you know this about Alvin?"

"He did time for assault. It's in the file. Analysis from the psychiatrist who evaluated him."

"Know that famous FBI profiler?"

O'Clair nodded but couldn't think of his name.

"He says when you look at childhood development characteristics of serial killers—three things keep coming up. They daydream all the time, they beat off, and they're isolated, alone and such."

"What's that have to do with it?"

"Young alone dudes create their own fantasy world."

O'Clair said, "How do you know so much about serial killers?"

"I got an MA in psychology at Wayne State two years ago."

O'Clair saw Alvin come out of the building and head down Cass toward Bookie's. "See him?" O'Clair said.

*

They stood in front of Alvin's apartment door again.

O'Clair saw DeAndre looking at him. "Why don't we do it right, get a warrant?"

"I've got a warrant right here," O'Clair said, taking a pick out of the pocket of his Sears wash 'n' wear suit coat.

DeAndre said, "Sarge, sure you want to do that?"

"Do what?" O'Clair slid the pick in the lock.

"We find something," DeAndre said, "it's not going to hold up in court. We're violating Alvin's rights."

O'Clair glanced at his spit-shined, dry-cleaned partner. "How about the dead girls, think their rights were violated?" He went back to work, angling the pick, finding the pin, and releasing the lock. O'Clair drew the Glock from a holster on his left hip and watched DeAndre draw his. He bumped the door open with his hip, going primary into the apartment, two hands on the weapon, barrel pointed at the ceiling.

In the bathroom, O'Clair found hair samples in the shower drain, picked them up with tweezers and put them in a small plastic evidence bag. There was a pubic hair on the rim of the toilet seat. O'Clair put it in a second evidence bag.

"Sarge, you better come in here, take a look at this,"

DeAndre called from the other room. O'Clair walked in the living room. DeAndre was sitting at the desk, rubber surgical gloves on, shuffling through polaroids, shots of Cynny and Peggy, dead at the scenes.

"Souvenirs," DeAndre said, turning the swivel chair toward O'Clair. "Helps the man relive his erotic sensations of violence in case his memory starts to go."

"Find any eyeballs?"

"No, but I found this," DeAndre said, holding up an X-Acto knife. "Box of blades with a few missing."

He handed the box to O'Clair and O'Clair shook one out, an angled silver blade that looked like a copy of the one he'd seen in Peggy Miller-King's eye socket. "Better put it back. We need a warrant."

DeAndre said, "Do I hear an echo?"

"I know a judge who might be sympathetic to our cause."

"We know what we've got," DeAndre said. "It's a wrap. Let's go get the motherfucker, get the bitch."

When he got excited, buttoned-up, college-educated DeAndre talked like he was back on the street. It made sense: find Alvin and hold him till they could secure a warrant.

They started at Bookie's, O'Clair standing at one end of the bar, DeAndre at the other end. O'Clair scanned the drinkers sitting there, six black men, four white men, and two black women—everyone hunched over shots of whiskey and vodka and bottles of beer—everyone smoking. He didn't see Alvin.

The bartender, a big grizzled white dude wearing a lot of turquoise and silver said, "What can I get you?"

O'Clair held up a photo. "Seen Alvin?"

"Not so far," the bartender said.

"When's the last time you saw him?"

"Yesterday afternoon. You a cop?"

O'Clair handed the bartender a card. "He comes back, call me."

"What'd he do?"

*

They went to Leftie's and Harry's and Honest John's. No sign of Alvin and no one had seen him for a day or so. They drove back to the apartment building, parked across the street, and waited.

"I was thinking about the photos of the dead girls. Alvin sees himself as powerful and controlling—thinks he has the power of life and death. Man's a plumber. Murdering these girls is the only power he's ever had, and he likes it. It feels good."

O'Clair saw someone walking on the sidewalk across the street. "I think that's our man."

DeAndre was turned in the driver's seat, looking out the side window.

*

When Alvin got within thirty feet of the entrance to the apartment building, he stopped and glanced at them in the unmarked, stripped-down Plymouth. It was Alvin Monroe, no mistake. Alvin had made them and took off running the way he'd come. DeAndre started the car, put it in gear, looking in the side mirror, waiting for traffic on Cass to clear, and made a U-turn. O'Clair saw Alvin climb a section of chain-link fence between two buildings and run down the alley. DeAndre stopped the car, glanced O'Clair.

"I'm going after him."

O'Clair, with his bad knee, couldn't run. He'd been shot by a bank robber, the nine-millimeter round shattering his knee cap. DeAndre, a former basketball standout at Pershing, took off after Alvin.

O'Clair got behind the wheel, went right on a residential street, colonials built in the twenties, some burned out and abandoned, others looking well-maintained, drove to the next block and took a left, just going by feel now. There were lights on in the houses on both sides of the street. O'Clair took out his cell phone, punched in a number. "Where the hell're you at?"

"Adelade, second block, east between the houses," DeAndre whispered. "Watch yourself, he's got a gun."

O'Clair turned around and drove back two blocks to Adelade, took a right and turned off the lights, creeping now. "I'm on the street, where are you at?"

"In back," DeAndre whispered. "Five, six houses from the corner."

"Where's Alvin?"

"Don't know. Lost him."

"I'm coming in," O'Clair said.

He got out of the car with a flashlight, slid it in his pants' pocket, drew the Glock, and moved toward the houses that were close together, maybe fifteen feet between them. One looked abandoned, the other one had first-floor lights on. It was nine-forty and almost dark. O'Clair felt claustrophobic moving in the narrow space between the houses, could hear himself breathing, could feel his pulse speeding up. Then he was in the backyard behind the houses, looked both ways, saw DeAndre approaching from the south, his silhouette against the faint glare of a quarter-moon. O'Clair signaled his partner and went north, a little unsteady on his bad knee, two hands on the Glock.

There was a tool shed behind the next house that had several broken windows and looked abandoned. He saw a foot in an athletic shoe sticking out from behind the shed. O'Clair aimed the Glock and said, "Alvin drop your gun."

"I do that, you're goin' to shoot me," Alvin Monroe said with a criminal's skewed logic.

"You don't throw it out I'm going to shoot you."

"I didn't do nothin'," Alvin said, sounding dumb.

"Then you've got nothing to worry about."

"Why's you comin' after me?"

"We want to talk," O'Clair said. "Give me the gun."

"Don't trust cops."

"Be straight with us," O'Clair said, "we'll be straight with you."

"Yeah, I heard that before."

DeAndre came up behind him, two hands on his weapon. O'Clair pointed to the shed.

Alvin said, "Who that?"

"My partner," O'Clair said. "You want to live or you want to die? It's up to you."

"Live." Alvin Monroe said it like he meant it.

"Throw out your weapon. Thumb and index finger on the grip."

"OK. Don't shoot."

O'Clair saw one of Alvin's arms come out and drop the gun on the hard, dry grass. Now Alvin Monroe stepped out from behind the shed. O'Clair aimed the flashlight, put the high beam on his face, saw him squint and bring a hand up to shade his eyes. "Get that out my face," Alvin said. He stumbled and went down.

O'Clair said, "Alvin, are you drunk?"

DeAndre moved on him, Alvin accepting the cuffs, hands behind his back, knowing from experience what was going to happen.

DeAndre said, "Gonna take my man to the car."

"It's two houses back. Here you go." O'Clair threw him

the keys and watched him escort Alvin between the houses. O'Clair swept the flashlight beam across the ground, held on Alvin's revolver that looked like a .38 or a .357. He bent over, slid a pen through the trigger guard, picked it up, and dropped the gun in his sport coat pocket. Now O'Clair shined the light around the outside of the shed and then behind it.

There was something on the ground next to the concrete foundation. O'Clair crouched and picked it up, a purple velvet Crown Royal bag with a drawstring top. He touched the bottom of the bag. There was something in it. He unloosened the string and pulled it open. At first he thought he was looking at marbles until he realized they were eyeballs staring at him.

TWELVE

Detroit 2006.

O'Clair and DeAndre watched Alvin Monroe through the two-way mirror, Alvin sitting at a table in an interrogation room.

"Now I know why they call the motherfucker Pinball, 'cause he was bouncing all over the place. Why'd he stop and hide? Should've kept going, he'd have gotten away."

O'Clair looked at Alvin. He seemed agitated, restless in the room with no windows.

DeAndre said, "Got a few things on his mind, you think?"

O'Clair said, "Murderers are usually relaxed, relieved they've been caught. You've seen 'em fall asleep, haven't you?"

"Not Alvin. Kills the ladies, thinks he's God."

"I get that, but why'd he take the eyes?"

"Souvenirs," DeAndre said. "Eyes must be important for some reason—something from his past."

"I had a whacko one time, killed four women, cut off their nipples," O'Clair said.

"Same kind of thing," DeAndre said straightening his bow tie in the mirrored glass. "Ready?"

O'Clair moved toward the door. They went into the interrogation room and sat across the table from Alvin.

"I'm Detective O'Clair, I want to ask you a few questions."

Alvin glanced at him with vacant eyes.

"How tall are you?" Start with some easy ones, get him loosened up.

"I be five feet nine inches in height."

O'Clair knew from Alvin's sheet he was only five seven and that was being generous. "How much you weigh?"

"Oh, you know, like one thirty or so."

"What's your address?"

"Nine four two Cass Avenue."

"Date of birth?"

"July the eighth, 1969."

"My man's an Aries," DeAndre said. "Enthusiastic and confident, dynamic and quick-witted, that describe you, Alvin?"

"Uh-huh," Alvin said, nodding, trying it out.

O'Clair said, "Why don't you do yourself a favor, Alvin, clear your head? Tell us what happened."

"What happened to what?" Alvin wouldn't look at O'Clair, glanced across the room, his expression blank.

O'Clair said, "Why do you think you're here? If you're in the game, you're fair fucking game."

"I'm not the person you think I am, you know? 'Cause I obey the law. I'm law-abiding." Alvin slumped down in the chair like he was driving a lowrider.

O'Clair stared at the tats on his arms sticking out of the sleeveless denim shirt, blue ink, words and symbols etched into light brown skin.

"You're law-abiding, huh? That's why you did thirty months for aggravated assault?" DeAndre getting heavy with him.

"I blame that on the love bug," Alvin Monroe said, like it was a secret he'd never told anyone.

DeAndre said, "What's that mean, you had a thing for Lakisha Brewer?"

"I was in love with that woman."

"You've got an odd way of showing it," O'Clair said.

DeAndre said, "Who falls in love with a hooker?"

"She was not a hooker. Was a person did drugs." Alvin slurred his words.

DeAndre said, "You gave her drugs, she gave you sexual favors, that the way it was?"

"I told her I loved her. She laugh, say I was nothin' but a fool."

O'Clair said, "You beat her up for that?"

"I was high at the time."

O'Clair said, "Like you are now?"

Alvin didn't react.

O'Clair said, "Let me try this one on you. Girl name Cyntree Johnson was murdered a couple weeks ago. Know something about that?"

Alvin shook his head. "They already axed me about that. You did too."

O'Clair said, "What about Peggy, lived in 2H?"

"Fixed their plumbing was all I did."

"You didn't kill them?"

Alvin looked at O'Clair for the first time and shook his head. "I'm going to take the fifth, don't have to answer this bullshit. Where my lawyer at?"

O'Clair thought instead of taking the fifth, Alvin acted like he'd had a fifth. "Tell us what you know."

"Don't know nothin'."

DeAndre said, "Killing those ladies made you feel important, didn't it Alvin? Like you were on top. Playing God. Got to decide, did they live or die?"

"Peggy and Cynny were shot with a .357 just like the one you were holding," O'Clair said.

"Wasn't mine did them."

"We'll let the lab tell us that." O'Clair pulled the Crown Royal bag out of his jacket pocket. "What about this?"

"It ain't mine, neither."

O'Clair said, "Why were you carrying it?"

"Who say I was?"

"I told you, if you're straight with us we can help you."

"Get me something to eat? Fried chicken dinner with cornbread, collard greens, and French fries. I'll think about it."

"Answer a few more questions," O'Clair said. "We'll see what we can do. Tell me about the bag."

"Somebody put it in my apartment, I wasn't there. I think somebody been comin' in, movin', rearrangin' things."

O'Clair said, "Why would somebody do that?"

"Make me think I'm crazy."

O'Clair wanted to say: you're handling that all by yourself. "What do you think's in the bag?"

"I wish it was whiskey, I'd have me a drink." He stared across the room, breathing through his mouth.

DeAndre said, "You open it and look in?"

"Yeah, I open it."

O'Clair said, "What was in there?"

"You know." Alvin wouldn't look at him.

O'Clair said, "Who put the bag in your apartment?"

"The devil."

DeAndre said, "This somebody you know?"

Alvin nodded. "Devil's trying to connect God's whole universe." Alvin was talking now like he'd lost it.

O'Clair said, "What're you saying?"

"Lucifer never mentioned the story of what he did to God."

O'Clair said, "Who's the devil, Alvin?"

"I call him the devil 'cause that might be his name." Alvin took a breath, staring at something across the room.

O'Clair said, "Who's eyes are in the bag?" Alvin was looking at the clock on the wall. "Want some fried chicken?"

That brought Alvin out of his trance. "Don't know."

They took a break.

DeAndre got Alvin a fried chicken dinner down the street, and when he finished, they had Alvin taken to jail.

*

The next morning O'Clair asked him to take a polygraph. Alvin agreed and passed with flying colors.

"What's it prove?" O'Clair swiveled his chair all the way, fixing DeAndre in his gaze. "Maybe Alvin fooled it, or maybe he thought he was telling the truth."

DeAndre said, "Why'd you have him do it then?"

"I was curious."

"Now what are you?"

"More curious."

O'Clair had Alvin's gun and the rounds in it tagged, and had everything submitted to the lab for a ballistics comparison. He wanted to see if they had the murder weapon, if the spent casings found at the two murder scenes had been fired from Alvin's gun, and as it turned out, they had not. O'Clair glanced at the evidence property list.

ET# E 3050402
1 .357, Smith & Wesson, model 65-3 revolver,
serial number AHJ 2576, classification 5 right 4" barrel,
6 shot.

"Does it matter that Alvin's gun isn't the murder weapon?"

"I guess you're right. Even without it the evidence is overwhelming, but Alvin sticks to his story, speaks with conviction."

"Says he's innocent, God-fearing, blah blah blasé," DeAndre said. "I don't believe a word he says but his name. If a polygraph was reliable, it'd be admissible in court. Doesn't matter, we've got everything we need to prosecute, put the case on a tee for the DA."

"Doesn't it all seem too good to be true?"

DeAndre gave him a questioning look.

"Does Alvin strike you as overconfident? A killer who's going to leave shell casings at the murder scenes?" O'Clair paused. "Like he's saying, if you're any good, come and get me."

"I think he's either crazy or working a con," DeAndre said. "You heard him. I thought he was going to start speaking in tongues."

"Maybe his dog told him to do it," O'Clair said. "Or maybe he's got a split personality. Alvin's the good guy. Pinball's the bad guy, makes him do things he doesn't remember."

DeAndre grinned. "There you go."

"I can't help but think something isn't right. It's all too perfect."

"You know how that works. Sometimes things fall into place."

*

"I didn't do it," Alvin Monroe said as he was bound over for trial. "You got the wrong nigger." Alvin continued to profess his innocence during the trial, and at the sentencing saying, "Yo, your honor, I's a God-fearing African American like yourself. I didn't do it. You got to help me."

"You've been found guilty—two counts of first degree murder—by a jury of your peers," the honorable Edwin Leshore said. "You are going to prison for the rest of your life without the possibility of parole. May God forgive you."

"I got two things to say your honor," Alvin said. "First, somebody should shoot my trial lawyer for doing such a poor job. And second, I didn't do it. Motherfuckers are makin' a mistake."

THIRTEEN

Detroit. Present Day.

O'Clair brought the files back to DeAndre's office and piled them on his desk. DeAndre, on the phone, leaning back in his chair, said, "I gotta go," and hung up. "Jaz says hi, can't believe you're here."

"You mean Detroit or homicide?"

"Both."

"Tell her I can't either," O'Clair said. "How are Jamiqua and Jacqui?" All the Jones girls' names started with "J."

"In high school," DeAndre said, sounding surprised.

"Come on, those little girls, used to visit you?"

"Jamiqua's a sophomore, Jacqui's a freshman."

"What's it like living with three women?"

"What do you think? Sometimes you can cut the PMS with a knife."

DeAndre picked up two framed photos off the credenza behind the desk and handed them to O'Clair. The cute little girls he remembered now looked like supermodels. "Wow. Watch out for the dudes, huh?"

"They're already circling like hungry dogs."

"Take off your jacket, let them see that." O'Clair nodded at DeAndre's holstered piece on the desktop.

"Boy comes to pick up one of the girls for a date I bring

him aside, don't say anything, take out the .40, put it in his mouth. What do you think?" DeAndre broke into a smile.

"That's subtle. I'm glad I'm not dating them."

"So what'd you find?" DeAndre said, indicating the files. "Any shocking new revelations?"

"I don't think Alvin did it, but I don't have a clue who did. I want to talk to him."

"You mean on the phone?"

"No, go see him, look him in the eye."

"What's he going to tell you, he hasn't already told you? Man was facing two counts of first degree murder. He had something, don't you think he would've said?"

"Maybe he didn't know he had it."

DeAndre frowned. "What the hell're you talking about?"

"I'll have to get back to you on that. But I need you to set it up. Call, tell them I'm coming, see if Alvin will talk to me. What do you say?"

O'Clair drove to Southfield, checked into a Holiday Inn on Telegraph, went to his room that looked worn out and smelled like cigarettes. He had a view of a Bob Evans restaurant, and cars in rush hour traffic, creeping by on Telegraph Road, the snow-covered ground and sky blending together, the same opaque white.

He pulled the spread down, propped pillows against the headboard, sat on the bed, and called Virginia. He missed her and missing a girl was something new for O'Clair. He liked the sound of her voice saying, "Pirate's Cove Motel, how may I help you?"

O'Clair said, "I want to reserve a room but only if you come with it."

"I don't know if you can afford me. I charge twelve hundred dollars an hour, two hour minimum." Virginia paused. "Seems like you've been gone for days and it's only been twelve hours. How's it going?"

O'Clair told her about reading the case files, coming to the same conclusion he'd come to during the investigation in '06. No new leads, no new direction.

"I just rented sixteen to a guy from Saginaw."

"What kind of car's he drive?" O'Clair was thinking of the Buick Hector Bos had seen near the trailer park.

"It's a Ford F150."

"How long's he staying?"

"A week, maybe longer," Virginia said.

"Find any more bodies?"

"Are you trying to be funny? 'Cause you aren't."

"You seen Holland?"

"He was here earlier, says he'll be back for the night shift."

"Did you clean the pool?"

"Jesus, you're worried about the pool?"

"You don't put enough chlorine in, we'll get algae."

"Algae, huh? I was hoping you'd say: 'How're you, Virginia? I miss you.'"

"I do," O'Clair said.

"When are you coming home?"

"Day after tomorrow, I hope."

"You better."

*

Alvin Monroe was in level-five security at the Ionia Maximum Correctional facility, I-Max, just outside a quaint little town with a population of about twelve thousand, an hour and a half drive across the Michigan hinterland from Detroit. He got there at nine-thirty, driving along the prison property, walls and gun towers set behind two twelve-foot wire stun fences topped with razor ribbon. O'Clair pulled into the complex and parked in the visitors' lot.

A guard escorted Alvin into the conference room. He

took short, clumsy steps trying to walk in leg irons connected by a fifteen-inch chain, his wrists cuffed to a leather transport belt. Alvin, in jail fatigues, looked older and heavier, dark hair now flecked with gray. The guard put him in a chair across the table from O'Clair. "Any problem, I'm right outside," the guard said and left the room.

The weight gain was muscle. O'Clair could see it in his neck, shoulders, and arms. "Alvin, how're you doing?"

"How the fuck you think I'm doing?" Giving him his hard-con stare. "What you want, come all the way here to see me?"

Alvin had added to his tat collection, arms now covered with ink. He was just able to lift his cuffed hands to the top of the table. O'Clair noticed a fancy tat on his ring finger. "What's that?"

"My wedding band. Got married last year. To a beautiful lady with a heart full of love."

O'Clair didn't expect that, but listened to the story of Alvin and his lady, Londie Moore, a librarian and poet, writing letters back and forth and falling in love. When Alvin finished, O'Clair said, "Tell me again who killed Cyntree Johnson and Peggy Miller-King."

"Wasn't me."

"I had doubts after we arrested you," O'Clair said. "I still do."

"Bullshit. I don't remember nothin' about no doubts. I remember 'Alvin, you're our man.' I remember 'Alvin you're being indicted on two felony murder counts in the first degree.' That's what I remember."

"Your pubic hairs were found on the bodies," O'Clair said. "How do you explain that?"

"I can't."

"You had the victims' eyes in a Crown Royal bag."

"I told you it wasn't mine. Someone left it on the kitchen counter in my apartment."

"Who?"

"I don't know. It was a set up."

"You lived in the 'hood, who were Peggy and Cynny's regulars?"

"I don't know, but the landlord was doing Peggy."

"Mr. Cooper."

"Uh-huh."

"How do you know?"

"Saw him pick her up on Woodward Avenue one time, Peggy with the short skirt and big legs, getting in Mr. Cooper's car."

"What was he driving back then?"

"Black Caddy."

"How'd you and Mr. Cooper get along?"

"Well, you know, pretty good. I fixed the plumbing in his two buildings. I also brought him hookers at the motel."

"What hookers?"

"Girls on the street. One time, Cynny for sure, and Peggy too."

"You were tried for murdering these women," O'Clair said, "and you didn't think to tell me this. Are you kidding?"

Alvin frowned. "I don't know, didn't seem important."

"Ever have a run in with Mr. Cooper, an argument, disagreement?"

"Not that I can think of."

"How often did you bring girls to him?"

"Once, twice a week."

"Man had a healthy appetite, huh? Where'd all this go on?"

"Here and there, you know, different motels and hotels. Viking on Grand River. Milner down near Harmony Park."

O'Clair said, "Why didn't he do it himself?"

"See, Mr. Cooper was respectable, didn't want to get himself arrested."

"You pick up the girls when he was finished?"

"That's right."

"He hurt any of them?"

"Not that I could see, or they said."

"No one complained, huh?" Alvin shook his head. "You think Mr. Cooper killed those hookers?"

"I don't know." Alvin kept his eyes on O'Clair. "You going to get me out of here?"

*

O'Clair drove back to homicide, dropped in on DeAndre, who looked up from his computer. "Thought you were going to I-Max."

"I spent an hour with Alvin this morning."

"How's he doing? You say hello for me?"

"I wanted to get some information, not piss him off." Alvin thought DeAndre had betrayed him. Brothers were supposed to stick up for each other. Like he'd broken some code. "You know he got married?"

DeAndre smiled. "Get the fuck out of here."

"Woman named Londie Moore, a librarian that went to the prison to read poetry to the inmates. She met Alvin and said there was something in his eyes. There was this remorse and sadness. She knew he was the one. They started writing letters and got married last year. He's got a ring tattooed on his finger, and refers to her as his lady."

"One of those crazies, falls for a convicted murderer. Probably abused as a kid. Knows *she's* in control 'cause he's behind bars and can't hurt her."

"The librarian quit her job and moved to Ionia to be closer to him."

"How romantic," DeAndre said. "Find out anything?"

"Alvin said he used to pick up prostitutes and take them to Henry Cooper."

"How 'bout that for service?" DeAndre said, "Henry Cooper. Why's that name familiar?"

"He's Alvin's former landlord," O'Clair said.

"That's right. Lives in the Boston-Edison neighborhood."

"I need to know if Henry's in the system." O'Clair paused. "Can you check AFIS, see if his prints are on file. Cooper evidently frequented prostitutes, and as Alvin's landlord, had a key to Alvin's apartment."

*

O'Clair was in a conference room downstairs thirty minutes later, going through the case files again when DeAndre came in carrying a computer printout, sat across the table, and slid the paper to him. "Henry was arrested in '02 for soliciting."

"That's why Cooper hired Alvin to bring the girls," O'Clair said. "The first time it's a misdemeanor, right? But get arrested for soliciting a second time and it would be a felony, which could mean jail time and a fine. Henry didn't want to risk a second arrest."

"Doesn't mean he's a murderer."

"Doesn't mean he isn't," O'Clair said. "Let's see where it goes."

"I'll check with motor vehicles," DeAndre said. "Find out if he's still living in the same place. Colonial on Boston as I recall."

*

DeAndre recalled correctly. They drove over, parked in the circular drive, got out, rang the buzzer, and knocked on the door. A tall blonde in tight jeans and a white blouse opened it and looked at them like they were there to rob her. DeAndre flashed his shield. "Detroit Police, we're looking for Henry Cooper."

"I'm Mrs. Cooper, may I ask what this is regarding?"

She was a good-looking woman, late thirties, short blonde hair.

DeAndre said, "Is Mr. Cooper home?" Breath smoking in the cold air.

"He's out of town on business."

"Be more comfortable we come in to have this conversation. You won't be heating Wayne County." DeAndre smiled, trying to be friendly.

Mrs. Cooper opened the door, stepped back, and they entered the house, standing in the vestibule that had dark paneling and dark tile with an iridescent finish.

O'Clair closed the door and rubbed his hands together, not used to the cold after three months in Florida, blood already getting thin. "Where's Mr. Cooper?"

"Atlanta."

"What kind of business?" DeAndre said, taking off his gloves, stuffing them in the pockets of his overcoat.

"Henry's father owned real estate in Detroit and Atlanta. When Robert died Henry inherited everything. He's trying to sell the properties."

O'Clair said, "Mrs. Cooper, how long has Henry been gone?"

"A couple weeks. He's coming home Monday."

O'Clair unbuttoned his coat. "He travel much?"

"All the time," she said.

DeAndre said, "Where's he staying in Atlanta?"

"The Ritz-Carlton in Buckhead. What's this about?"

"There was an armed robbery at your husband's apartment building on Bethune," O'Clair said. "We're investigating. Do you mind answering a few questions?"

Mrs. Cooper led them down a hallway to a big room with a dark wood floor and a huge Oriental rug covering most of it. The furniture looked well made and expensive. The room had touches of old-world craftsmanship: ornate moldings, wainscoting and leaded glass windows. The house was a gem probably built in the early 1900s and looked as solid as the Fisher Building.

"Have a seat," Mrs. Cooper said, indicating a big over-stuffed couch.

They sat and she sat across from them in an old maroon leather chair with an ottoman, receiving them like a couple of insurance brokers selling whole life.

"What do you want to know?"

O'Clair stared at the deer head on the wall, looking strangely out of place in a formal living room.

"Henry caped that whitetail out himself. He believes in preserving the game and the memory of the hunt."

"He did that?" O'Clair's voice was full of surprise.

"Henry has been stuffing and mounting animals since he was a boy. His grandfather was a taxidermist in northern Michigan. He usually sends the hides out to be tanned then he does the mount himself."

O'Clair glanced across the room. "Beautiful home you have." He wanted to meander for a while. "How long have you lived here?"

"Henry bought it in 1998, the year we were married."

"They don't build them like this anymore," O'Clair said.

"We paid fifty thousand dollars. It would be worth two and a half million in Bloomfield Hills."

DeAndre sat and listened, let O'Clair run the show.

"Where'd you and Mr. Cooper meet?"

"Nemos, after a Tigers game. I had a date with a guy who wasn't paying attention to me. I was sitting at the bar and Henry sat next to me. We started talking and hit it off. I thought he was cute." Mrs. Cooper smiled. "He bought me a couple of beers and ended up giving me a ride home. We started dating seriously after that and got married a year later."

O'Clair said, "You both from Detroit?"

"Born and raised. I grew up in Birmingham, an only child. I went to Seaholm, the local high school, and Albion College." She took a breath. "Henry grew up in Troy, went to Troy High and Eastern Michigan. Henry was adopted. His parents couldn't have kids."

O'Clair said, "What was his name on the original birth certificate?"

"I don't know and I don't think Henry does either. He's never mentioned it."

DeAndre said, "So Henry never met his biological mother?"

"I thought you were here about a robbery," Mrs. Cooper said. "We're getting a little off track, aren't we?"

O'Clair said, "Do you own a 2011 Buick Lacrosse?"

"You must know we do."

"Is it here?"

"No, Henry drove to the airport."

"Do you know where he parked? We want to take a look at the car," O'Clair said. "There was a silver Lacrosse parked on the street the night of the robbery."

"You don't think Henry . . . ?" She paused, gears in her head turning. "When did this happen? I don't remember seeing anything on the news or in the paper."

"Day before yesterday," O'Clair said.

"It couldn't be ours, Henry was out of town and he's the only one who drives it."

"We'd still like to take a look, if you don't mind."

"I have no idea where he parks. Why don't you call him?"

*

Back in the car, DeAndre glanced across the interior at O'Clair. "You want to tell me what that was all about?"

"The guy who killed our maid drove a silver Lacrosse. I looked at the motor vehicle report, saw that a car just like it had been registered to Henry Cooper."

"I saw it too, but didn't think about it 'cause you didn't say anything."

"I wanted to check the trunk for hair and fibers, check the odometer. See if he could've driven to Pompano Beach and back."

"She said he's been gone a couple weeks. Who leaves their car at the airport that long? I'll send someone to Metro in the morning, try valet first and maybe we'll get lucky."

When they got back to the station O'Clair called the Ritz-Carlton in Buckhead. He asked for Henry Cooper and was connected to the room. A voice said, "Hello."

"Henry?"

"Yeah, who is this?"

O'Clair hung up. Okay, so he really was in Atlanta.

FOURTEEN

O'Clair went back to the Holiday Inn. It had been another long day and he was already tired of the grind. He showered and called Virginia, felt better hearing her voice and wished he could see her and hold her. He told Virginia about visiting Alvin at I-Max and a possible new lead in the case.

"This means you're not coming home tomorrow, doesn't it?"

"I think it's going to be a few more days. Believe me, I want to. It's freezing here."

"And you miss me."

"And I miss you." O'Clair paused. "Guy I went to see, Alvin, is in a singing group with four other cons. They call themselves Unit Five, referring to their security level, five being the tightest. Alvin said they sing without accompaniment, 'You know, acapulco.'"

Virginia laughed. "He did not."

"I'm serious."

"That's good."

"Alvin got married to a librarian who writes poetry. She's pregnant and they don't allow conjugal visits."

"Sounds like you're having a good time."

"I wouldn't go that far. What's going on there?"

"I hired a couple girls to replace Jady. Two twenty-year-old Haitians, and they only speak French."

"That shouldn't be a problem, you're bilingual, aren't you?"

"*Ou est la bibliotheque.*"

"I'm impressed."

"You should be. That's one of about six lines I remember from high school."

"Did Holland keep an eye on things last night?"

"Yeah, but it doesn't feel right without you."

"I'll be back soon."

*

In the morning O'Clair stopped and bought coffee, a Danish, and a *Free Press.* He parked across Boston Boulevard from the Cooper residence with a clean angle on the house and garage. It was January 7, twelve degrees at eight fifteen in the morning, going up to a high of twenty. He kept the car running and the heat on, skimming the newspaper, drinking coffee, watching the house.

At eight forty-five a black Chrysler sedan backed out of Cooper's garage and rolled down the driveway. O'Clair followed it to the St. Regis Hotel on West Grand Boulevard. Mrs. Cooper pulled up in front, left her car with valet. O'Clair parked on the street and followed her into the hotel and across the lobby to the salon. It looked like she was having her hair done and would probably be tied up for a couple hours.

O'Clair drove back to the Cooper house, parked, walked up the driveway to the back door, and rang the bell. He waited a couple minutes and rang it again. It was cold standing there. He could feel the chill go right through him, fingers losing feeling as he brought the pick out of his pocket and unlocked the door, went in and closed it. He was in the kitchen, industrial stainless steel appliances, black-and-white tile floor, cabinets painted glossy white. He noticed the security keypad on the wall next to the phone, but the bulb that should've been lit up, wasn't on.

O'Clair walked into the dining room, looked up at the twelve-foot ceiling trimmed in ornate molding. There was a long antique wooden table you could seat twenty people at. There was another deer head on the wall, liquid eyes staring at him. O'Clair walked out of the dining room, crossed the hallway, and glanced into the living room where Mrs. Cooper had talked to them the day before. Further down the hall was the paneled den or office, with an antique desk and a brick fireplace, four stuffed game birds on the mantel.

O'Clair sat at the desk and opened each of the three drawers, found Henry Cooper's checkbook, bank, brokerage and credit card statements, cell phone bill and call log. O'Clair folded the call log and put it in his coat pocket. He found tax returns going back five years. Henry and Amanda Cooper's 2012 joint federal tax return that said they'd earned $86,000. He found the lease agreement for a 2012 Buick Lacrosse. The lessee was Henry R. Cooper, the lessor was Ally.

O'Clair went upstairs and checked the bedrooms. Two of the five had adjoining bathrooms, and looked like someone was using them. Henry's clothes and toiletries were in one closet and bathroom, her things were in the closet and bathroom of the adjoining second bedroom suite that was larger than all of the other rooms and had a fireplace. It had to be the master.

So they didn't sleep together. O'Clair checked Henry's walk-in closet. Scanned the laundered white and blue dress shirts, the suits and pants and sport jackets on hangers. Shoes were lined up on angled shelves. He found a box of Trojan ultra thin lubricated condoms in the top drawer of the built-in dresser.

He checked the bedroom and the bathroom, didn't find

anything. Walked down the hall, checked Amanda Cooper's bedroom, closet and bath, and didn't see anything out of the ordinary. O'Clair went downstairs and found the door to the basement, walked down and heard the furnace chugging, big old thing that burned oil. He crossed the concrete floor, paint fading on white cinderblock walls, exposed pipes overhead, and walked through the dark cavernous rooms, an old ping pong table in the corner of one, a locked door in another.

O'Clair opened the door and turned on the light, saw a workbench and power tools, deer heads on the walls, eyes staring at him, a couple stuffed birds in various stages of completion, shelves filled with plastic containers, things he'd never heard of: epoxy sculpt, antler in-velvet preserver, big game hide paste, deer stick, replicator white, antler stain. Most of the products were from Jim Allred Taxidermy Supply, worldwide distributor in Saluda, North Carolina.

There were two plastic skulls on the work bench along with chain hooks, scissors, a scalpel, sewing needles, paints, and airbrushes. He opened one of the bench drawers and saw sets of eyes: bird eyes in red, yellow and brown, flex bird eyes with glossy pupils and moist red lids, and packages of brown deer eyes that looked wet and real. O'Clair scanned the shelves one more time and saw the gun box and brought it down from the shelf. He opened it, looking at a matte black Beretta .380 Cheetah, and a Colt Python .357 Magnum with a six-inch barrel. He grabbed a rag, wrapped it around the Colt's grip and slid the revolver in the deep side pocket of his coat. It fit, but just barely.

O'Clair put the gun box back on the shelf, walked out, turned off the light, closed the door, and went back upstairs, relieved to be out of Henry Cooper's taxidermy room. He knew one thing, Henry had the skill and equipment to remove a person's eyes. O'Clair should've dug a little deeper, been more thorough the first time around, taken a closer look at Cooper. That was obvious now, but at the time they'd made a decision based on the evidence they'd had, and it had been overwhelming.

It looked like Henry had set up Alvin Monroe to keep Homicide off his trail. Henry, the serial killer, overcome by the urge to kill, couldn't help himself and hit too close to home. He panicked, thinking the police would figure it out, and there was Alvin.

*

O'Clair put the Colt on DeAndre's desk.

"What's that?"

"A Colt Python .357 Magnum."

"Okay we agree so far. Where'd you get it?"

"Henry Cooper's basement. Unless I'm mistaken this is the gun that killed Peggy and Cynny. I need you to do ballistics comparisons with the casings found at the murder scenes."

"I have to tell you something. We don't break in someone's house and steal a piece of evidence like the old days."

"What do you do?" O'Clair said.

"This is gonna shock you. We get a search warrant and do it right. Which is what I'm gonna have to do if this gun's the murder weapon."

"Where's the evidence at from the 2006 murders?"

"You hear what I'm saying?"

"No."

"It's still at 1300."

"How long will it take to do the test?"

"I don't know. I'll see what I can do to speed it up."

*

O'Clair drove downtown to the Office of Vital Records in the Coleman A. Young Municipal Center. He asked for Trayce Fenton, an old friend who'd worked there forever. She came to the lobby, smiling, a pretty girl with dark hair and bangs to her eyebrows. She looked the same as the last time he'd seen her in '06.

"I don't believe it." Trayce kept coming and hugged him. "To what do I owe . . . ? No, let me guess, you need a favor."

"I wanted to see if you were available for lunch."

"It's two-thirty."

"So, you've eaten?"

"Oak, come on, I know you. Tell me why you're here."

"I need a birth certificate. Suspect in two felony murders."

"I thought you were retired, living in Florida. Didn't I hear that?"

"Guy's name is Henry Cooper."

"You're sure he was born in Wayne County."

"I think so."

"What's his DOB?"

"I don't know. He's forty-three. Adopted."

"You have Mr. Cooper's consent, right?" Trayce winked at him.

"Of course."

"I'll see what I can do, have a seat," she said and walked back to the offices.

*

O'Clair saw a folded *Detroit News* on an empty chair. He was reading a front page article about a rich guy from Grosse Pointe who was arrested for killing his wife when Trayce came back out.

"Here you go."

She handed him an eight-and-a-half-by-eleven sheet of paper, a Xerox copy that said:

STATE OF MICHIGAN,
DEPARTMENT OF PUBLIC HEALTH,
CERTIFICATE OF LIVE BIRTH

The child's name was Henry Robert Cooper, a single male born March 25, 1970 at 4:54 p.m. Harper Hospital, City of Detroit, Wayne County. There was a doctor's signature verifying the time and place of birth, and the registrar's signature. The mother's maiden name was Carol Jean Kelton and the father's name was Robert James Cooper—both parents born in the state of Michigan. The certificate was signed and stamped by the City Clerk.

"It's straightforward," Trayce said. "If Henry was adopted, you can get a copy of the original birth certificate as long as the biological parents have given consent, or they're deceased. The law divides information in adoption records into two categories. Non-identifying and identifying. Non-identifying gives you just about everything you want to know. Time and place of birth, hospital, city, county, state. An account of the health, psychological and genetic history of the adoptee, and the biological parents. You'll get the given name of the adoptee, and the ages and sex of the siblings if there are any. You'll get the adoptee's racial, ethnic, and religious background, and a general description of the birth parents, their level of education, athletic or artistic achievements, hobbies, special interests, but no names.

"Identifying information is just what it suggests. You get the names of each biological parent and their most recent address or addresses."

"Who's got it?"

"The Family Independence Agency, Central Adoption Registry."

O'Clair said, "They're going to give me what I want?"

"Are you kidding? This is the epitome of bureaucracy. You've got to fill out forms, go through the proper channels. It could take months." Trayce paused. "Or you can petition the court where the adoption was finalized—for the appointment of a confidential intermediary."

"I've got a couple days," O'Clair said. He told her about Alvin Monroe and the homicides in Pompano Beach.

"Why don't you go to a judge? Get a warrant."

"I'm an ex-cop with no authority." He paused. "Come on, you know someone who works for the agency, don't you? I've got to cut through the bullshit and get some names."

"This is sensitive stuff. I could lose my job."

"Someone could lose their life," O'Clair said, overdoing it for effect. He kept his eyes on her, and went from deadpan to a half smile.

Now Trayce grinned. "Okay. I'll make a call. How do I get in touch with you?"

FIFTEEN

The first night had been the strangest, being in the big bed all alone, door locked, Roger Holland—who she hardly knew—sleeping in the living room on the couch she'd made up with sheets, a blanket and pillow.

Holland had arrived just before *American Idol* started. Virginia saw him pull up in the souped-up VW, come in the office wearing Levis and a Drive-By Truckers T-shirt, holstered Glock on his hip, carrying a gym bag. Holland spent the night, stayed till around seven, and drove home.

They watched *Idol*, sitting at opposite ends of the couch, making small talk, getting to know each other like it was their first date. It was odd and she was uncomfortable at first.

"How long have you been a cop?"

"Three years, four months, and three days."

"Are you kidding?"

"I'm a numbers guy. I remember dates and times, like the day I graduated high school and the police academy. The day I became a detective, June 10, 2010."

"Why's that important?"

"I don't know. I just remember dates. I can tell you when I've gone out to dinner, what I had to eat, and how much the check was."

She hoped he wouldn't, and tried to change the subject. "I don't see a ring, but aren't you married?"

"August 22, 2009 was our wedding day. We got married at six p.m. I don't wear a ring 'cause I work on cars a lot and get my hands all greasy. I'm a tuner."

"Oh yeah, the car. I wondered. So you race, huh?"

"Solo. You run a course, race against the clock. I made it to the finals in Lincoln, Nebraska last year at Air Park, a seriously awesome course. I finished second. The winner beat me by a hundredth of a second, the closest margin of victory in SCCA history."

"What's SCCA stand for?"

"Sports Car Club of America. It's been around since 1948."

"You must be good."

"I'm okay."

"What's your wife do?"

"Julie's a court reporter, works for Official Reporting Services. She spends most days at the Broward Judicial Complex in Fort Lauderdale. That's how we met."

After *Idol* Virginia excused herself, said she was going to bed. She went in the bedroom and locked the door. She washed her face, brushed her teeth, and got in bed. Watched *Dateline* for twenty minutes and turned off the light but couldn't sleep, thinking about O'Clair, hoping he'd be back soon.

Virginia got up at six forty-three, wondering if she'd slept at all, dressed and walked through the living room to the kitchen. Holland was asleep on the couch. She made a pot of coffee. He was sitting up, stretching when she came back in and handed him a cup. "How'd you sleep?"

"Not bad. I'm going to have to pass on the coffee. I'm late. I'll see you tonight."

"Thanks for everything."

"I didn't do anything."

"Well, you're here aren't you? It makes a difference, believe me."

Holland picked up his gym bag and went outside. She heard the low rumble of the high-performance engine as he started the car and drove off.

*

Virginia looked at the sun rising over the water and made a visor with her hand. She scanned the beach, saw a couple joggers go by. She lined up the lounge chairs, skimmed the pool, tested the water, and added chlorine. When she was finished she went back to the apartment and had blueberry yogurt, an English muffin, and another cup of coffee.

*

The Haitian maids showed up at eight forty-five in straw hats and bright-colored island skirts and blouses like Jady wore. They were fifteen minutes late, slow to arrive and slow to clean, but they were cute and friendly and spoke French with a Caribbean accent. Virginia liked them and they only charged nine dollars an hour.

At ten twenty-three the Dudleys, Dee Dee and Bobby, an elderly couple from St. Paul, Minnesota walked in the office. They wanted to rent a room. Virginia took them upstairs to unit fourteen, showed them the kitchen, the living room, and then let them see the ocean view.

Bobby Dudley said, "Will you look at that."

"Oh fer gosh."

"Seven hundred square feet of living space," Virginia said. "This is one of our larger units. The bedroom has a king-size bed, and the dining-living area has two queen-size sleeper sofas in case anyone comes to visit you. There's a full kitchen with a frost-free refrigerator, microwave, oven/

range, coffee pot, blender, toaster, TV, and air conditioning."

"We're not gonna need no tuque and sorel here," Dee Dee said. "I'll tell ya."

"So you'll take it?"

"Oh yah," Bobby said. "Mother, what do you think?"

"Yep. You betcha," Dee Dee said. "All we need now's some grow-shrees."

From what Virginia could understand they wanted to rent it for two weeks. The motel was now at eighty-five percent capacity. She couldn't wait to tell Oak.

At twelve thirty a big, tan, dark-haired guy came in the office in a guayabera shirt and stood at the counter. He was Oak's height, but bigger through the shoulders, and muscular. He took off his sunglasses and smiled, reminding Virginia of Sylvester Stallone, a younger version when he was in Rocky, the original. This guy had the same kind of raw energy.

"You remember me?" Deep voice, Spanish accent.

"You're the driver." She was sitting in the back of the Mercedes sedan on the way to Jan Arquilla's house, seeing part of his face, dark eyes in the rearview mirror. And the smell of his cologne, thinking he could've cut it by fifty percent and still it would've been too much.

He nodded. "My name is Chano. I am happy they not hire you."

"How'd you know where to find me?"

"I follow."

Hearing it gave her the creeps. "What do you want?"

"Wait—"

He left the office quickly and came back with a bouquet of roses, handing them over the counter to her.

"For you." He smiled. "*Te quiero. Me gustaria salir contigo.*"

"I don't know what you're saying." She didn't want to know.

"I have this feeling for you."

Virginia was stunned, he'd driven her from Bayside to Coral Gables and back. They'd barely talked and this big Cuban was acting like he was lovestruck. "That's nice but I have someone."

He lost the smile and looked like she had put a knife in him.

"I'm sorry," Virginia said.

Chano slapped his hands over his chest and backed away from her like an actor in community theater. He turned and walked out of the office. What was that about? Virginia came around the counter, moved to the door and saw him get in a big Mercedes that looked like the one he'd picked her up in. He drove to Fifth Street and took a right. She glanced the other way and saw a silver car parked on the street in front of the Surf Side condos. Oak had told her a silver Buick was seen outside the trailer park the morning Jady was kidnapped.

Virginia went back inside, walked through the office into the apartment, opened a drawer in the table next to the bed, and picked up the Glock. She went back outside, holding the gun down her leg, walking toward the silver car. When she was twenty yards away, the car that she now recognized as a Buick, made a U-turn and took off speeding north. She ran back to the apartment and called Holland and told him what had happened.

"Stay inside. I'll be right there."

*

Virginia was in the office behind the counter when Holland came in ten minutes later, the Glock on a shelf under the countertop.

"You okay?"

"Yeah. I don't even know if it's the guy, but when I walked toward the car he took off."

"You see him?"

"Just a shape behind the windshield."

"What was he doing?"

"I don't know."

"What kind of car?"

"Silver Lacrosse."

"Did you get the tag?"

"No, but I'm sure it was a Florida plate."

"I'll have a patrol car parked in front."

"Then he'll know we're onto him."

"I think he already knows."

"He's not going to walk in here in broad daylight and try something?"

"He took Jady Martinez in broad daylight."

"But she didn't have this." Virginia gripped the Glock and brought it up to show Holland, expecting a reaction, and she got one.

"Jesus, where'd you get that?"

"Oak gave it to me."

"You know how to use it?"

"Point, depress the trigger and safety at the same time, and shoot. I think fifteen rounds is enough to do the job, don't you?"

Holland smiled. "Well, I feel better all of a sudden. But, I'm going to have a car come by here every thirty minutes or so, and I'm going to check on you myself. The main thing is to be aware. If you leave the office lock the door. If you're going to leave the property, call me."

Holland left and the phone rang. It was Dee Dee Dudley in fourteen.

"I's makin' a hot dish and the dreen's plugged."

"What?"

"It's the dreen."

Virginia didn't know what she was saying, it was something in Minnesotan. "OK, I'll be right up."

SIXTEEN

He parked the Lacrosse in the Publix lot on Atlantic Boulevard. He'd stolen it six days earlier from long-term parking at Fort Lauderdale airport. He'd brought clean-up bleach with him and sprayed and wiped down the interior. After the girl had walked toward him, somehow recognizing the car, Frank knew he had to get rid of it.

He went over the bridge, crossed Atlantic, and walked down Riverside Drive to NE Ninth Street. He'd rented a house on a corner lot with a two-car garage and a pool in the backyard. He went in, put on a pair of Ray-Bans, got in the Ford Escape he had stolen from the Gardens Mall in North Palm Beach, and drove back to the Pirate's Cove. There was a Pompano Beach police cruiser parked on the street just in front of the motel, two cops in front. He zipped by, went back to A1A, and parked at the public beach. He got out, opened the trunk, grabbed the beach bag and lounge chair, and walked south along the water's edge to O'Clair's motel. He found a secluded spot, put his gear down, and turned the chair so he could watch the action at the pool.

*

The morning before he'd watched O'Clair come out of the motel office, carrying an old suitcase. O'Clair put it in the trunk, got in the Seville, and took off. Frank had followed him to the airport, watched him park and walk into the terminal, watched him stand in line at the Delta counter, and watched him check his bag. When O'Clair walked away from the counter, Frank approached the ticket agent. "That big guy who was just here, I think he's an old friend of mine named O'Clair; I haven't seen him in years. Can I ask where he's going?"

The Hispanic woman in her blue polyester uniform looked at him and said, "Detroit."

*

Now Frank had his shirt off, leaning back in the lounge chair. He'd watch young cuties in bikinis walk by, and then glance at the motel. He saw Virginia come out to the pool, carrying a tool box. She knelt next to the Jacuzzi, took out a screwdriver, and removed a metal plate on the side of the tub. He got up, put his white Lacoste shirt on, then walked up to the motel, opened the gate, and moved across the pool enclosure. The girl looked up at him as he approached. She worked a wrench, loosening a bolt. There were discarded parts on the concrete patio next to her.

"What're you doing?"

"Replacing the motor." She looked up at him. "Can I help you?"

"I was just walking by and noticed your place. It looks nice. I'm staying half a mile down the road at the Ebb Tide. I wanted to check your rates."

The girl got up and said, "I'll be right back."

He watched her spectacular ass as she walked to the office, went in, came out with a folder, and handed it to him.

"I'll check it out, give you a call. You do have rooms to rent."

"There're a couple, but I can't guarantee they'll be available. I'll hold one if you're serious. I'm Virginia."

She offered her hand and he shook it.

"I'm Frank."

"Nice to meet you. I run the place with my boyfriend. Where're you from?"

"The East Coast. Pike Creek, Delaware. Listen, I've got to run." He held up the folder. "I'll check this out, give you a call. Good luck with your project."

If she recognized him, he saw no sign of it. He drove home, had a Stouffer's Salisbury steak for dinner, and watched the evening news. When it was dark, he drove to the Pirate's Cove and parked across the street from the office, cracked the side window a couple inches, and turned off the car. It was seven seventeen. He could look through the breezeway and see lights around the pool.

At seven forty-seven Holland's tuned VW rumbled up and parked in one of the tenant spaces. Holland got out with a gym bag in his hand, glanced around, and knocked on the office door. Virginia opened it and Holland went in. What the hell was this? He wondered if Holland had something going on with the girl while O'Clair was out of town.

At eight thirty-five he was getting antsy and got out of the car, crossed the street, and went through the breezeway to the pool. The lights were still on but no one was around. The ocean was flat and calm. He walked around the pool to the office that was dark inside. He looked in the window of the apartment. The white slatted blinds were closed tight, but there was a narrow gap where two of the slats didn't fit together. He could see Holland and Virginia sitting on a couch, watching TV.

He wasn't going to break in with an armed detective sitting there, but sooner or later Holland would have to leave.

Frank went back to the car and fell asleep, waking at first light. The tuned VW was still there.

At seven fifteen the detective came out of the motel office in the same clothes he'd worn the night before. Holland was leaving, but a truck had pulled up, a guy was stacking boxes on a hand truck, delivering pool supplies. Frank looked through the breezeway and saw two couples sitting at a table, drinking coffee. This wasn't going to work, he'd have to catch Virginia another time.

Holland got in the VW, revved the engine a few times, backed out, and took off. He followed the detective west on Atlantic Boulevard out past the turnpike. Holland lived in a treeless subdivision of single-story prefab houses with white concrete driveways. He watched Holland park, open the garage door with a remote, and drive in.

There was a red Honda Civic in the second space. A few minutes later a blonde in a blazer came out, carrying a briefcase. She got in the Honda and drove off. Frank tailed her to the county courthouse in Fort Lauderdale, parked a few spaces away, followed her in the building, and into one of the courtrooms. Her name was Julie Holland. She was a court reporter.

He sat and watched ten people plead not guilty to drunk driving, a female judge with a stick up her ass sentencing all of them to serve time in the Broward County Jail and pay a fine. The guilty were handcuffed and taken into custody. Jesus. What was the world coming to; you couldn't have a couple drinks and drive home?

He arrived back at the Pirate's Cove at ten forty-seven, no police cars or tuned VWs. Virginia came out of the office at three minutes after eleven and locked the door. Frank followed her to a Home Depot in North Lauderdale, parked, went in, and tracked her to aisle ten.

He wheeled his cart past back splashes, bakeware, cabinets, carts, islands and utility tables, cleaning supplies, and countertops. Virginia stopped at Disposers & Accessories. He was across the aisle with his back to her but could see her in a kitchen mirror on display. She picked up an InSinkErator, read the description on the back of the box, and put it in her cart. She moved on to kitchen faucets, selected one, and wheeled her cart to the cashier lanes.

He was in the car when she came out of the store with her new purchases. There were too many people, too many cars pulling in and out, to go after her now. He watched Virginia get in her Toyota and he followed her back to Pompano.

Holland was waiting in front of the office in an unmarked Chevy Malibu. Virginia pulled in next to him, got out, and met him at the office door. They talked for a couple minutes and went inside.

Frank drove by and went to the public beach and changed into a bathing suit in the restroom. He carried his beach bag and umbrella down to the Pirate's Cove, found a secluded stretch, and set up: spread out a towel, stuck the umbrella pole in the sand, sat and scanned the motel with a pair of binoculars. He saw Virginia come out of the office with a toolbox and the disposal under her arm, and watched her walk up to one of the second-floor rooms.

She reappeared half an hour later, coming down the stairs, carrying the toolbox and a broken disposal. He watched Virginia go in the office and wondered if he should get a room, keep an eye on her from close range, and wait for an opportunity. But then the stolen car would be parked there and police cars were cruising by every thirty minutes. No, he decided, it was better to keep his distance.

Frank went home and napped till dinner. He was tired from the night before. Woke up, had a chicken pot pie and a couple glasses of wine, watched the evening news hoping the stories about the escort and the Honduran maid would continue, but they'd been replaced by a Pompano man who had reported his wife missing, and the husband was the prime suspect.

*

He drove back to the Pirate's Cove and parked across the street. He was reclining in his seat when Holland pulled up in the tuned VW and got out with the gym bag and knocked on the office door. It was clear now, Holland would stay over again, and probably every night until O'Clair returned.

*

Frank went back to the house and watched TV. At two in the morning he went to the garage, grabbed the crowbar and glass cutter, and got in the car. He pushed the button on the remote and the door retracted and he drove out. He didn't pass another car on the way to Atlantic Boulevard and only a couple on the way to Holland's subdivision, which was dark and quiet at two twenty-two in the morning.

No lights on at Holland's house or the houses next door, and no moon. He parked in front, picked up his tools, and got out of the car. The grass was wet and he could hear his shoes squishing as he walked along the side of the house, looking in windows, but it was too dark to see anything.

There was a small concrete patio in back with a table and chairs, grill, and terra cotta planters filled with flowers. The neighbor's house was across a stretch of lawn thirty yards away.

French doors opened to a family room. He affixed the suction cup to the center of a glass pane, heard the scratchy sound as he traced a score line around it with the cutting tool, and popped out a perfect circle of glass. He reached through the opening and unlocked one of the doors. He left the cutting tool on the patio, picked up the crowbar, opened the door, went into the house, and listened. He didn't hear anything, not a sound.

He moved across the tile floor of the family room, holding the crowbar in his right hand. His wet running shoes made too much noise, so he took them off and walked into the kitchen in his socks. The digital clock on the stove said two forty-six. He walked along a tile hallway to the bedrooms. The first one was set up as an office. He walked in the second room, moving toward the queen-size bed, headboard against the far wall, the shape of Holland's wife on her side under the covers. He could hear her slow, easy breathing and smell her perfume. He studied her face in sleep, blonde hair covering her forehead, sweeping across one of her cheeks. She was attractive but not pretty. He brought the crowbar up over his head, thinking: *Want to really make things interesting?*

SEVENTEEN

Bill Cheslin handed O'Clair a copy of the original birth certificate. Henry Cooper was born Francis Meldrum on March 25, 1970 at 4:54 p.m. Harper Hospital, City of Detroit, Wayne County. His mother's maiden name was Donna Marie Meldrum, and where the father's name should've been it said: *Unknown.*

Cheslin said, "How do you know Trayce?"

"We met when I was with Homicide."

"Ever go out?"

Cheslin sounded like he was jealous. "Not the way you're thinking," O'Clair said. "We're old friends, that's all."

According to Trayce, Cheslin was a former high school math teacher who'd taken a job with the Family Independence Agency. They'd met at a state conference years earlier and had an affair.

Cheslin had stuck sunglasses on top of his head and had probably forgotten they were there. He wore a brown shirt and a light green tie, and looked like an assistant manager at Olive Garden. O'Clair had driven to Lansing first thing the morning of his third day in Michigan, and now he was in a conference room at the FIA.

"The birth mother never gave consent, but has since died," Cheslin said. "That's why I can give it to you." He paused. "Looks like somebody else was inquiring about Donna Meldrum back in June 1988."

"Is there a name?"

"John J. Remington III; he's an attorney."

"Who was he working for?"

"Doesn't say."

"When was Donna killed?"

"A month later. The sixth of July."

O'Clair was thinking she was only sixteen when she had the first boy. "What happened to her?"

"According to Detroit Police she was murdered."

"Does it say where she lived?"

"Thirty-six Milwaukee Street. Do you know where that is?"

O'Clair nodded. "What'd she do?"

"Doesn't say."

"Parents address?"

"Doesn't say."

"Donna have any other kids?"

"Another boy named Gary, born November 10, '71, father's name unknown. Gary was also given up for adoption."

*

"A woman named Donna Meldrum was murdered in 1988. Donna is Henry Cooper's real mother." O'Clair said, sitting across the desk from DeAndre Jones back at homicide.

"Where'd it happen?"

"I don't know. She lived on Milwaukee. Where would the file be?"

"1300," DeAndre said. "I suppose you want me to call ahead, tell them you're coming."

"If it's not too much trouble."

An hour later, O'Clair was sitting in one of the old interview rooms on the fifth floor with the case file on Donna Meldrum. This is where he'd worked as an investigator for fifteen years. Homicide had moved across town to Grand River and Lesure in 2006.

O'Clair was thinking about the murderers he'd questioned and got talking, got confessions from in this very room. O'Clair's theory, unless you were a psychopath or sociopath, if you murdered someone you wanted to talk about it, relieve yourself of the guilt.

He remembered this skinny, soft-spoken hit man named Verlon Showers, six two, one thirty. Verlon had been hired by a crack dealer named Rasheen McClain to kill Rasheen's wife, Lorraine, aka Lo-Lo. Verlon had been on homicide's watch list for several months, O'Clair aware of six contract hits Verlon had fulfilled, but couldn't prove any of them without a witness and a murder weapon. Now he had the man across the desk, and Verlon's demeanor surprised him. "Can I get you something to drink?"

"Got a Mountain Dew?"

O'Clair stood up, left the room and walked out to the lobby, put a dollar in the vending machine and brought a green plastic bottle back to Verlon.

"Thank you," Verlon said in a soft, quiet voice that sounded like Michael Jackson—almost like a kid talking. Verlon twisted the cap off the top and took a long drink. "Oh, that's good."

O'Clair was thinking about the contrast, a hit man, a killer drinking green soda pop.

"Tell me what happened."

"Tell you I feel bad about it." Verlon sipped his soda. "Dust was steppin' out on Lo-Lo."

"Who you talking about?"

"Rasheen."

"For the record, what's his full name?"

"Rasheen McClain."

"Why do you call him Dust?"

"He sold angel dust mixed with crack, product called space base or rocket fuel, 'cause you smoke it, it send you to an outer fuckin' galaxy."

"What was his problem with Lo-Lo?"

"She in the way. Dust was steppin' out with a lady name of A'Lea. Axed me, would I do Lo-Lo?"

"What'd you say?"

"Where do I find her and such?"

"So you agreed?"

"Uh-huh." Verlon sipped his Dew, eyes on the table. "Paid me ten grand, I followed her up for a couple days, learnin' her routine. I's layin' out for her in her house, she pull in the drive, I think was a Camry. I walked out, lit her up."

"How many times you shoot her?"

"Five."

"Lorraine McClain was taken to St. John Hospital and pronounced dead on arrival. Cause of death was multiple gunshot wounds."

"I feel bad about it," Verlon said. "See, I like women. I like my momma. I like my sister, Dejeuner. Thinkin' back, I shouldn't a done it."

O'Clair couldn't believe it, a hit man with a conscience, or maybe there was something in the Mountain Dew.

Verlon also confessed to murdering six others, giving up dates and details in his soft, high-pitched voice. Admitted he deserved whatever punishment the judge was to give him, which was seven consecutive terms of life in prison, and if he lived to be three hundred, the gun possession charges would kick in.

*

O'Clair opened the Donna Meldrum case file and took out the investigator's report. She was Caucasian, thirty-four, five five, 118 pounds. Eye color: unknown. What did that mean? He read the description of the crime scene, and studied the crime scene photographs. Donna was found fully clothed on the floor of her apartment at Thirty-six Milwaukee Street in the city of Detroit. Her body was faceup, eyes closed, arms at her sides, legs straight. No sign of sexual assault.

Donna had been strangled. There were photos taken by the medical examiner showing the trauma to her neck, the shapes of the assailant's fingers embedded in her skin.

Donna Meldrum's body had been taken to the Wayne County Medical Examiner's Office and placed on morgue file number 73-462. Dr. Gerald Fine performed the autopsy. The cause of death was manual strangulation (vascular obstruction), the manner of death was ruled a homicide.

During the autopsy, Dr. Fine discovered that the victim's eyes had been removed. The report had been signed by Sgt. Leo Wall, Officer in Charge, badge number S-6148, Homicide. The murder had been committed in 1988, which ruled out Alvin Monroe. He would've been about seven years old at the time. O'Clair was surprised by the grisly similarities to the Peggy Miller-King and Cyntree Johnson crime scenes, eighteen years separating the murders. What was the thread that linked them?

He looked at Donna's criminal history. She'd been arrested half a dozen times from 1972 to 1988 for possession of dangerous drugs, possession with intent to sell, and prostitution. There were mug shots of her with long hair and short hair, she'd been a blonde, a brunette, and a redhead at various times. The shot of Donna with long blonde hair reminded him of someone. He studied her face and pictured Gloria McMillen. There was a definite similarity. O'Clair slid the photograph in his shirt pocket. The last item in the file was a criminal bench warrant for failing to appear on one of the prostitution charges.

EIGHTEEN

DeAndre said, "Where you gonna start?"

"I want to talk to Leo Wall, retired Homicide detective. He was the lead investigator on the Donna Meldrum murder."

"That's easy. I'll have Na'Tae look him up."

"I have to find out if Donna's parents are around. They might still be living in Garden City."

"Write their names down, I'll have Na'Tae check into that too. Anything else?"

O'Clair shook his head.

"You got something to do for thirty minutes or so? Come back, we'll see what's up."

*

O'Clair went downstairs to a conference room and called Holland.

"Hello."

"It's O'Clair."

"How's it going?"

"It's going. I'm trying to wrap things up but I keep finding new leads."

"You don't get back soon I'm going to need a divorce lawyer. After being out two nights in a row, my wife is starting to wonder."

"Hey, I'm doing this for you, remember?" O'Clair paused. Although he was doing it more for himself. "It's colder than a bastard and I miss Virginia. I'm thinking another day maybe two. Anything new on your end?"

"During the autopsy the ME found a metal rod in the maid's vagina. Why's he doing this?"

"I don't know, but I have a feeling he's not going to stop. Just keep an eye on Virginia, keep her safe till I get back."

O'Clair hung up and called the motel, listening to it ring, wondering where she was, and then he heard her voice: "You've reached the Pirate's Cove in Pompano Beach, please leave a message and we'll get back to you as soon as possible." He tried her cell, same result. She was probably fixing something and couldn't hear the phone.

*

"Here you are," DeAndre said, handing O'Clair a piece of notepaper that said: *Lieutenant DeAndre Jones, Homicide, Detroit Police Department* in the top left corner. "Leo Wall, seventy-seven, retired in 1988, the year Donna Meldrum was murdered, lives in Harper Woods."

There was a photo of a dark-haired guy with sideburns that had to have been taken thirty years earlier.

The Meldrum parents had both passed; Mr. in 2004 and Mrs. In 2007.

*

It was a little after four when OClair parked in front of Leo Wall's small brick house in an old, middle-class Detroit neighborhood. Leo didn't look anything like his picture. He was practically bald, and what hair he had left was gray. He led O'Clair into the kitchen that smelled of cigarettes and they sat at a round table with a view of the snow-covered backyard, and beyond it, the neighbor's yard and house.

O'Clair gave him the background, told him about the double in Detroit in '06 and the recent murders in Pompano Beach, and asked him about the Donna Meldrum homicide.

"I remember it," Leo said. "An apartment building that had seen better days. A neighbor smelled something bad and called the police."

"Who killed her?"

"Somebody with a grudge." Leo took a pack of cigarettes out of his shirt pocket and lit up.

"You mean because she was strangled?"

"Or the missing eyeballs. Take your pick. Here's something else, her eyes were two different colors. One was blue, the other was hazel. It's called heterochromia iridium."

"You think that's why they were taken?"

"I don't know."

"What else do you remember about her?"

Leo had a liquid cough that came up from the depths of his lungs. "She was born in 1954, lived in Westland, got pregnant her junior year, quit school, had the kid, and gave it up for adoption."

"You remember all that?"

"I've got copies of my files. I familiarized myself with the case after you called."

"Did Donna go back to school?"

"I don't think so," Leo said, blowing out smoke.

"What about the parents?"

"Their names are Fred and Jean. He worked the line at the Wixom Assembly Plant, making Lincolns. She waited tables at a Ram's Horn on Telegraph across from Detroit Diesel."

"Did you interview them, ask why their seventeen-year-old daughter had become a stripper and then a hooker, giving up two kids for adoption?"

"They couldn't control her. The mother said, 'That girl has a mind of her own.'"

"Like that explained it, huh?"

Leo put the cigarette out in a small glass ashtray filled with butts.

"Donna have any brothers or sisters?"

"An older brother named Larry, a real piece of work."

"How come none of this was in the file?"

"I'm surprised there is a file. You know how long it's been?"

"What do you know about the brother?"

"Donna's best friend said Larry was the one who got her pregnant. He started sneaking into Donna's bedroom when she was fourteen. He'd touch her and she'd pretend she was asleep, eyes closed tight. Larry fondled her at first and then it escalated to full-blown rape. Donna never told anyone until she was showing and didn't have a choice."

"Do you remember the friend's name?"

"Mary Cataldo."

"How do I get in touch with her?"

"I don't know, but what good's it going to do now?"

Leo was right, it was way too late. "Did you question the brother?"

"I tried. He didn't give me much. I said, 'Larry, are you the father of your sister's first born?' He looked at me and said, 'Go fuck yourself.'"

"Do you know where he lives?"

"Howell, but that was in 1988. I have no idea where he is now, or if he's still alive. He'd be around sixty." Another liquid cough.

"You okay?"

"Fine."

Leo didn't sound fine. He sounded like he was going to croak any minute. "What'd the brother do for a living?"

"He was a carpenter, worked on a crew that built tract homes."

"Was he ever a suspect?"

Leo Wall shook his head. "No."

"Let me shift gears for a minute." O'Clair paused. "Donna was a hooker working the New Center area, right? Did she have a pimp?"

"His name was Ernest Davis, street name Nemo. I talked to him. Ernest said he didn't know who done Donna but somebody owed him a white hooker could fuck like a mink."

"What about the neighbor, Denise Dunn seeing a young white guy coming out of Donna's apartment? Could it have been the brother?"

"Too old. Larry Meldrum was thirty-six at the time. The guy the neighbor saw was described as having dark hair, five eleven, and about nineteen or twenty. We had a sketch of him drawn and showed it around the neighborhood. Then we looked at the case from a different angle, thinking because the eyes were missing maybe it was a med student. I took the sketch to local clinics and hospitals, but nobody recognized him."

"Were there any other prostitutes killed that way in 1988?"

"No, that was it, an isolated case." Leo paused. "You're telling me this is somehow related to one you solved in 2006, but you got the wrong guy?"

"I think the Pompano Beach homicides are too."

"Why'd the killer take a break for twenty-some years? And what the hell was he doing between 2006 and now?"

*

O'Clair got in the car and called DeAndre, told him what Leo Wall had said. "Can you search AFIS, find out if there's anything on a Lawrence Meldrum, lives in Howell, or did. He's Donna's older brother and might be the father of Henry Cooper."

"You serious?"

"Leo thinks so."

"I'll check it out. You coming back to the office?"

"It's too late. I'll see you in the morning."

O'Clair put the car in gear and headed for 696. He took out his cell phone and tried Virginia on the way, grinning when he heard her voice.

"Pirate's Cove Motel."

"You know how much I miss you?"

"Who is this?" She laughed. "How much do you miss me?"

"More than I can put into words."

"I didn't know you were so romantic."

O'Clair didn't either.

"Tell me you've wrapped things up and you're coming home."

"Almost."

"What does that mean?"

"I'm getting close."

"Are you talking two more days, a week? I could use your help."

"I doubt that, and I don't know. How're you?"

"A couple from Minnesota burned out the disposal in fourteen."

"You got to fix something, so you must be happy."

"We're at eighty-five percent capacity."

"Well, alert the media."

"You don't really care, do you?"

O'Clair let it pass. "How're you and Holland getting along?"

"Fine. Just come home, will you?"

"I have to or I'm gonna go crazy thinking about you."

NINETEEN

The next morning O'Clair drove to South Lyon, a small town forty-five miles west of Detroit, to the Woods Mobile Home Park. DeAndre had given him Larry Meldrum's address and criminal history. Larry was in the system, arrested twice for drunk driving in 1987 and '90, on probation for twelve months for the first offense and two years for the second. In 1993 he was arrested for assault, and did 120 days in the Oakland County Jail. Man had a temper and liked to drink.

DeAndre had said, "Be careful this dude looks like trouble. Want me to come with you?"

"He's sixty. How much trouble could he be?"

O'Clair found Larry Meldrum's double wide, and saw his Ford F150 in the attached carport. He could see a man in the window, looking at him. O'Clair parked behind the pickup, got out, moving toward the front door that opened as he approached. A big man with a heavy gray beard stood, pointing a shotgun at him.

"I told you assholes I don't have the money. What don't you understand? I'll make a payment when I'm able."

"I'm not here for money."

"What the fuck do you want?"

"I'm with Homicide, Detroit Police."

"I ain't been to that shithole in twenty years, so I don't know what the hell we've got to talk about."

"Your sister."

"Ain't got a sister."

Larry Meldrum swung the door closed and O'Clair heard the deadbolt slam home. He had a feeling it was gonna go that way, or maybe worse. Larry didn't have to talk to him and knew it. O'Clair went back to his car, drove out of the snow-covered trailer park, and pulled into a wooded area across the road. It was nine fifteen.

At eleven twenty-eight he saw Larry Meldrum's pickup drive out the entrance. O'Clair followed him to a strip mall, watched him go into a liquor store and come out carrying a grocery bag against his chest, two hands under the load. O'Clair was standing next to Larry's truck as he approached.

"Who murdered Donna?"

"How the fuck do I know?"

"You *talk* tough. Put the bag down let's see if you can back it up."

"I got nothing for you—you son of a bitch, and ain't nothing you can do about it. Now get the hell out of my way."

O'Clair raised his fists. He could see a couple women look over, probably wondering what was going on, seeing two old guys ready to duke it out. Larry crouched and placed the paper bag on wet snow-covered asphalt, reached in, brought out a fifth of Jim Beam, unscrewed the cap, took a long pull, and blew out air and spittle, looking at O'Clair with a red face and watery eyes.

"All right, get in the truck."

Larry screwed the cap back on the bottle, put it in the bag, picked the bag up, and carried it to the truck. O'Clair opened the driver's door and moved around the front of the truck and got in on the other side. Larry sat behind the wheel, closed the door and retrieved the bourbon, taking another long drink, and stuck the bottle between his thighs. He glanced at O'Clair, his rage defused by sour mash.

"I don't know who killed my sister. Why's Detroit Police Homicide give a shit what happened to a white hooker twenty-some years ago?"

"Why'd she quit school during her junior year?"

"Got knocked up," Larry said, looking at the bottle of Jim Beam between his legs, hands shaking as he reached for it.

"Who's the father?"

"Some guy she was seeing, I don't remember his name."

Larry unscrewed the cap and took another long drink, the bourbon already a third gone.

"It wasn't you?"

"Where'd you get that pile of horse shit at?"

"Donna's best friend."

"Yeah, who was that?"

"Mary Cataldo. She said you started molesting your sister when she was fourteen, snuck in her bedroom at night for two years."

Larry's face tightened and he squeezed the neck of the bottle like he might swing it into O'Clair's face, but instead he took a drink.

"Kids will be kids."

"What does that mean?"

Larry ignored him, screwed the cap back on the bottle and lit a cigarette, burning through it like he couldn't get the nicotine in his system fast enough.

"Tell me about Donna."

"There isn't a whole lot to tell. She was a regular girl, got knocked up, quit school, had the kid."

"You were what, three years older than her? Were you still living with your parents when Donna gave birth?"

"I'd moved out by then, took a job working construction."

Larry unscrewed the cap and guzzled bourbon.

"How often did you see your sister?"

"Donna? Not much. She run off at seventeen, worked in

a strip joint on Eight Mile Road called Foxxy's. I seen her on stage one time, taking it off."

"What was that like?"

"Weird."

"I'll bet."

"Heard she got knocked up again, had that kid. Then got introduced to coke and heroin, started hooking, lived in a dump near Woodward and Grand Boulevard."

"Ever try to help her go straight?"

"How exactly would I've done that?"

"Donna's neighbor said she saw a young dark-haired guy about twenty outside Donna's apartment. That sound like anyone you remember?"

"Could be. One of Donna's bastards showed up at Mom and Pop's, and then here."

"What was his name?"

"I don't know that he said."

"How'd he find out about you?"

"Beats the hell out of me. He was looking for his mother. I said, 'She didn't want you, what the hell you want with her?'"

"What'd he look like?"

"The way you described him. Said he wanted to get to know his family. I said, 'We ain't your fucking family.' I said, 'Your mom's a whore.' Then he asked, did I know who his daddy was. I said, 'He was some john. Why don't you go downtown look around, maybe you'll find him.'" Larry grinned thinking about it, unscrewed the cap and took a drink.

"You tell him where Donna lived?"

"I think so."

"Why didn't you mention this to the police after your sister was killed?"

"What the hell for?"

Larry took another drink and looked dazed now with half a fifth in him, and that was the end of it.

TWENTY

Holland got home at seven thirty-nine, parked in the drive-way, opened the garage and saw Julie's Honda, which meant she was running late. He picked up the newspaper and went into the kitchen, made a pot of coffee, poured himself a cup, stirred in a little cream, and went into the family room. He sat and drank his coffee and read the sports section until he noticed something on one of the French doors.

Holland put his cup on the coffee table, got up, moved closer to the doors and saw there was a hole where the glass had been cut out, and the door was unlocked. He looked outside and saw the circle of glass on the patio and drew the Glock, moving toward the bedroom. The bathroom door was closed and he could hear the shower on, nervous now, blood pumping, not sure what he was going to find. Holland opened the door and steam escaped. The shower curtain was closed, but then his wife's head appeared.

"I thought I heard something." She noticed the gun now. "Roger, what're you doing?"

"Somebody broke in last night."

"Come on."

"I'm serious, put some clothes on and I'll show you."

"What're you going to do?"

"Get Morgan over here." He holstered the Glock.

Julie turned off the water and pulled the shower curtain back, grabbed a towel off the rack and wrapped it around herself, and wrapped another one around her hair. "You're scaring me."

"I hope so."

Seeing his wife like this reminded him how vulnerable she was. He pictured the killer in the bedroom watching her, and felt sick to his stomach. If anything happened to her . . .

"You think this is who you're looking for?"

"I don't know." Had the killer followed him, or was this a random home invasion? He'd have to see if anything was stolen.

"Well, whoever it was left that." Julie pointed at a crowbar that was leaning against the wall. "It was on the countertop when I came in this morning. I thought you put it there and I couldn't figure out why."

The perp was going out of his way to make it obvious, playing with him. "I think you should call in, take the day off."

"I'm in the middle of a trial."

"Somebody else can fill in for you."

"I'm not going to be a prisoner in my own house."

"At least let me take you and pick you up."

"I'll be fine. You know how many cops are at the court house. It's the safest place in town."

Holland couldn't disagree, but he didn't want to let her out of his sight. "It's getting from here to there that worries me."

He called Morgan, the latent print expert, and told him what had happened. When Julie was dressed, he opened the drapes covering the door wall, flooding the room with morning sunlight, saw his neighbor, Kim Curran, picking up toys on her patio.

He could hear Julie drying her hair in the bathroom while he searched the room, pulling out dresser drawers, looking

under the bed and in the closet. Holland heard the hair dryer turn off and his wife walked out of the bathroom in a
skirt and blouse, hair teased, face made up, looking as sexy
as ever.

"You've got to be aware, keep track of cars, who's behind
you, make sure nobody's following you."

"Roger, don't worry, I'll be fine."

Holland couldn't help himself, he'd seen what the guy did
to the escort and the maid, couldn't get the images out of his
mind. He followed her into the kitchen. Julie filled her travel mug and grabbed her purse.

"I'll pick up something for dinner."

"No, you won't, just come home." Holland paused. "I
want to show you something." He led her into the family
room, pointed at the French doors. "I want you to take this
seriously."

She stared at the circle cut out of the glass pane and her
expression changed. "Oh, my God."

Holland put his arms around her and held her close. She
was crying now and he felt her body tremble. Holland was
crazy about her and this situation made him nervous, scared
the hell out of him. "You going to let me give you a ride to
work?"

Julie nodded, opened her purse, took out a Kleenex, and
dried her eyes.

*

When he got back, John Morgan's car was in the driveway.
Morgan, walking along the side of the house, stopped,
crouched, and put his fingerprint kit that looked like a tack-
le box on the ground, opened it and took out a tape mea-
sure. He pulled it open measuring something on the grass
and glanced back at Holland. "Do you wear running shoes?"

"I don't run, I drive."

"Well, somebody does."

Morgan grabbed a camera from his kit, and shot several photos of the shoe print from different angles. Holland came up and saw the tread pattern in the soft grass. "Does it look familiar?"

"What're you talking about?"

"I remember one just like it at the Jady Martinez crime scene."

"Right, it was behind the lounge chair. I'll do a comparison."

The shoe prints went all the way to the patio, but now Morgan was more interested in the French doors. He opened the kit and took out a container of powder and a brush and went to work, dusting the door handles and the pane with the cut out circle.

"Anything?" Holland said.

"Oh, I got a couple beauties here. At first I thought this guy was a pro. You don't see home invaders use cutting tools very often. But now I'm not sure. You should've worn gloves, pal." Morgan paused. "If he's in the system, we'll have him."

"Maybe that's why he didn't worry about leaving fingerprints, he's not in the system, or the prints aren't his."

Morgan found a few more: one on the inside of the door handle, faint running shoe tread marks on the orange tile floor, and prints on the crowbar.

Holland said, "Do you think he forgot it?"

"Are you kidding?" Morgan paused. "Roger, I've got to tell you, seeing all this and knowing what this freak did, I'd say Jules is incredibly lucky."

"If he wanted to kill her he would have. He did it to keep me home at night."

"Why?"

"So he can go after Virginia, the girl at the motel."

TWENTY-ONE

"It's a match," DeAndre said. "Lab confirmed it yesterday. The cartridge cases found at the Peggy/Cynny crime scenes were fired from the weapon you brought from Henry Cooper's house, and are caliber compatible to fired projectiles on lab sheet FR-1275E."

"You probably have enough evidence to arrest Henry and reopen the case." O'Clair took off his overcoat and sat across the desk from him. "Did you talk to the DA?"

DeAndre, with his elbows on the desktop, made a steeple with his hands. He was wearing a pink shirt with gold cufflinks and a maroon and gray striped tie. "There're two problems. First, Henry's dead."

"What?"

"After I found out it was the murder weapon I called Atlanta PD and asked them to detain Mr. Cooper, we'd send someone down to collect him. Cooper and an escort were taken out in the man's hotel suite, both shot and killed. No leads. Nobody heard a thing."

DeAndre slid the file across the desktop to him. O'Clair opened it, scanned the investigator's report, saying that a hotel maid had knocked on the door. There was no response so she entered, went into the bedroom and observed blood on the wall over the headboard and a man on the bed who appeared to have been shot. She immediately left the room and contacted Mr. Erickson, the manager, who phoned Atlanta PD.

O'Clair read the description of the crime scene:

> We were dispatched to an executive suite at the Ritz-Carlton Hotel at 3434 Peachtree Road in Atlanta, Georgia, where we discovered the body of Henry Cooper, a forty-three-year-old Caucasian male on the king-size bed. He was on his back, wearing a head-strap and ball gag, his wrists and ankles were secured by leather restraints. There was a bullet hole in his forehead. It is the investigator's opinion that the shooter stood at the end of the bed and shot Mr. Cooper. There was spatter on the headboard and on the wall consistent with a single gunshot to the head. On the carpeted floor next to the bed was a broken champagne flute and spilled champagne. Across the room on a small round table was a half bottle of Perrier Jouet. The body of Linda Stubblebine, a twenty-eight-year-old Caucasian female, was naked on her side on the adjoining bathroom floor, arms spread apart, legs bent. She appeared to be running, trying to get away from her assailant. She was shot once in the upper back, right side, through-and-through, and once in the back of the head. There was spray on the tile floor, glass shower door and wall consistent with the gunshots.

There were morgue photos, close-ups of the dead girl's face. O'Clair took the shot of Donna Meldrum out of his pocket, compared it to the morgue photos and glanced at DeAndre.

"Got something?"

"Linda Stubblebine, aka Taylor, looks a lot like Donna Meldrum, and Gloria McMillen, the escort I found on the beach in Pompano. They could be sisters."

"Read the next page, Linda was a known Atlanta hooker, worked for A-List Escorts. Henry e-mailed them, filled out an application, gave his contact info and his credit card number. She was supposed to show up at eleven, and it looks like she did."

O'Clair went back to the report. There were three spent casings—stamped *.40 SW EXT SHK Arms Corp Philippines*—at the scene, one at the foot of the bed and two on the bathroom floor. There were accompanying photos that appeared to coincide with the crime scene description. No one working the night desk remembered seeing Mr. Cooper or Ms. Stubblebine enter the hotel. None of the hotel guests heard or saw anything. No sign of forced entry. No witnesses, suspects, or apparent motive. Mr. Cooper was wearing a gold Rolex wristwatch and his wallet contained $1,057 in cash. Ms. Stubblebine had three $100 bills in her purse and a string of pearls around her neck. The bodies were taken to the morgue to be autopsied. The report was signed by Detective Tocco investigating the scene.

O'Clair read the medical examiner's opinion, the calculated time of death based on the state of rigor, and the manner of death, which O'Clair thought was obvious looking at the bodies. There was a note. Laboratory analysis revealed traces of Zolpidem in Henry's system. "What's Zolpidem?"

"What they use in sleeping pills like Ambien to put you out."

O'Clair closed the folder.

DeAndre said, "You know Henry was into S&M?"

"It wouldn't surprise me."

"See anything relates to the '06 homicides?"

"Spent casings."

"Yeah but they came out of a semiautomatic."

"So why not pick 'em up? Would you leave evidence at a crime scene on purpose?"

"If that was my thing, if I wanted to fuck with the police.

I don't see anything else that's relatable. No rebar in her jay-jay, and they still got their eyes, unless the ME missed it."

"The question, who else was invited to the party?" O'Clair paused. "Well, we know one thing, in spite of all the evidence pointing at him, Henry isn't our man."

"How do we know that? Henry had the murder weapon. Henry has a connection to the dead hookers in 2006, and based on what you saw in his workshop, Henry had the tools and skill to take out someone's eyes."

"Based on what I found in Henry's basement, he's our man, but he didn't shoot himself from across the room." O'Clair looked at DeAndre. "So if it isn't Henry, who is it?"

"I look clairvoyant to you?"

"Has Mrs. Cooper been informed about her husband's death?"

"I just found out myself."

"Who's going to tell her?"

"I thought we'd have you do it," DeAndre said with a half smile.

"Maybe we should both go."

"I was putting you on."

"Maybe she knows something."

"Maybe she does." DeAndre got up and fit the black fedora on his head, taking his time till he got it just right. He knew how to wear a hat. He took a black cashmere overcoat off the coatrack and slipped it on.

Walking to the parking lot, O'Clair said, "What's the second thing you were going to tell me?"

"The gun you found in Henry's basement, know who it's registered to?"

"Don't tell me Alvin Monroe."

"Richard King. Purchased it in June 2004, reported it missing September 2006. Know he owned a firearm?"

"This doesn't make any sense but it's getting good. I met

King, did a Q&A, and wrote him off. You think he was the trigger?"

"I can see him doing his wife, man's distraught, little lady's out buying crack with hard-earned funds from the joint cash management account. Why'd King kill Cynny Johnson? And how'd Henry get King's gun?"

"What connects them," O'Clair said, "is Peggy. She knew Cynny and she took the gun for protection. You can see that, can't you? She was with Henry in a motel, had the gun in her purse, he found it."

"Why'd King have a gun in the first place?"

"Why don't we ask him."

"Who killed Henry?"

"We'll ask him that too."

TWENTY-TWO

The front door opened, Amanda Cooper looked at them, frowned and said, "Jesus, now what?"

DeAndre said, "Can we come in?"

"What do you want?"

"It's about your husband," DeAndre said.

She led them to the living room. They sat on the couch, overcoats folded in their laps, looking, O'Clair imagined, like two guys about to deliver bad news.

Amanda Cooper said, "Are you going to tell me what this is about, or do I have to guess?"

"Your husband was murdered in Atlanta," DeAndre said. "Mr. Cooper was shot."

The news didn't seem to affect her, she sat calm and relaxed, legs crossed on the ottoman. There was a sexiness, a bawdiness about her that he hadn't noticed the last time they talked to her. She reminded O'Clair of Kathleen Turner in *Body Heat.* "Atlanta Homicide is investigating."

"Anyone with him?"

DeAndre glanced at O'Clair and then at Amanda Cooper. "A young lady was also murdered."

"You mean a prostitute, don't you? What a shocker."

"We don't know much about her," O'Clair said, wondering why Henry went to prostitutes when he was married to this sexy woman.

"You obviously don't know much about Henry."

"We're sorry for your loss, Mrs. Cooper." DeAndre looked uncomfortable, situations like this were difficult and she wasn't making it easy.

"Sorry for my loss? Come on."

"Do you know who killed your husband, Mrs. Cooper?" She fixed her cold stare on O'Clair but didn't answer. "Do you know anyone who had a grudge against Henry?"

"You mean other than me?" She paused. "He was a slumlord, what do *you* think? Do you know what it's like living down there? I'll bet you do," she said staring at DeAndre, "don't you?"

"I live in Grosse Pointe," DeAndre said, sounding defensive, wanting her to know he'd made it.

"Well, I'm impressed."

O'Clair said, "Did you kill your husband, Mrs. Cooper?"

"If I was going to kill him, and believe me I've thought about it, I wouldn't go to Atlanta, I'd do it right here. Shoot him when he walked in the door, shoot him when he was in bed asleep," she said it calm and matter-of-fact, no anger in her voice. "There're guns downstairs in Henry's studio. I prefer the .380 Beretta over the .357, but I'm proficient with both."

"Atlanta PD wants you to fly down, identify the body of your husband," DeAndre said.

"What's the point?"

O'Clair said, "They can't release Henry until he's been positively identified by a member of the family. Forms have to be signed."

"You have to go to the Fulton County Medical Examiner's Center. You'll get an official report of the findings and a death certificate." DeAndre took a sheet of paper out of his pocket, unfolded it, and started to read.

"'Concerning the death of: Henry Robert Cooper, the Fulton County Medical Examiner Investigator is: D. V.

Wolfe. Please contact the investigator directly for specific questions regarding the investigation. The investigator will try to answer any questions you have, or make sure you are able to contact someone who can answer the questions for you. You should choose a funeral home.'"

"Okay, I understand. You don't have to read anymore." Amanda Cooper uncrossed her legs and sat up straighter in the chair.

DeAndre looked down at the sheet of paper. "You have to bring photographic proof of your identity and relationship to your loved one."

"'*Loved one*,' that's good. Not exactly how I would describe Henry."

DeAndre leaned to his right and handed the paper to her.

"Are you coming with me?" She looked at O'Clair when she said it.

He glanced at DeAndre not sure what to say.

"You can have a family member accompany you."

"I don't have any family members and I'm not going alone. You're so interested in Henry, here's your last chance to see him. When they ship him back I'm going to have him cremated."

O'Clair didn't know what she was up to, but said, "All right."

"Excuse us for a minute," DeAndre said. He glanced at O'Clair, got up and draped his coat over the back of the couch. O'Clair got up, did the same, and followed him down the hall to the kitchen.

"The fuck're you doing? It isn't our responsibility."

"It's a nice gesture, good PR, and I might learn something."

"You're no longer with Homicide, remember? And I'm sure as hell not going to pay for you to fly to Atlanta."

O'Clair said he'd pay for his own flight, anything to get the investigation over with and get back to Virginia.

On the way to the living room, he glanced in Henry Cooper's study and saw a humidor on the desk. O'Clair went in and opened it, looking at rows of Montecristo cigars, the same wrapper as the one he found in the field outside Jady's trailer park.

*

That evening they stood on the front porch of a red brick colonial, O'Clair rubbing his hands together. It was cold, dark, and quiet. Earlier DeAndre had called General Motors and talked to Richard 'call me Dick' King, and had made arrangements to stop by his house in Bloomfield Village. DeAndre rang the bell and the door opened, King was standing there in Levis and a black turtleneck.

"Come in." He glanced at O'Clair, gave him a look. "I remember you. Sergeant O'Clair, right? Or have you risen up through the ranks?"

DeAndre looked at him and grinned.

King took them into a paneled room and they sat at a round captain's table with leather chairs. King looked nervous, but most people were in the presence of cops.

"Tell us about the gun," DeAndre said.

"I didn't realize it was missing until September twenty-third."

O'Clair said, "Why September twenty-third?"

"I was thinking of going to the range. I hadn't fired it in more than a year."

O'Clair said, "Why'd you buy a Colt Python?"

"I don't know. I like cop shows; I thought it was macho."

King needed all the help he could get, O'Clair thought. "What'd Peggy say when you came home with a high-caliber revolver?"

"She thought I'd lost my mind. She hated guns, told me she didn't want it in the house."

O'Clair said, "Where'd you keep it?"

"A gun box in the basement."

O'Clair said, "Peggy know where it was?"

"I don't know. She never mentioned it again."

DeAndre said, "How do you know Henry Cooper?"

"Never heard of him. Who's Henry Cooper?"

"Peggy's landlord," O'Clair said. "Why would he have your gun?"

"I don't know, unless Peggy gave it to him or sold it to him. Doing what she was doing, I'd say anything's possible."

"You know how this looks?" O'Clair said. "Your wife killed with your gun."

Dick King took a breath. "What're you going to do?"

TWENTY-THREE

Virginia brought the binoculars to her eyes and scanned the street to the north from the window of a vacant second-floor room. She adjusted the focus and closed in on a car parked down the street, looking to see if anyone was inside watching the motel. She was paranoid, on guard, and couldn't wait for Oak to get back. This is how she started her day, walking up the outside stairs to the vacant room, sitting in the window, looking for someone in a car who looked suspicious.

There was a man in the driver's seat of a Mustang across the street, in front of the Surf Side Motel. The widow was down and he was smoking a cigarette. Virginia could hear the twangy chords of a country tune on the radio. From this angle she couldn't see his face, just his left hand hanging, holding the cigarette over the edge of the door, and the blue tattoo, the figure of a woman on his biceps.

The small pool enclosure in front of the motel was empty at nine forty in the morning. She glanced south, down the street toward the public beach access, and saw a silver sedan that didn't appear to have anyone in it. She came back to the Mustang as a blonde in a sundress opened the door and got in. The driver dropped his still-lit cigarette on the street, it sparked and rolled, and the Mustang pulled away.

Satisfied there was no one outside the motel waiting for her, Virginia went down to the apartment, took the Glock out of her bedside drawer, slid it in her purse, locked the office door, and left a note saying she would be back soon.

She drove to Oceanside, parked in the big lot. If he followed her, if he was out there, he'd have trouble keeping an eye on her. It was crowded, cars pulling in and out, people everywhere, walking and pushing shopping carts. Virginia got out of the car and went to the cleaners to pick up Oak's Tommy Bahama shirts. At first she could tell he didn't like them, but now he wore them all the time. His favorite was the blue one with palm trees. She'd been thinking about him since he left. She liked him 'cause he was real, no surprises. What you saw is what you got. She liked his big shoulders and big hands and the way he held her. She felt safe when he was around and that was the problem. She liked watching him eat, seeing the look of pleasure on his face when he liked something. And she liked seeing him deal with the renters and their problems, seeing him suffer through stupidity and small talk.

Virginia didn't know where their relationship would go from here. She couldn't picture O'Clair with kids, didn't think he had the patience or desire, and wondered if she did. They had never talked about it.

She went back to the car and drove to a hardware store on Federal Highway, making mental notes of the cars she'd seen earlier, and the cars around her in traffic. She parked, went in, and bought a faucet for the kitchen sink in unit six.

Back in the car, Virginia noticed a white Ford SUV with blacked-out windows parked in the lot a couple rows away. She'd seen it earlier, driving behind her on the way to the store. She backed out of the space, floored it, and took off fast. Got back on Federal Highway, racing now, weaving in and out of traffic, glanced in the rearview mirror, didn't see the SUV and felt relieved.

Virginia drove back to Pompano, thinking maybe she'd

overreacted until the SUV appeared again, following her over the bridge. Virginia went straight to the public beach, pulled in and parked, reached for her purse and gripped the Glock. Her heart was racing. The SUV rolled through the parking lot and kept going, heading north now on A1A. She took off after it, followed it to NE 14th Street, and went left.

The SUV pulled into a driveway. Virginia parked on the street in front of a small white house about fifty yards away. She picked up the binoculars and trained them on the SUV, wondering if the driver was still in the car, or did he get out without her seeing him and go in the house? Maybe she wasn't being followed, she was imagining things.

Virginia glanced to her right and saw a silver-haired woman in the window, looking at her from the house. Now a guy about her age came out the front door, wearing a tank top and cargo shorts, smoking a cigarette. He came down the sidewalk and walked around to the driver's side of her car and tapped on the glass. She pressed the button and the window went down halfway and she stopped it.

"Can I help you?"

He blew cigarette smoke through the opening. Virginia fanned it with her hand. "Why do you think I need help?"

"Well, for one thing you're on private property. What're you doing with those binoculars, spying on us?"

She glanced through the windshield. The SUV was gone. She put the window up and left the man standing there and drove back to the Pirate's Cove. There were several messages on the answering machine. The air conditioning was out in unit twelve. The toilet was plugged in unit nine. And Mrs. MacGuidwin found another centipede on the chesterfield.

Virginia phoned Holland and told him what happened.

"You see someone you think's following you, don't wait till you get home, call me wherever you're at."

"I wasn't positive. I'm still not. I thought maybe I was being paranoid."

"I don't care how trivial you think it is, call me. Another thing, you're supposed to let me know when you leave the motel. Didn't we agree to that? Why're you taking foolish chances?" There was a sternness in his delivery she'd never heard before.

"I have things to do. I don't think about calling you every time I have to go somewhere."

"How can I keep you safe? You know what I'm saying?"

Virginia felt foolish. "You're right. I'm sorry."

"Don't let it happen again." This time he lightened up a bit. "What kind of car was it?"

"A white Ford Escape."

"You get the license number?"

"I never got close enough."

"Was it a Florida plate?"

"I think so."

"Where's the house at?"

She told him.

"I'll check it out and get back to you. Planning to go any-where else today?"

"I don't know."

"What're you gonna do before you leave?"

Virginia felt like she was back in grade school, getting scolded by a teacher. "Call you."

"Well, all right. I think you've got it. I'll stop by a little later to check on you. Heard from the big guy?"

"He's trying to wrap things up, wants to come home. No offense, Roger, but having him back would sure make life easier."

"For both of us."

"What's your wife think?"

"Pretty much what you do, wants me home. If Julie saw you, she wouldn't let me out of the house."

After all that Holland was paying her a compliment.

*

When O'Clair's girl turned left on A1A and parked in the public beach lot, Frank knew something was wrong. Why would she go there when she had a beach of her own a couple blocks away? The second red flag, she didn't get out of her car. Something was definitely wrong. He cruised through the lot that was almost full and kept going north on A1A.

He turned on a random street to see if she was following him and she was. He decided he could outrun her or throw her a curve. He pulled into a driveway, sitting in front of a yellow single-story house with a white tile roof, hoping the home owner didn't see him and come out.

Frank saw her park down the street. She wouldn't have the nerve to come any closer, although she had the nerve to follow him. He'd have to be more careful.

*

Holland stopped by a little after two, came in the office and said, "Man who lives there where you saw the Ford SUV is an eighty-two-year-old widower by the name of Nelson Ewald. Doesn't own a white Ford Escape. I asked Mr. Ewald, did he have any friends drove a vehicle like that and he said he didn't. I asked Mr. Ewald if he had any deliveries this morning a little after eleven. He said he didn't. So there we are."

"Based on that, I think somebody was following me."

"Next time he's not gonna be in a white SUV, trust me on that, and I'm gonna be right behind you."

TWENTY-FOUR

O'Clair booked a seat on a Delta flight that took off at nine thirty the next morning, and cost him $570 round trip. He met Amanda Cooper at the gate and sat in an aisle seat several rows behind her. An hour and a half later they landed at Hartzfield International Airport and took a cab to the Fulton County Medical Examiner's Center on Pryor Street SW.

On the way, O'Clair said, "Why'd you think the woman with your husband was a prostitute?"

"That's what Henry does. You don't get it at home—and Henry hasn't gotten anything for a very long time—you get it somewhere else. We haven't shared a bed together in ten years."

O'Clair furrowed his brow.

"You don't understand, do you?"

O'Clair looked at her but didn't say anything.

"I don't either. He was never very interested in sex with me. I found condoms in the pocket of a pair of pants he threw in the laundry years ago. So I followed him for a while, saw him check into cheap motels in Detroit, and have this little black guy bring him girls."

"What black guy?"

"I didn't know him; we never met."

"What did he look like?"

"A little guy with tattooed arms."

O'Clair pictured Alvin. "Why didn't you get a divorce?"

"I don't know."

Now O'Clair wondered if Amanda Cooper could've been involved in the murders of Peggy and Cynny in 2006. By her own admission she had access to Henry's guns. She also had access to Henry's taxidermy tools. "Ever help Henry with the animals?"

"What do you mean?"

"Are you into taxidermy?"

"When we were first married, but I never liked it. Are you kidding, it creeps me out."

O'Clair could see her murdering Peggy and Cynny with Henry's gun, leaving a trail of evidence to frame her philandering husband, have him put away. That might've been more satisfying than divorcing him. If Henry was in prison serving two consecutive life sentences, she'd likely have control of the estate. He'd have to talk to an attorney, find out if that's the way it worked. The thing that didn't make sense: how could she be involved in the Pompano murders? Unless she had someone helping her.

The cab stopped in front of the Medical Examiner's Center. They got out and went in. Amanda Cooper had called ahead and talked to D. V. Wolfe, the investigator assigned to her case, who took them to a viewing room. In the old days you'd go into the morgue operating room that smelled of antiseptic and spoiled meat, and the body would be on a metal table covered by a sheet. Now you sat in a comfortable chair and watched it on a flat-screen monitor.

There was a bank of square stainless steel refrigerator doors. A morgue assistant opened one of the doors and slid out a metal tray with a body on it covered by a sheet, feet sticking out one end. A camera zoomed in on the toe tag that listed:

Name: Cooper, Henry R

SSN: 387-45-0977
DOB: March 25, 1970
AP: Dr. Richard Carsen

Now the camera zoomed in on the disfigured gray-blue face of the deceased, head resting at an odd angle, O'Clair guessed because a piece of his skull had been blown off. There was a small, jagged entrance wound in the center of his forehead.

D. V. Wolfe, the unseen investigator said, "Mrs. Cooper, is this your husband?"

Staring at the TV screen, she nodded and said, "Yes, that's Henry." She was calm and unemotional.

"Are you positive?"

"Look at his eyes. One's blue and the other one's green."

*

A few minutes later Wolfe came in the room and confirmed it. "Mr. Cooper has heterochromia."

Amanda said, "Do you understand what he's saying?"

O'Clair nodded. He remembered Leo Wall telling him Donna Meldrum also had two different colored eyes.

"A postmortem examination was performed. You can request an official report of the findings, which will be available in six to eight weeks, as well as a death certificate signed by the chief medical examiner. Because Mr. Cooper's death was ruled a homicide, Atlanta PD Homicide Division is still investigating. Mrs. Cooper do you have any questions?"

"Who's the prostitute they found in the room with my husband?"

The investigator wasn't expecting that. "I don't know, you would have to talk to Atlanta PD Homicide. I can give you their number."

"That's okay."

"You can request Mr. Cooper's personal property, or I can give it to the funeral home and they will make it available to you at a later time."

"I'd like to take it with me."

*

In the cab on the way back to the airport, O'Clair watched Amanda Cooper open the envelope that held Henry's personal effects. She poured out the contents in her lap. O'Clair said, "That must've been tough seeing your husband like that."

"Not at all."

She picked up Henry's wallet, opened it, looked at the credit cards: American Express and Visa, fanned and counted the money, at least ten crisp $100 bills. She put the wallet back in the envelope and held up a three-pack of condoms, glancing at O'Clair.

"At least he used protection, but it didn't help him, did it?"

She put the condoms in the envelope and handed him a gold Rolex.

"Want a watch? I gave it to Henry for our tenth anniversary."

"No thanks." He handed it back.

"You'd turn down a seventy-five-hundred-dollar Rolex just like that?"

"It's not me. I'm a shot and a beer guy." O'Clair didn't want a dead man's watch and couldn't understand why she was offering it to him. Being with her made him uncomfortable. Maybe she'd made Henry feel the same way, that's why he didn't want to sleep with her.

"I feel I should repay you for coming with me."

"That's okay," O'Clair said. "You don't owe me anything. I wasn't expecting a reward."

*

O'Clair followed her through security and walked her to the gate, thinking about Virginia—he could be back in Pompano in an hour, spend the night with her and fly to Detroit in the morning. O'Clair knew if he saw Virginia he wouldn't want to leave, and if he went back to Detroit for a couple more days he could wrap things up.

Their seats weren't together, but the plane was wide open, and O'Clair felt obligated to sit near her and took a seat across the aisle. Once they were airborne he ordered a Makers on the rocks and she had a vodka.

"You married, Detective?"

"Divorced."

"When did you know it wasn't working?"

"The day I proposed."

"Why did you go through with it?"

"'Cause I'm a dumbass."

Amanda Cooper smiled. "You mean 'cause you're loyal."

O'Clair sipped his drink. "I'm living with someone."

"You're going to try matrimony again?"

"We'll see what happens." He put his drink on the tray. "Are you going to stay in Detroit?"

"I'll probably sell the house and move somewhere warm, like Florida."

He hoped it wasn't near Pompano Beach. O'Clair sipped his drink. "Remember the first time I stopped by with Lieutenant Jones?"

She looked up from her vodka.

"I asked you if Henry had ever met his biological mother. You never answered the question."

"What difference does it make now?"

"Then why don't you tell me."

"Henry said he saw her one time, but they didn't meet."

"When was that?"

"He was eighteen."

O'Clair was thinking, so twenty-five years ago, 1988, the year Donna Meldrum was murdered. "What about Henry's brother?"

She drank the last of her vodka, sucking on ice cubes. "Evidently, he contacted Henry, but Henry wasn't interested in meeting him. That's all I know."

"Did you think it was odd that Henry didn't want to get to know him? If you found out you had a sister, wouldn't you be excited to meet her?"

"We're not talking about me. Henry's a weird guy."

"What's the brother's name?"

"I don't remember."

O'Clair didn't believe her. His guess was the brothers did meet. What happened beyond that, he had no idea.

TWENTY-FIVE

"Free for lunch?" O'Clair said. He was on his cell phone in the rental car driving south on Woodward Avenue, passing the Art Institute and the Detroit Public Library.

"You must really want something," Trayce Fenton said.

"Where do you want to go?"

"The Rattlesnake Club. We'll start with champagne and caviar," she said, sounding serious like she was going to sock it to him.

He hesitated before saying, "Anywhere you want."

"Oak, I'm kidding. Did you lose your sense of humor? Pick me up in ten minutes, we'll go to the Mercury Bar. That sounds better, I'll bet. First tell me what you need."

"Remember, I was asking you about Henry Cooper? You gave me a copy of his birth certificate, but that's when he was given up for adoption. Henry was born Francis Meldrum. His birth mother was Donna Meldrum, father unknown. The mom gave birth to a second boy named Gary in November 1971. He was adopted and I want to know by who."

*

O'Clair could read:

STATE OF MICHIGAN,

DEPARTMENT OF PUBLIC HEALTH,
CERTIFICATE OF LIVE BIRTH

at the top of the page that was on the table in front of
Trayce, a bottle of Lite Beer blocking part of it.

"Thanks for doing this," O'Clair said.

Trayce Fenton said, "You owe me: a cheeseburger and
fries, and probably another beer." She paused. "All right,
here you go. The child's name is Walter Kindred, a single
male born November 10, 1971, two thirty-eight in the
morning, Receiving Hospital. The mother's maiden name
is Dolores Katherine Robinson, and the father is Gordon
Alexander Kindred." Trayce picked up her beer and took a
drink.

"Know where they live?"

"Bloomfield Hills, but that was more than forty years ago.
Are the parents still there? Who knows."

Trayce handed him the birth certificate. O'Clair folded
it and put it in his pocket. Their burgers came and they
ordered two more beers.

"What's the story with you and Cheslin?"

"We're friends."

"You shack up once in a while you told me."

"Where are you going with this?"

O'Clair had a mouthful of burger and couldn't talk.

"How come *you* never asked me out?"

O'Clair swallowed and said, "I didn't think you were
interested."

"I was."

"You were married."

"How about you, Oak?"

O'Clair broke into a grin. "Divorced, but I'm seeing
someone."

"Even tough guys fall in love, huh?"

O'Clair phoned DeAndre from the car.

"Your boy, Walter Kindred's driving a 2011 BMW 5-Series, what do you think of that?"

"I'm impressed."

"I imagine so, material possessions being so important to you and all." DeAndre took a breath. "His driving record's spotless, not even a parking ticket. Lives in Birmingham."

O'Clair took out a pen and wrote down the address. It started snowing again as he drove to the expressway, passing fast food restaurants and stretches of abandoned storefronts. Detroit looking gritty under the gray overcast sky, nearly dark at seven minutes after five. He took 696 to Woodward and went north about five miles.

Walter Kindred lived in a townhouse on Merrill Street, middle of the block, two-car garage in back. O'Clair parked in front, got out of the car, walked to the front door and rang the bell. He waited, looked in the front window, glanced at the bronze mail slot in the door, crouched and opened it, looking in at a pile of envelopes and magazines on the carpeting.

O'Clair moved along the side of the house, walked up the driveway to the garage, crossed the snow-covered patio to the back door, took out his tools, picked the lock and went into a well-furnished family room with a fireplace, and walked through to the kitchen. He opened the refrigerator, looking at three bottles of Miller High Life, a jar of Vlasik Kosher Dills, mustard, barbecue sauce, a moldy wedge of cheddar, a rotten three-pack of Romaine, a can of Coke, and five eggs.

O'Clair walked down the hall to the front door, crouched, scooped up the mail and took it to the kitchen, piled it on the table and shuffled through the mail—everything addressed to Walter Kindred: Consumers Power, DTE, City of Birmingham, Comerica Bank, AAA. Checking the postmarks it looked like Walter had been gone since early December.

There were two rooms and two baths upstairs. One was used as a bedroom, the other as an office. He checked the bedroom first. There was a king-size bed against the wall, and two overstuffed chairs in front of the fireplace. He opened the closet, scanned the rack of shirts and pants on hangers, shoes lined up on the floor. He opened the drawers of the built-in dresser, ran his hands under the neatly folded clothes. There was nothing out of the ordinary, nothing of interest.

O'Clair walked into the second room, went to the desk and sat, opening drawers, found a passport in one, opened it, looking at forty-two-year-old Walter Kindred: curly dark hair, big nose, blank expression. Something familiar about his face, and like flipping a switch, it hit him. Walter looked like Henry Cooper, same nose and hair. O'Clair wondered if these two adopted brothers had ever met, and had they ever met their mother?

O'Clair found 2011 bank statements in a nine-by-twelve manila envelope. There were monthly deposits of fifteen thousand dollars, the checks originating at Merrill Lynch. He opened the Apple laptop that was on the desk and booted it up. First he went through the e-mails. There were 108 new ones. He scrolled down: *United Nations, Your payment is ready, For Singles Only, New Affordable Insurance, Barrister Musa Hassan—Get back to me regarding your payment.* It was all junk, spam. He checked *Deleted Items*: It was empty. He clicked on *Safari*, and when it opened, checked *Bookmarks*. Saw ESPN and CNN listed. So Kindred liked sports and news. He clicked on *History*. It opened and he went to *Show All History*. At the top of the screen it said, *Vacation Rentals by Owner*, and under that was a list of vacation houses in South Florida. There was a description of each house, the amenities, general location, and the name and e-mail address of the owner or real estate company handling the rentals. O'Clair printed a copy and put it in his shirt pocket. He checked *Sent* mail. It was empty. He checked *Trash,* nothing there. He turned off the computer and went to his car.

*

A black maid in a uniform escorted O'Clair through the big house to the kitchen. "Mrs. Kindred, Detective O'Clair."

The good-looking, gray-haired woman standing at the island counter said, "Thank you, Gladys."

She reminded O'Clair of the happy, vital seniors you'd see in commercials for retirement communities, everyone active and having fun. "Mrs. Kindred, I'm investigating a cold case, a homicide."

"As you said on the phone. Would you like coffee, Detective?"

"Please."

"How do you take it?"

"Black."

Mrs. Kindred turned, opened a cupboard and took out a coffee cup and saucer, and placed them on the counter. She poured a cup and handed it to him. "Why don't we sit."

Dolores Kindred picked up her cup and saucer and led him to an oval table next to a bay window with a view of a snow-covered backyard the size of a football field. There was a swimming pool beyond the patio, and beyond that was a tennis court. She sat and O'Clair went around the table and took a seat across from her.

"Well, you've got me curious, I'll say that. Now what's this all about?"

"I'm investigating the murder of Donna Meldrum, your

son's biological mother. She was a prostitute strangled in an apartment near Woodward and Grand Boulevard in 1988."

"Oh my."

Dolores seemed to be looking past him at something in the backyard. She wore a gray Nike warm up with pink trim.

"What does this have to do with me?"

"Did you ever meet Donna Meldrum?"

"No."

"Does Walter know he was adopted?"

"He found out when Gordon passed away. It was at the reading of the will at the lawyer's office. I was there with Walter and Gordon's brother, Howard."

"When was that?"

"June 4, 1988." Mrs. Kindred paused. "Howard was a gambler who had gone through all his money. Gordon didn't approve of him and only left Howard ten thousand dollars. When he heard that Walter inherited the bulk of the estate, $4.7 million, Howard blew up and said something like: 'I get ten grand and the orphan boy, who isn't a real member of the family, get's almost five million? This is a joke, right?'"

"You'd never told Walter he was adopted?"

"I looked at him and said, 'Walter, I couldn't have children. We loved you and raised you as our own.' Walter said, 'Why didn't you tell me?' I told him we didn't think there was any reason to."

"How did he react? Was he upset?"

Dolores Kindred sipped her coffee and put the cup back on the saucer. "Walter told me he was lucky." She smiled. "He said he had the best parents in the world."

"He wasn't curious about meeting his real mother?"

"I'm his real mother and Gordon was his father," Dolores said, taking offense. "We raised him, took care of him when he was sick, helped him with his homework. We made him into the man he is today."

"Walter never tried to find his birth mother?" O'Clair drank his lukewarm coffee.

"Why would he? We gave him everything he needed."

"Who was Gordon's attorney?"

"John J. Remington III. He's also my attorney. But, if you're thinking of calling him, he's not going to know any more than what I just told you."

"Do you know that Walter has a brother?"

"A man at the adoption agency mentioned it. No names or anything just that his birth mother had had another child who was also given up for adoption. Walter never had any interest in meeting him."

"Do you know the brother's adopted name?"

"Why would I?" Dolores Kindred sipped her coffee and made a face. "It's cold. Would you like some more?"

"No thanks."

Dolores took her coffee cup to the island counter, filled it, and came back to the table. She reached for the cream, poured some in her coffee, and stirred it with a spoon.

"How often do you and Walter get together?"

"Not often since he moved out."

"When was that?"

"About two years ago. He bought a townhouse in Birmingham that I've never been invited to."

"Did something happen?"

"Walter started going out with this girl."

"What's her name?"

"Carol Noonan. After he met her, everything changed. I'd rather not talk about her, if you don't mind."

"Did they get married?"

Dolores didn't answer and O'Clair decided not to press the issue.

He was thinking of the description of a nineteen-year-old white male outside Donna Meldrum's apartment the night she was killed. "Do you have pictures of Walter growing up?"

"Do I ever. Stay there. I'll be right back."

Excited now, she got up, walked out of the room, and came back a few minutes later with a photo album. She sat and opened it, and turned it toward O'Clair. There were eight black-and-white photographs of Walter as a baby, Walter in the tub laughing.

"Wasn't he cute?"

The next one showed Walter posing in a diaper, holding his arms up, trying to make muscles.

Dolores smiled. "I remember that."

O'Clair was getting worried, thinking he'd have to look at every picture in the goddamn book. The next one was Walter's at the end of the hall naked, looking over his shoulder.

"That was our game." Dolores smiled. "It was called *I'm going to get your fanny*. Walter would get out of the tub and run, and I'd chase him."

It was getting hard. He turned a couple pages, wanting to speed ahead, skip the trip down memory lane. O'Clair turned the page. Walter was in a Cub Scout uniform, and then playing Little League baseball.

Dolores Kindred smiled again. "Walter was a terrific athlete. He was the best hitter on the team."

Then finally, Walter was in a cap and gown, posing with his parents in a medium shot. "There's one of me, Walter, and Gordon in 1988."

O'Clair was studying Walter's features: big nose, long, dark curly hair. He looked so much like Henry, O'Clair wondered if it was the same guy. He closed the photo album.

"Oh, don't you want to see the rest? I haven't looked at these pictures in years."

"I have to go." O'Clair paused. "Tell me, what does Walter do for a living?"

"As I mentioned earlier he has a trust fund from his father's estate. Walter has never had to work, and probably never will."

"I've called his house several times without success. Is Walter out of town?"

"He's on vacation. Walter told me he was renting a house in Florida for a couple months."

"Do you know where?"

"He didn't say."

O'Clair was thinking about the rental properties he'd seen on Walter's computer. "Can you give me his cell number?"

"I don't know that he has one."

TWENTY-SIX

Virginia knew something was wrong as soon as Holland walked in the office, the look on his face giving him away. He stood on the other side of the counter and told her what had happened.

"How's your wife?"

"Better than I am. I had to get someone else to stay with you tonight, a patrolman named John Forrest. He's a good guy, you'll like him. He's also the Broward County Sheriff's pistol champ, three years running. I'm sorry, I can't leave Julie."

"Don't be. This whole thing's crazy and getting crazier."

"I'm going to step up the patrol car presence and come by more often myself." Holland paused. "Now I'm going to go to the courthouse to pick up my wife and drive her home."

Virginia could see that the break-in had really affected him. She could see the tension and worry on his face. Virginia could relate.

"I'll bring Forrest over later and introduce you." He paused, looked distant, like he forgot what he was going to say. "Oh, and I left O'Clair a message explaining what happened, so I think you'll be getting a call any time."

She did a few minutes after Holland walked out the door. Her cell phone rang. She said, "Hello."

O'Clair said, "You all right?"

Hearing his voice had a calming effect. "Yeah, I'm fine.

Someone broke into Holland's house, Roger thinks it was the guy who killed Jady and the escort."

"Did Holland explain what happened?"

"Whoever it was used a glass cutter and entered the house. Holland's wife was asleep, never heard a thing. They were able to get prints, but he isn't in the system."

"So there's no way he's going to be staying with you."

"He got a sheriff's deputy to cover for him, the reigning Broward County pistol champ."

"Keep the Glock handy anyway. I know you don't want to shoot anyone, but it might come to that."

"I don't want to think about it."

"You want to end up like Jady and Gloria?"

"There's something I didn't tell you. I saw a man in a silver Buick parked in front of the condos next door yesterday."

"What?"

"I went in and got the Glock and walked toward him, but he took off."

"Are you out of your mind? Why didn't you call Holland?"

"I did and he came right over."

"You see the guy?"

"Not really."

"How about the license plate?"

"I think it was Florida."

"Why didn't you tell me?"

"I didn't want you to worry."

"Holland told me they found a silver Lacrosse in the Publix parking lot that had been stolen at the airport seven days ago." O'Clair paused. "What else have you been holding back?"

"This Cuban guy, driver for the escort service, came by."

"Came by for what?"

"He wanted to ask me out. I told him about you, made it clear I wasn't available and wouldn't be." She decided to leave out the part about the flowers and the guy professing his love.

"What'd he say?"

"Nothing, he just left."

"How'd he find you?"

"He said he followed me from the parking garage at the mall in Miami. Don't worry, he's gone. I'll never see him again."

"Anything else?"

"I miss you. I wish you'd finish up and come home."

"I'll be back tomorrow night, late. Tell the pistol champ not to shoot me, and don't you, either."

"Are you getting anywhere on the case?"

"I know Alvin Monroe's the wrong guy."

"Are they going to let him go?"

"First I've got to prove he's innocent."

"Do you know who the right guy is?"

"I think so. I'm still trying to piece it together. You see a 2011 BMW with a Michigan plate, get Holland on the phone, fast."

"Who is it?"

"Guy's name is Walter Kindred. Let's just say at the moment he's a person of interest."

"How's it feel to be back in the Motor City?"

"Like I never left, and I want to. Just be careful, if anything happened to you . . ." He didn't finish but the meaning was clear.

"I love you," she said.

"Me too."

He couldn't quite say it, but she knew he did. He wasn't very good at communicating his feelings. Hearing his voice was enough, it made her feel good.

"All right, I'll see you tomorrow."

Virginia hung up, went in the bedroom and got the Glock, put it in her purse, locked the office and taped a piece of paper to the door that said, *I'll be back in thirty minutes, call if you have an emergency*, and included her cell number. No way she was going to call Holland after what had happened.

She turned and scanned the street, memorizing the cars and where they were parked, a red Kia and a white Toyota across the street in front of the Sea Breeze Motel. Looking north, she saw a dark GMC SUV next to the condos, and to the south a convertible—she didn't know what make—in front of the vacant lot.

She got in her car and drove to the bank to get cash to pay the maids, checking the rearview mirror to see if anyone was following her. No one appeared to be. On the way back she stopped at Publix. The lot was packed; she parked and got out, looking around.

*

Frank spotted her in the produce section, squeezing and smelling cantaloupe melons. She selected one, put it in her cart and moved on, stopped and picked up grapes and bananas. He was thirty feet behind her, looking at plastic containers of prepared foods: fried chicken, barbecue ribs, pot pies, macaroni and cheese—getting hungry.

When he glanced back over, she was gone. He pulled the cap down low over his eyes, hiding his face, and went after her. He caught up to Virginia in dairy, watched her put milk, eggs, butter, and yogurt in the cart, watched her open the stainless steel freezer and take out two quarts of Haagen-Dazs. *Jesus, don't eat too much of that, turn into a goddamn whale.* Although, once he put his plan into motion, she wouldn't have time.

He followed her to the checkout lanes. While she was in

line, he walked away from his cart and went to the newspaper rack, picked up a *Miami Herald* and paged through
it, keeping an eye on her. After she paid, he followed her
outside to her car and watched her load everything in the
trunk. He was thinking of running up and pushing her in,
but there were too many people around.

TWENTY-SEVEN

Carol Noonan was head of account services at the Blue
Moon Group, an ad agency in Birmingham. They met in
her office on Woodward above Cosi, a chain coffee shop.
Carol got up from behind her desk and greeted him at the
door. She was a plump Irish girl with red nails and a hard
handshake, overdoing it.

"You have older brothers, don't you?"

"Five. How'd you know?"

"You've got a grip like a teamster," O'Clair said. "I'll bet
you can throw a curve ball too."

"We'll have to play catch sometime."

Carol sat behind her desk that had an Apple MacBook
Pro and an iPhone in a pink shell case and half a dozen small
silver photo frames turned toward her.

"Okay, don't keep me in suspense any longer. What's this
all about?"

"I'm a retired former homicide investigator helping the
Detroit Police solve a cold case."

"I used to love that show."

"What are you talking about?"

"*Cold Case*. It was on TV. Detective Lilly Rush used her
understanding of the criminal mind to crack old cases that
were never solved."

Carol was excited now and reminded O'Clair of Irish
Catholic girls he knew in grade school and high school.

"A prostitute named Donna Meldrum was murdered in Detroit in 1988, no suspects, no witnesses, no motive."

"I've never heard of her and I was four years old when it happened."

"You've heard of Walter Kindred though, haven't you?"

Carol Noonan's face went blank.

"Donna is Walter's biological mother. She gave him up for adoption in 1971."

"He never mentioned it. I thought he was a blue blood, drove a BMW and seemed to have a lot of money."

"You dated him, what's he like?"

"Nice at first and then—" She threw it out, but didn't explain.

"Where'd you meet?"

"The bar at Forte." She pointed south. "A restaurant that was right down Old Woodward. It's a steakhouse now. I was having a drink after work with our Bentley client, an Englishman who had a dinner engagement. When he got up to go, a nice-looking guy on the other side of him was smiling at me. He said, 'Hi, I'm Walter, can I buy you a drink?' He looked ten years older than me at least, dark hair starting to go grey, but he had this boyish charm." Carol Noonan paused. "I'd had two glasses of wine and hadn't been on a date in six months. He moved over next to me, started talking, and we hit it off."

"What'd you talk about?"

"Everything. Walter was an excellent conversationalist. He had a lot of interests. That's the thing, he drew me in initially."

"What did he do for a living?"

"He said he owned a couple apartment buildings in downtown Detroit."

"Did he say where?"

"Vaguely. I think there was one behind Henry Ford Hospital, a few blocks north in a neighborhood with a lot of abandoned buildings. I can't remember where the other one was. We had a couple more drinks and I was smashed by then. He invited me to dinner but I passed. I gave him a card and said, 'Call me.'"

Her cell phone rang. She picked it up and looked at the screen, pushed a button on the side and looked at O'Clair.

"Sorry, I turned it off." Carol paused. "Where was I? Oh yeah, so the next morning I'm sitting here hungover and a guy delivers a dozen roses. The card said, 'great meeting you, Walter Kindred.' He called a couple hours later and invited me to dinner at the Capital Grille."

"What'd you think?"

"I was nervous, excited. I couldn't wait."

"How was your date?"

"Wonderful. Walter was interesting, attentive, funny. I have to say I was smitten. No one had paid that much attention to me for a long time. We started seeing each other a couple times a week and within a month it was almost every day. He'd spend the night occasionally."

"Where'd he live?"

"Bloomfield Hills."

"Ever go to his place?"

"No, and I finally asked him why. I thought maybe he was married. That's when he told me he lived with his mother."

"Think it was odd?"

"Odd? Are you kidding? Hell-o. I convinced him to get his own place. I said, 'How many guys your age live with their mother?' It was as if he'd never considered it. I went online and searched real estate listings and found a townhouse in Birmingham. It was $1.3 million and Walter didn't bat an eye."

"Did you move in with him?"

"He never asked me to, but I spent a lot of time there before we broke up."

"When did it start to go wrong?"

"After a few weeks I began to notice little things. He was always coming down with something. He had a sore throat, or pulled a muscle in his back, or he ate something and thought he had food poisoning."

"You didn't believe him, huh?"

"He was looking for attention. I was giving it to him anyway so it didn't make sense."

"Did he ever talk about the relationship with his mother?"

"I got the impression she was strict and kept Walter in line like he was still a little kid. It was weird. He was always going back home to help her with something, or make her dinner, and she had full-time help."

"How'd you get along with her?"

"I didn't. Dottie didn't make me feel welcome or comfortable. She'd talk to Walter; they'd have a conversation like I wasn't there."

"What'd they talk about?"

"Having fun at their cottage in Petoskey, or trips they took to different places. Dottie would bring out a photo album and they would reminisce. I'd sit there like I was invisible."

"Did you say something to Walter?"

"Yeah, he'd blow up and then apologize." Carol Noonan paused. "Here's when it really started getting weird. I had a framed photograph of me and this guy named Craig I'd dated for about a year. It was my last significant relationship before Walter, and he didn't like it. He'd hide the frame when he came over. I'd say to him, 'Come on, Walter, I did have a life before I met you.'"

"Didn't Walter mention his past relationships?"

"I don't think he had any."

"You were his first?"

"I know, it's too weird. One time he got mad and hit me in the face and knocked me down, almost knocked me out. I told him to leave. That was it. I said to myself, if he hits you once he's going to do it again. I saw my father do it to my mother, and I wasn't going to live like that."

O'Clair could see she was upset and he didn't blame her, Carol's pale Irish face was turning red.

"He wouldn't give up, kept calling and sending flowers for a few days." Carol took a breath. "I told two of my brothers what happened and they went over and said if he contacted me again they'd break his legs. Walter stopped calling after that. I haven't heard from him since."

"When was this?"

"The second week in December."

O'Clair was thinking that's when he probably took off, that's when his mail started piling up.

Next on his list was the lawyer, John J. Remington III. O'Clair called and made an appointment. He told John J. the same thing he'd told Carol Noonan about investigating the cold case murder of Donna Meldrum.

"Did Walter Kindred hire you to find his birth mother?"

"Walter came to see me a couple weeks after the funeral. He was curious, wouldn't you be? Walter wanted to find out what his biological parents looked like and where they lived. He wanted to know if they had any more kids, did he have brothers or sisters."

"Did Dottie know Walter was doing this?"

"No, and I tried to talk him out of it. I said, 'You might not like what you learn.' But he insisted."

"What'd you find out?"

"Walter was born Gary Meldrum. He had a brother who was a year older. His grandparents Fred and Jean lived in

Westland, and Walter had an uncle Larry. I tried to find Donna Meldrum's address and couldn't. I checked with the Secretary of State, Department of Motor Vehicles, and the Internal Revenue Service. Donna Meldrum didn't drive a car and didn't pay taxes. I talked to her parents and they hadn't seen her in years and had no idea where she lived or if she was alive. And she wasn't for too much longer."

"Did Walter ever find his mother?"

"I don't know. But I gave Walter his brother Henry Cooper's address in Troy."

"Did he look up Henry?"

TWENTY-EIGHT

O'Clair met with John Brennan, the psychologist who'd helped profile murderers when O'Clair was with Homicide. Since then Dr. Brennan, a blue collar guy who'd put himself through college, had done well—now treating rich suburbanites with problems, and by the look of things business was good.

Brennan was tan in January, well-dressed, and had a slick suite of offices in Bloomfield Hills. O'Clair sat across the desk from him. "You've come up in the world. I feel like I should check your ID, make sure you're the same guy."

Brennan grinned. "I've done okay, but it's not as interesting as what we used to do. My patients are overindulged housewives who feel unappreciated, and dissatisfied entrepreneurs who have everything but they're not happy."

"Do you feel sorry for them?"

"Are you kidding?" He paused. "Tell me about this woman who was murdered in 1988. You think she was raped by her brother, huh?"

"It was never proven. That's what a good friend of Donna Meldrum's told Leo Wall, the lead investigator on the case. Say it's true, does it have anything to do with what happened to her?"

"It could have everything to do with it. Donna had an incestuous relationship with her brother. Imagine being introduced to sex this way. It's wrong, as wrong as it gets.

It's disgusting, forbidden, but it's also pleasurable—an endorphin high for the brain." Brennan picked lint off the front of his black sweater. "Donna was taken advantage of, but probably blamed herself. Someone introduced to sex this way is not going to have a normal sex life."

"You think that's why she started hooking?"

"It's a similar dynamic. Prostitution is wrong and dangerous, just like being with her brother, but she also likes it. Carl Jung said we're born with genetic markers, a collective unconsciousness—children know incest is wrong before they're told it's wrong."

"Donna had a son by the brother and gave him up for adoption. She had another boy the next year and gave him up too. The first kid's name is Henry Cooper."

"Does Henry know he was adopted?"

"His wife said he does."

"Did Henry try to find his real mother?"

"His wife didn't know, but didn't think so; although I'm not convinced she was telling the truth. Here's something else you might be interested in. Henry frequented prostitutes. Years ago he was arrested for soliciting."

"His mother didn't want him; Henry felt rejected, worthless. Henry found out where she lived and went to meet her, and saw what she was. It sounds classically Freudian; Henry used prostitutes as surrogates because of his desire to sexually possess his mother."

"Come on."

Brennan looked at him and smiled. "I know. It sounds like bullshit, but given what we know it's a plausible conclusion."

"We don't have to worry about Henry anymore; he and an escort were murdered in a hotel room in Atlanta a few days ago."

"Tell me about the second boy."

"His name's Walter Kindred. He was adopted by a wealthy couple in Bloomfield Hills. His father died when he was in high school."

"Did Walter know he was adopted?"

"I guess he found out a week after his father passed away."

"How'd the father die?"

"A brain aneurism. Gordon, the dad, and Walter were playing tennis. The kid hit a shot, his father ran for it, fell over, and died."

"I'm sure Walter blamed himself for his death. He was grieving, and after the funeral he found out his parents weren't really his parents. It's more significant where the mother's concerned. Imagine you're a teenager, you find out your mother isn't really your mother. The woman who carried you and gave birth to you, rejected you. Everything you thought was right is wrong." Brennan sipped his coffee. "There's great psychology in adoption: 'How bad was I that my mother didn't want me?' That's a lot for a teenager to handle. My guess, Walter would try to find his birth mother, there's an emotional connection, he wants to meet her. Every kid craves unconditional love from their mother."

"He hired an attorney to find Donna."

"Did Walter meet her?"

"I don't know. Donna was murdered right about that time. It was in July 1988. Her neighbor saw a young, dark-haired white guy outside Donna's apartment."

"How old was Walter?"

"Seventeen, but looked older."

"How was Donna killed?"

"Strangled, and her eyes were taken out."

"She came at the kid for sex, got him excited, and he was overwhelmed by his own disgust."

"How do you explain the eyes?"

"He's horrified. The last thing she sees is his face. He takes the eyes out so he can't be identified."

"She's dead."

"In Walter's mind it makes perfect sense." Brennan picked up the coffee cup, brought it to his mouth, and hesitated. "Let me ask you something, did the brothers know each other?"

"Amanda Cooper said they didn't."

"But you don't believe her. You think Walter killed Henry?"

"It looks that way, but maybe we're missing something." O'Clair paused. "I've got one for you. Why'd he take a break for seven years?"

"How do you know that he did?"

"Why'd he come down to Florida? There are plenty of hookers in Detroit."

"He obviously wants you involved. You arrested the wrong guy in 2006 and he's rubbing your face in it. B. F. Skinner said, 'Once man has tasted the success of a kill, he's going do it again.'"

"Why?"

"He enjoys it. It's an endorphin rush, a feeling of exhilaration, ecstasy, and he wants to keep feeling it."

TWENTY-NINE

Virginia had been at the motel all day fixing things and doing chores, and now, in the late afternoon, felt like a prisoner. She had to get out for awhile, decided to walk down the beach to a bar and have a beer and a burger. It was only a couple hundred yards and Virginia didn't think there was much, if any, risk.

The sun was fading as she walked on wet sand along the water's edge, beach deserted except for an occasional jogger or dog walker. She carried her sandals and wore the Prada knock-off with the Glock in it over her shoulder.

The bar was on the corner of Briney Avenue and Atlantic Boulevard. She went in, it was loud and crowded during happy hour, a Marvin Gaye track playing over the din.

She sat at the far end of the bar, an empty seat next to her. Virginia wasn't looking for companionship or conversation. She ordered a beer and a cheeseburger and kept the menu to give her something to do. She saw someone take the empty seat to her right, but wasn't paying attention until he said, "So, did you fix the hot tub?"

Virginia glanced at him, a man in his mid-forties with salt-and-pepper hair and a big nose, nothing remarkable about him, but something vaguely familiar.

"I stopped by the day you were fixing it."

Yeah, she remembered him now. "You asked for rates but I guess you changed your mind."

"It was going to be too much of a hassle to move. I mean the beach is the same, right? Can I buy you a beer?"

"I've got one, thanks."

He got the bartender's attention and ordered a glass of chardonnay. "Where did you learn to fix things?"

"My father. He'd look at something and know what to do. He had a knack."

"I'm Frank by the way, and you're Virginia, right?"

"You've got a good memory."

"I've seen you around."

"What do you mean?"

"I saw you at Home Depot one time, buying a disposal. And I was at Publix picking up a couple things, I look over and there you are."

Virginia had a bad feeling about Frank. He'd obviously been following her. She sipped her beer, slid off the bar stool, and grabbed her bag.

"Where're you going? You just got here."

"The ladies room." She had to get away from him. She walked through the dining room to a hallway where the restrooms were. There was a window in the ladies, but it was too small to climb out. She went into a stall and called Holland's cell and it went to voicemail. Virginia was going to leave a message but the restroom door opened. She looked through a crack and saw a girl walk into the stall next to her.

Virginia went back in the dining room and glanced at the bar. Frank was gone. She walked to the front door and went out. He was smoking a cigarette. "Looking for me?"

"I've got to go."

"What about your burger? Bartender just brought it."

"I have to get back to the motel. There's a plugged up toilet I have to take care of."

Frank made a face. "Sounds like an emergency. I'll give you a ride, my car's right over there."

"That's okay." She started down Briney Avenue, pulse racing, trying to get away from him without making it look too obvious. It was dark now. She looked over her shoulder. He was gone.

Virginia was halfway to the Pirate's Cove when a tan Honda with blacked-out windows appeared, creeping along next to her, front passenger window down. She looked through the interior and saw him behind the wheel. The car stopped and Frank got out, looking over the roof. "Hop in, I'll take you the rest of the way."

Virginia was so afraid she could barely talk. "I'm fine." Her hand was shaking as she reached in her shoulder bag and gripped the Glock. If he came toward her, she'd shoot him.

"Take care, I'll see you later." He got back in the car and drove away. She tried to read the license number but it was too dark.

The only way Virginia could keep it together was thinking about O'Clair, knowing he would be home in a few hours and everything would be okay. She opened a beer and took it in the living room, sat on the couch and watched the evening news, but couldn't concentrate, kept picturing Frank's menacing expression and crazy eyes holding on her.

At seven thirty there was a knock on the office door. Virginia got up and went to the window, pulled up the slats and saw Holland and another guy. She opened the door and they stepped in the room.

"Virginia, this is Deputy John Forrest, John, meet Virginia Delaney."

"How do you do, ma'am, it's a pleasure," Forrest said. He was tall and thin and had a nice smile.

"You're in good hands," Holland said.

Virginia said to Holland, "Where's your wife?"

"Stayin' with a neighbor till I get back." Holland paused. "I didn't see that you'd called till a few minutes ago. My phone ran out of juice, I had to charge it. So what's up?"

"I saw him, the man you're looking for. He was right out front."

She wasn't going to tell him she went to a bar. "Asked if I fixed the hot tub. I was rebuilding the motor a couple days ago when he walked up from the beach and asked how much it cost to rent a room. I gave him a rate card and he left."

"Why didn't you tell me?"

"It didn't seem important."

"Why did it tonight?"

"He said he'd seen me around, which means he's been following me, and he's not worried about admitting it."

"My god in heaven," Holland said. "I'm going to step up the patrols, and I promise I'll have my phone with me at all times. Deputy Forrest will be here with you."

"Oak's coming home tonight, should be here before midnight."

"That's her boyfriend, the ex-homicide guy I was tellin' you about. I'll call, check in periodically."

Holland left; Virginia locked the door and led Deputy Forrest into the living room. He wore jeans and a dark brown Broward County Deputy Sheriff's golf shirt out, covering his belt and semiautomatic holstered on the left side. He was tall, towered over her, had to be six three at least.

"I appreciate you keeping an eye on me. As I said, my boyfriend's coming home a little later, don't shoot him."

"Don't worry."

"I'm going to go in my room and try to relax. If you want something to eat or drink, help yourself, kitchen's right over there."

THIRTY

O'Clair stopped at homicide on the way to the airport. DeAndre was putting his overcoat on, getting ready to leave for the day.

"I think you got what you came for, but now what?"

"I have to find Walter."

"At least you know who you're looking for." DeAndre paused. "We've got to do something about getting Alvin out of I-Max. I talked to the DA, said I had my doubts about the case, but I couldn't mention your name, you understand."

"What'd he say?"

"'You don't have enough to do, you're looking at old cases? Jesus, this one solved with an overwhelming amount of evidence.'"

"I'll *bet* he's wondering. It is a little hard to believe, even when you know the backstory," O'Clair said.

"I hear you, but we fucked up and we've got to make it right."

"We will. I'll let you know how it's going." O'Clair paused. "When it's over, you've got to bring the girls down to Pompano. You're my guest, stay as long as you want, or bring Squad Three down; I'll take care of you."

"Homicide's innkeeper. I'll throw it out at the next meeting."

*

The plane landed in Fort Lauderdale at five after eleven. The lead flight attendant got on the intercom and said, "Another Delta on-time arrival." Forget that they were three hundred yards from the terminal, and it took fifteen minutes to get there. O'Clair picked up the old plastic Samsonite suitcase at baggage claim and walked to long-term parking.

He called Virginia twice on the way to the car and got her voice mail both times. He tried her again when he got in the car—same result. He tried the motel line, it rang quite a few times and then the answering machine kicked on and he heard Virginia's recorded voice say: "You've reached the Pirate's Cove in Pompano Beach, please leave a message and someone will get back to you as soon as possible."

O'Clair figured Virginia was asleep, tired from running the place the past few days. He took I-95 and drove fast, getting to Pompano a little after midnight. Coming east on Atlantic Boulevard the town looked deserted. He went right on Briney Avenue, put the window down, felt a warm breeze, and smelled the ocean. He was happy to be back, excited to see Virginia.

The neon Pirate's Cove sign was turned off and the street was quiet. He parked in a space next to Virginia's Toyota in front of the office, and saw a light on inside. He got out of the car, opened the trunk, took out his suitcase, and carried it to the office door, unlocked it and went in. The desk light was on, and he could hear a TV in the living room next door.

O'Clair opened the apartment door. The coffee table was on its side and there was a tall, dark-haired guy on his stomach on the carpeting in front of the couch, blood pooling under him, a shell casing on the floor five feet away. O'Clair had left his .38 in the glove box. He crouched next to the man, touched his neck, his skin was still warm, a good sign, touched his carotid artery and got a pulse. O'Clair took the guy's wallet out of his right rear pocket, opened it, staring at his Florida driver's license. His name was John Forrest, six three, 180, age twenty-six, lived in Margate. Forrest, the Broward County pistol champ, never got his gun out of the holster. O'Clair released the clasp and slid out the deputy's Glock. He felt his stomach churning, hoping he wasn't going to find Virginia in the same condition.

The bedroom door was closed but not locked. O'Clair opened it and stepped in the room. There were signs of a struggle, but no sign of Virginia. The covers were in a pile on the floor at the end of the bed. There was a roll of duct tape on the bedside table, and the Glock he'd given Virginia was in the drawer. Walter, if that's who did it, had come in and surprised them.

O'Clair checked the bathroom, went back into the bedroom, opened the drapes and the sliding door and went out to the pool area. He was thinking about Gloria McMillen and Jady, knowing he had to find Virginia fast. The lights were out but the moon was almost full. There was nothing on the deck or the tables or the lounge chairs.

O'Clair ran to the beach, scanning stretches of sand in both directions. He ran up the beach to the vacant lot, the building site that was surrounded by an aquamarine chain-link privacy fence, climbed up and looked over. There was nothing but sand. O'Clair went back to the office and phoned Holland, who picked up on the third ring.

"I just got back. Your man, Forrest, has been shot but he's alive, and Virginia's missing."

*

Eighteen minutes later the street behind the motel was filled with police cars, lights flashing, and an EMS van.

Deputy Sheriff John Forrest was lifted onto a gurney by two EMS techs and rushed to North Broward Medical Center. A deputy sheriff questioned O'Clair, writing down his answers in a pocket-size, spiral-bound notebook.

"What were you doing in Detroit?"

"Looking at an old homicide case file."

"You're a PO?"

"I was."

Then Holland walked in, wearing an SCCA T-shirt and cap.

"It's okay, J. D., I'll take it from here."

The deputy nodded and walked out of the room.

"What can you tell me?"

"His name's Walter Kindred. He's rented a house in the area, needs privacy to do what he does to these women."

"We're gonna find him and Virginia too, I want you to know that."

O'Clair glanced at him and said, "Give me a minute, will you?"

He went outside and got his .38 out of the glove box, slid it in his pants' pocket. O'Clair stood in the middle of Briney Avenue, his back to the police cars, lights blinking shadows on the pavement in front of him. There weren't any cars parked on the street to the south. He could see several of his renters huddled in the breezeway, looking at him.

O'Clair turned, moving past the police cars, looking north now at cars parked on both sides of the street, and gawkers from nearby motels and condos, drinking beer, smoking, and watching the action.

"Hey, what happened?" someone said.

O'Clair ignored him, scanned the crowd and went back to the Pirate's Cove. He could see a group of renters out by the pool. He told them what happened. They all said nice things about Virginia, and said she would be in their prayers. Everyone, including the Dudleys from St. Paul, and the fisherman from Pittsburgh, were going to be leaving in the morning. O'Clair said, no problem, he understood. He asked if anyone had seen anything. No one had.

Holland was waiting for him when he walked in the office.

"Listen, I'm sorry. I feel responsible. I should've been here."

"Don't do that to yourself. You didn't have a choice. You couldn't leave Julie alone. I'd have done the same thing."

"Whatever it takes, we're going to find Virginia. I want you to know that. You've got the full support of the Broward County Sheriff's Department behind you. That I promise."

Holland's words didn't exactly reassure him, but O'Clair didn't say anything. An evidence tech was dusting the coffee table for prints. "You see the casing?" he said to Holland.

"I've got it, and a bullet frag we found in the wall."

O'Clair handed Holland a photo of Walter he'd taken from the townhouse, and told him who Walter was and what he'd done.

"Doesn't look like the type," Holland said, rubbing his eyes.

"What type are you talking about?"

"You know what I mean; he looks like a regular guy."

"They all do."

"Does Walter have a record, is he in the system?"

"He's never even had a parking ticket, drives a gunmetal BMW 5-Series. It has a Michigan tag unless he stole a plate or registered the car here. Have your deputies on the lookout for it." O'Clair ran his tongue over his front teeth.

"How much time you think we have?" Holland's face turned red. "Sorry, I didn't mean it that way."

"It's okay. I was thinking the same thing. But I don't know the answer."

"According to Hector Bos, your maid walked out of the trailer park a little before eight the morning she was abducted. The ME estimated her time of death at four a.m., so she'd been kept alive for about twenty hours. According to the valet, Gloria McMillen left the W Hotel in South Beach at nine thirty-seven, drove to the Publix in Pompano on Atlantic. Gloria used a Visa to buy groceries at ten forty-three. We know she was abducted in the parking lot shortly after that. Her car was still there the next morning. The ME calculated her time of death around three thirty, so she was kept alive less than four hours."

"I went to Walter's house, turned on his computer, and checked his e-mail history. Walter had been on a web site looking at vacation rental properties in South Florida." O'Clair took a piece of paper out of his pocket and handed it to Holland. "I don't know if he rented any of them, but you ask me, this is the place to start."

Holland studied the list. "They're all in the area at least."

O'Clair went online and started pulling up the houses Walter had selected. "*Waterfront estate on Intracoastal, sleeps six.*" There were shots of the exterior, the pool and kitchen, master bedroom, and views of the Intracoastal.

"Look at this one," Holland said, reading over his shoulder. "*'Paradise in Pompano, a stunning three-bedroom oceanfront home with walled, security-code gated entrance, spectacular views from every room.'* You say Walter's rich, this is the kind of place he's gonna rent."

O'Clair went down the list. There were thirteen more houses. All appeared to be private and secluded, and all had calendars that showed what weeks and months the houses were booked. Every house on Walter's list had been rented through the months of December and January.

There was also contact information, the owner's name and e-mail address, or the real estate agent who was renting the property. Holland said, "You're sure Walter didn't e-mail the owners of any of these places saying he was interested?"

"If he did, he deleted them. We'll start with Pompano, and if we strike out, move on to Hillsboro and Lauderdale-by-the-Sea, keep going north and south till we find him." O'Clair paused. "Now do me a favor, will you? Go home to your wife."

Holland left and O'Clair went out to his car and brought back a map of Hillsboro, Pompano Beach, Lauderdale-by-the-Sea, and Fort Lauderdale. No street addresses had been listed, but photographs of the houses showing their proximity to the ocean and Intracoastal helped O'Clair determine some of their locations. He put an X on the map in orange marker next to where he thought each house was. It was almost four a.m. when he finished. The sun would be up in about three hours and he'd start looking for Virginia.

The computer beeped. O'Clair saw a new e-mail had arrived. He scrolled down to the stamp icon, clicked, and clicked again on *Inbox*. The message was from wkindred@aol.com. There was a jpeg. He clicked on it and an obituary filled the screen. At the top it said: *IN REMEMBRANCE*. Under that was the name *DELANEY* positioned over a photograph of Virginia with her eyes cut out. He thought she was already dead until he read the text: *Virginia J. Delaney, 26, of Pompano Beach, passed away January 12, 2013, at 11:03 p.m.* It was tomorrow night. Walter was telling him when he was going to kill her.

He had seventeen hours to find Virginia.

THIRTY-ONE

Frank was standing behind two young guys drinking beer when he saw O'Clair appear, coming out of the shadows, moving toward the crowd that had formed just north of the Pirate's Cove. A young guy with a cooler offered him a beer and now he looked like he was one of the gang, holding a can of Miller Lite in his hand.

Somebody said, "Jesus, what the hell's going on? All the cops in Pompano are here."

"Let's go rob a liquor store," someone said.

The beer drinkers laughed.

Someone else said, "Hey Officer, can you tell us what happened?"

O'Clair did look like a cop, but instead of coming closer, he turned and went back to the motel, disappearing in the shadow of the building. "I'll bet somebody had a heart attack," the guy next to him said. Frank moved away from the crowd, walked north a couple buildings, went down to the beach and circled back to the Pirate's Cove, sitting on the sand behind the motel. The pool area was all lit up at one-thirty in the morning, the renters standing around, talking until O'Clair came out and addressed them.

He would've given anything to hear what O'Clair was saying. Seeing a subdued O'Clair talking to the people staying at the motel was quite a contrast to the showboating detective he'd watched at Jacoby's after Alvin Monroe's trial—Alvin professing his innocence to deaf ears in the court-room. O'Clair, who'd arrested and helped convict the wrong guy, was boasting, overdoing it. 'We hunted Alvin, caught him, and put him away. That's what we do in Squad Three.' The cops around him cheered and hooted. O'Clair had screwed up big-time, but that afternoon he was a hero.

Earlier, Frank had taken a cab to the West Palm Beach airport, and walked through long-term parking, checking cars, trying to find one that had a spare key hidden in a wheel well or under the front or rear bumper.

He'd tried a dozen cars, hands covered with grease and dirt, getting frustrated. It usually didn't take this long. Number thirteen was a tan Honda Accord. He slid his hand through the lowest vent under the grill and felt the box. He gripped it and pulled it away from the flat steel undercarriage. The box was covered with road grime. He slid the top back, turned it upside down, and the key fell out in his hand.

He drove back to the house and sat on the patio, looking at waves, white caps coming in. The property had two hundred feet of beachfront, and extended on the other side of the main road to the Intracoastal. The ad for the place said: *The best of both worlds. Relax in your seaside mansion and dock your yacht right behind it.* The neighbors to the north and south were barely visible behind layered walls of sea grape and stucco.

Frank had a Stouffer's baked stuffed pepper and a glass of red and took a nap. He got up at two thirty, walked the beach, and sat by the pool, thinking about what he was going to do that night, seeing himself subduing the cop and surprising Virginia. He couldn't wait, tried to contain himself.

When it was dark, Frank drove to Pompano, passed the Pirate's Cove and was approaching the public beach, Virginia on his mind as usual, when he saw her walk across the street and enter the bar. He couldn't believe it. It was almost as if he had conjured her up, made her materialize. He had been looking for an opportunity the past few days, and there she was.

He usually avoided Irish pubs during happy hour, but this was too good to be true. He went in and looked around, saw her at the bar, an empty seat next to her. He went over, sat down and started talking to her, could see right away she was uncomfortable, trying to fake it.

When Virginia slid off the barstool he knew she wasn't coming back. He watched her walk through the dining room to the rest rooms and got an idea. He went outside and smoked a cigarette, standing several feet from the front door when she came out, saw him, and just about shit her pants. He toyed with her, offered a ride he knew she wouldn't accept. She was afraid, wouldn't look at him. He'd go get the car and give it one more try.

*

He drove by the Pirate's Cove at seven thirty in time to see Holland and another cop arrive in separate cars and knock on the office door. The second man was tall and lanky, wearing Levis and a golf shirt. Holland came out and got in his car a few minutes later, and now Frank understood, the tall lanky cop was Holland's replacement.

He sat in the Honda down the street from the Pirate's Cove, cracked the side window a couple inches, feeling the ocean breeze, and waited. Every thirty minutes a Broward County sheriff's deputy cruised by and Frank ducked down in his seat.

At eight twelve the cop stepped outside and lit up, wandered down to the breezeway and stood by the pool, smoking, and looking out at the ocean. The cop walked back to the office a few minutes later, dropped his cigarette on the asphalt parking space, stepped on it, and went inside. He came out to smoke at nine thirty-seven, and again at ten forty-two, walking a little farther from the motel each time. At eleven nineteen the cop came out, put a cigarette in his mouth, cupped his hands against the wind, lit up, and walked down to the public beach access, and that's when he made his move. Got out of the car, gripping the handles of a beach bag, crossed the street, and opened the office door. He went in and listened, heard a TV on in another room.

When the cop returned, closing and locking the door, Frank was in the closet on the far side of the living room. The sliding door was open a couple inches. The cop sat on the couch and turned on the TV. Frank had a silenced Smith & Wesson .40 in his hand, debating whether to come out firing or wait till the next smoking break.

At eleven forty-five he was restless and uncomfortable, unable to move in the narrow closet. He slid the door open and stepped into the room, raising the pistol. The cop was watching a Western, hearing the sounds of gunshots and dynamite and didn't seem to notice Frank till he was halfway across the room. The cop reached for his gun, but not in time. Frank shot him in the chest. The velocity of the round blew him back against the couch, then he tumbled forward, knocking over the coffee table, and landing on the floor.

Frank went to the closet and got the tape and rope out of the beach bag, moved to the bedroom door and tried the handle, it was locked. He knocked and heard Virginia say, "What is it?"

"Sorry to bother you, Ms. Delaney, one of your guests needs to talk to you right away."

"Just a minute."

Frank heard the lock turn and the door opened. Virginia saw him and tried to close it. He blocked the door with his foot and pushed his way into the room. Virginia turned and ran. He caught her and threw her on the bed, tried to pull her arms behind her back. She kicked and fought and screamed till he turned her body around and put his hand over her mouth. She tried to bite him. Frank pulled his hand away. She went for his face, his eyes. He punched her and rocked her head back. Her arms went limp and dropped to her sides.

Frank pulled a long strip off the roll of duct tape and wrapped it around her wrists, and then wrapped another strip around her ankles.

He went out to his car, got in, and backed across the street to a parking space in front of the office, opened the trunk, went inside, glanced at the dead cop, and walked through to the bedroom. Virginia was on the floor, struggling to free herself. He pulled the top sheet off the bed, spread it out, and rolled it around her.

She fought as he dragged her through the apartment to the door, and opened it. She kept fighting as he picked her up and carried her to the trunk and closed the lid. He went back inside the office and turned off the lights, walked out and locked the door.

*

Virginia was curled up in the small trunk, struggling to free herself. Her jaw ached where he had hit her. She could smell a cigar burning and hear the loud hum of the tires on asphalt. They drove for about ten minutes. The car slowed down and then picked up speed. She felt the vibration and heard the metallic whine as they went over a bridge.

A few minutes later, the car slowed down again and turned right. She heard a garage door retract. The car drove in and the door went down and made contact with the concrete floor. She heard the engine turn off, heard a car door open and close, and his footsteps.

The trunk popped open. He said, "Smile." He held up his phone. She saw the flash and heard the *click*, as he took three shots in quick succession. "Now I'm going to take you inside. We can do this the easy way or the hard way, it's up to you. You fight me, I'm gonna hurt you."

He took a knife out of his pocket, opened it and cut the tape on her ankles, and pulled her out of the trunk. It was a four-car garage. There was a silver BMW in one of the spaces, and she remembered Oak mentioning that the suspect drove a car like that. Frank held the knife point against her neck and walked her in the house.

THIRTY-TWO

O'Clair glanced at the map that had red X's marking the approximate location of each rental property. Holland would have a team contacting the owners or real estate companies handling the rentals first thing in the morning. From what he'd read, reserving and securing a place required a down payment, which was typically accepted by check or credit card.

He studied photos of the first house on the list that was described as *a spacious retreat with loads of charm and its own swimming pool*. It was located in the heart of Pompano Beach, across the street from the Intracoastal Waterway, three blocks from the beach, and walking distance to shops and restaurants. There were exterior shots of the house and pool, an aerial shot showing the neighborhood and the house's proximity to the ocean and Intracoastal. He thought the place was on 5th or 6th Street and Riverside Drive.

O'Clair yawned and rubbed his eyes, stood up and stretched, and went into the bedroom, staring at the covers on the floor, telling himself Virginia was okay. He took the Glock 21 he'd given to her, propped pillows up against the wicker headboard, got on the bed and leaned back, resting the semiautomatic in his lap. It was a couple minutes to four. O'Clair closed his eyes, God he was tired. He tried to clear his head, tried to fall asleep. Just twenty minutes, but there was no way.

He got up and made coffee. Drank a cup, standing by the pool, staring out at the dark sky and ocean. He should've come back a day earlier. If he hadn't gone to Atlanta he would've been with Virginia; he would've prevented this from happening. O'Clair went back in and poured another cup of coffee and took it into the bathroom. He showered and put on shorts and a Tommy Bahama shirt Virginia had picked up from the cleaners, still in the plastic. It was loose and hung down over his waist and would hide the gun.

At five he got in Virginia's Toyota, thinking it would be less noticeable than his fifteen-year-old Seville that had a hole in the muffler. He brought binoculars, photographs of the rental houses, and a detailed map of South Florida. He took Riverside Drive north off Atlantic Boulevard, heading to the first house on the list. What he was doing was dumb. Somebody was going to see him and think he was a prowler and call the police, but he couldn't just sit around and wait for something to happen.

There were no addresses. He had to study different exterior shots of each house, and look for landmarks to try to figure out the location. The first one was several blocks farther north than he had calculated on NE 9th Street. O'Clair parked and sat behind the wheel, studying the property. There was a simple all-white house right behind the rental, facing south, and another neighbor directly east about fifty feet away. It wasn't private or secluded, and O'Clair doubted Walter would've brought Virginia here. He was thinking like a homicide investigator again, senses on full alert.

He could see light breaking on the horizon, driving to the second house, a secluded two-story mansion with a pool, neighbors bordering the property to the north and south and the Intracoastal on the east. Based on how the house was positioned near the water, it had to be off SE 28th Avenue. It took awhile, but he found it. There was a wall of tall, heavy shrubs surrounding most of the property, and there was a metal gate across the driveway, flanked by brick columns.

O'Clair found a way in, pushing through a narrow opening where the shrubs had withered and died, scratching his arms and face in the process. He knelt on a strip of lawn and scanned the back of the house with the binoculars, and then scanned the lower level and pool area. He didn't see anyone.

O'Clair was looking in a rear window when he heard the *whir* of a motor, and moved around the side of the house and saw the gate open and a car drive in. It was a white sedan with the name of a security company on the side that wasn't legible from his angle.

He pushed his way back through the shrubs and there was a security man in a blue uniform, pointing a semiautomatic at him, two hands on the weapon, arms extended like he knew what he was doing. The guy was older than O'Clair, gut hanging over his belt, probably a former cop.

"Hands on your head." Southern accent.

"I got him," the security man said into a collar mic.

The man patted him down and found the Glock.

"You, my friend, are in a whole lot of trouble. You want to tell me what the hell you're doing on someone's private property before the sun's even up?"

"I'm looking for my girlfriend."

"Oh, that's good, that's rich. I don't believe I've heard that one."

O'Clair felt like a fool. He wasn't gonna be taken by this senior citizen security man. First he tried to reason with him. "Call Pompano Beach PD, ask for Detective Holland, he'll vouch for me."

"I'm gonna do better than that, I'm gonna take you there myself, and I'd say you're gonna be there awhile too, just on the concealed weapon charge. Then see, does the homeowner want to charge you with trespassing in addition? Put your hands behind your back."

The security man tried to cuff him, and O'Clair turned and drove his fist into the man's gut. The guy groaned and bent over, dropped his gun, and went down on the grass, curling up into a ball, holding his stomach. O'Clair retrieved the Glock, threw the security man's gun in the Intracoastal, and cuffed him.

"Roy, where you at?" A voice whispered into the fallen man's collar mic.

O'Clair moved to the hedgerow and saw him, gun drawn, on the other side, waited as the second security man came through the same opening he'd used. O'Clair took his gun, threw it in the water, brought him over to Roy, cuffed them together back to back by their wrists, and left them on the wet grass.

*

Holland burst through the office door forty minutes after O'Clair got back to the motel. "You outta your mind? Sneakin' on someone's property. Why didn't you tell me what you were gonna do?"

"I didn't know what I was gonna do."

"And why in hell did you give 'em my name?"

"So they wouldn't think I was a burglar."

"Yeah? Let me tell you, that went over well."

"I tried to reason with them but they were a couple hardasses."

"You made them look like amateurs, and they're pissed off, want us to arrest you."

"They are amateurs." O'Clair paused. "We can talk about this later if you want. Right now I'd like to find Virginia."

"I can't involve you anymore," Holland said. It was obvious he was embarrassed. "I'm in deep shit. I'm lucky I still have a job. My boss came down the hall and reamed me a new one."

"You've got a short memory. I just got back from Detroit after four days, looking up an old case for you. Any of this sound familiar?"

"I know you were trying to help."

"If I hadn't gone, we wouldn't be having this conversation. I'd be eating breakfast with my girlfriend. Now cut the bullshit and tell me what you've got."

"We've been able to contact eight of the fifteen property owners on Walter's list. He rented a house in Bay Colony."

"Where's that?"

"North Fort Lauderdale. It's a gated community, expensive homes built on canals that all connect to the Intracoastal."

"Let's go."

"Did you hear anything I just said?"

"I've got thirteen hours to find Virginia before she ends up like the others. Are you with me or not?"

*

The house was Mission Style, white stucco walls and orange tile roof, 7,640 square feet. It was surrounded by a wall of hedges and built on a peninsula, bordered on three sides by Intracoastal canals.

O'Clair walked up the brick driveway, Holland next to him wearing a tan suit and sunglasses; O'Clair, in the pitted-out Tommy Bahama, squinting in the morning sun. Holland had arranged to get a key from the real estate office even though it was still being rented.

"He could be watching us," Holland said. "This is crazy, we should have backup."

"We don't need backup. He's in there, I'm gonna rip his head off."

Holland was worried about keeping his job, but in O'Clair's mind, finding Virginia was a little more important. "I'm gonna go around to the other side. Come through the house and let me in." He didn't want Walter, if he was in there, running out the back door.

There was a balcony that ran along the rooms on the second story, a terrace below it, and below that, a pool, built thirty feet from the canal. There was a speedboat tied to the dock behind the house. He walked by the pool and up the steps to the terrace. O'Clair put his face close to the floor-to-ceiling window and saw Holland walking through the house, coming toward him. Holland opened the sliding door and O'Clair stepped into the family room. It was hotter inside than it was out.

"Anybody home?"

"Doesn't look like it."

O'Clair led the way, two hands on the Glock, barrel pointed up at the ten-foot beamed ceiling. Holland was behind him, two hands on his weapon as they moved through the dining room into the kitchen. Holland opened the refrigerator. It was empty. They went down a hallway with a terrazzo floor that dead-ended at a bedroom and bath. It was a guest room maybe, or servant's quarters. There was a queen-size bed with four posts and a view of the canal on the north side of the property. The quilt was wrinkled, looked slept on. O'Clair studied the scene, noticed a couple long, dark hairs on one of the white pillows, thinking they could've been Virginia's, but then decided they were too dark and he thought of Jady, pictured her long, straight jet-black hair. Holland picked them up with tweezers and put them in a plastic evidence bag.

They went through the rest of the house room-by-room. They went upstairs, checking closets and drawers, and didn't find anything incriminating or out of place. No sign that anyone was living there.

Holland said, "If this guy Kindred was staying here, you'd see evidence of it, wouldn't you? Clothes in a suitcase, a toothbrush, shaving cream and a razor in the bathroom. Something."

Back downstairs, O'Clair said, "We better check the garage." It was off the kitchen. O'Clair opened the door, turned on the light and walked down two steps. The floor was concrete, the two-car space was empty, nothing in it but two green trashcans on wheels, and cleaning supplies on built-in shelves against the back wall. O'Clair took the tops off the trashcans, one was empty, the other had a black zip-tied trash bag in it. He grabbed the end of the bag and lifted it out, put it on the concrete floor and opened it, seeing Styrofoam carryout containers and smelling the sharp reek of spoiled food. He upended the bag and dumped out the trash, eyes focusing on the length of nylon rope that curled through the debris like a green snake. "Let me have the tweezers."

Holland handed it to him. O'Clair crouched, pinched a section of rope, and pulled it out, upending pieces of trash in the process. He pictured the ligature marks he'd seen on Gloria McMillen's and Jady Martinez's wrists and ankles, and hoped they'd be able to get a print. Holland took O'Clair back to the motel before he brought the forensic team to the house to do a broader search for evidence.

All the cars were gone. The renters had cleared out. In a way he was relieved, it was one less thing he had to worry about. O'Clair turned on the *No Vacancy* sign and went in the apartment and leaned back on the couch, tired, nerves frazzled, thinking about Virginia, wishing he could slow things down. It was eleven thirty. His phone rang and he took it out of his pocket and said hello.

"Walter Kindred rented another house," Holland said.

THIRTY-THREE

Frank studied his face in the mirror as he brushed his teeth. His hair was getting grayer and he wondered about having it dyed. He rinsed his mouth, spit in the sink, and went to the kitchen to make coffee. He was excited. This was the fun part, trying to figure out how it was going to end. He filled a cup and walked down the hall to the bedroom in his socks and underwear, went in, and sat at the desk.

He booted up the computer. The bullet camera he'd had installed on the back wall of the dressing room was hooked up to his laptop. He opened with a wide-angle shot. Virginia, in panties and a T-shirt, was on her back on the air mattress. He zoomed in on her face, snoring lightly. He looked at her for a while, but it wasn't very interesting watching someone sleep. Although it was exciting to think she was his captive and he could do anything he wanted to her.

He yawned and stretched, got up and went to the kitchen, poured another cup of coffee and made breakfast. He fried bacon, cooked scrambled eggs in the bacon grease, and toasted sour dough. He ate at the table in the family room, looking out at the ocean. The house and grounds were spectacular: four bedrooms upstairs, two on the first floor, ocean views from almost every room, private beach, swimming pool, and lots of space. Perfect for his purposes.

After breakfast, he rinsed the dishes and put them in the

dishwasher. It was time to check on Virginia again. He felt a rush of excitement, walking through the house to the bedroom.

*

Virginia opened her eyes and breathed through her nose. It was completely dark. The left side of her face hurt where he'd hit her. She brought her bound hands up and touched the swollen cheek. The tape had been wound around her head, covering her mouth. She was on an air mattress, ankles taped together like her wrists.

She brought her arms over her head and tried to feel what was behind her—there was nothing there. She touched carpeted floor on either side of the mattress, touched a bottle of water on the right, a metal bedpan and a roll of toilet paper on the left. So he was going to keep her alive for a while, or at least make her think he was. Virginia brought her arms up again and touched the tape that was wound around her head, felt for a seam, and found it behind her head. Dug a fingernail under the tape, pulled up a corner, and kept pulling till she could grip the tape with two fingers and heard the adhesive give way sounding like Velcro. She kept unwinding until the tape caught her hair. She pulled harder, eyes watering from the pain, yanking long strands out of her head, and wincing as she pulled the tape over her mouth and damaged cheek, now taking deep breaths.

She was thinking about how he'd surprised her. She should've been faster, should've had the gun with her. Virginia reached for the water bottle, unscrewed the top, and guzzled it. What did this freak want with *her*? What was he going to do?

He watched her sit up and bend her legs. She found the seam and unrolled the duct tape from her ankles. Got on her knees and reached out. He didn't know what she was doing, and then it occurred to him. She couldn't see anything and was trying to get a feel for where she was, the size of the space. It was more exciting than he thought it would be. Like watching a movie. It reminded him of the *Collector*, but his intentions were considerably different than Frederick Clegg's.

Now she moved a few feet from side-to-side, touched a wall and then stepped over to the built-in, floor-to-ceiling shelves on the other side. She stood up, raised her arms, nothing there. She walked straight ahead six paces and touched the wall under the camera, looking up at the lens but didn't see it. He studied her face in close up, wondering what she was thinking. Then Virginia turned, arms out in front like she was sleepwalking, went ten paces the opposite way and touched beveled wood, moved her hands left and right, and felt the door handle.

*

Virginia, from what she could tell, was in a big closet or a dressing room. He had blindfolded Virginia before he brought her in the house. She got on her knees and ran her fingers under the door. A towel had been stuffed in the opening; as she pushed it out, light filtered in, and she could see the dimensions of the room now. It was five feet by ten feet with a high ceiling. There was a light switch on the wall, she flipped it and nothing happened. He wanted to keep her in the dark, keep her afraid, and his plan was working well.

She thought about the young cop, Forrest, the pistol champ, assuming he'd been killed, and felt terrible. The poor guy was doing Holland a favor; he shouldn't have been involved, none of them should have. She thought about O'Clair, knowing he'd be going crazy looking for her. She thought about the short drive from the motel, no more than fifteen minutes to wherever he had taken her. Virginia remembered smelling the ocean when he pulled her out of the trunk and brought her in the house.

Now that she could move around, all she thought about was escaping. She came up with a plan. It was risky, 'cause if it didn't work he'd probably kill her, but he was going to anyway. She felt vulnerable in her underwear and Guided by Voices T-shirt—not exactly the outfit she'd have chosen to take on a psychopath.

Virginia put her face on the floor and tried to see through the opening under the door, but couldn't. She smelled coffee and bacon, wondering when he'd be coming for her, and knew she had to be ready.

Sometime later, Virginia heard footsteps, the squeaky sound of athletic shoes on hardwood. She heard the jiggle of keys and the lock turn and felt her pulse take off.

*

That Virginia had freed herself didn't surprise him. If she could replace a disposal and repair a Jacuzzi motor, she could unroll duct tape. He inserted the key, heard the bolt slide, and opened the door. He saw her arms swing forward, gripping the bedpan, and felt the warm liquid splash his face, stinging his eyes. He was blinking, couldn't see. She bumped him coming out of the dressing room. He reached out and tried to grab her, got an arm, squeezing, trying to take her down, and he felt something hard crash into his forehead. Dazed, he let her go and fell back against the door frame.

*

Virginia ran out of the room, down a hallway, and through the kitchen toward the wall of glass, the floor-to-ceiling windows and sliding door that opened to the pool and patio. She got there and pulled on the handle, it was locked.

She looked over her shoulder, didn't see him, unlocked the door and tried to slide it open, but it wouldn't budge. She heard a lawnmower, looked out and saw a little dark-skinned guy in a green uniform, cutting the small section of grass around the patio. Virginia waved and pounded on the glass. "Help." But he didn't see or hear her.

She looked down and saw a piece of wood in the door track. Looked behind her and saw him coming through the kitchen now. Virginia crouched, grabbed the piece of wood out of the track, and swung it with two hands like a base-ball bat as he came at her, driving it into his shoulder. The blow didn't seem to have any affect. He knocked the wood out of her hands and wrapped his arms around her upper body, pulling her from behind. Virginia tried to fight, tried to resist, but she was off-balance and he was too strong. He dragged her back to the bedroom, pushed her in the dressing room, and locked the door.

She kicked and pounded on the door, and he banged on it from the other side.

"I know what you've been doing in there and you're wasting your time. You can't get out."

"What do you want?"

"O'Clair. But is he smart enough to figure it out?"

"What does that mean?"

"Is he going to be able to find you in time?"

"How much time do I have?"

He didn't answer.

"Are you there?"

He kicked the door and startled her. Virginia felt her heart racing, and then heard his shoes squeaking on the hardwood floor, the sounds trailing away.

THIRTY-FOUR

The next house was at the end of a street on the Intra-coastal, neighbors to the north and south. The house was in the center of Pompano Beach, and yet, it was somewhat secluded. They sat in Holland's unmarked department-issue Malibu. There was noise and movement around them: a landscaping crew mowing and trimming a lawn down the street, and boats moving by on the Intracoastal—engines rumbling in low gear—slowing down as they approached the bridge at Atlantic Boulevard.

"Why would Walter rent two places?"

O'Clair glanced at him. "I don't know." He spit his gum out the window. "What'd the owner say about him?"

"Seemed like a nice guy. Sent his check in right away, and this was in the envelope."

He handed O'Clair a folded piece of paper that had a black-and-white copy of Walter's Michigan driver's license.

They got out of the car, trying to appear casual as they approached the house, Holland looking like a Jehovah's Witness in the tan suit, and O'Clair like an off-duty barten-der in the Tommy Bahama.

He walked around to the Intracoastal side, same drill as before. If Walter was there, O'Clair would make sure he didn't try to sneak out the back. There were apartment buildings across the water, senior citizens under wide-brimmed hats, parked in lawn chairs, watching boats go by, the sun high and hot.

The house had a swimming pool and a half-moon-shaped patio. There was a round table with an umbrella through the center and four chairs. He stood at the French doors waiting for Holland, saw him come through the big room filled with rattan furniture, and unlock the door.

Holland scratched his goatee. "Nobody's here. No sign anyone's been here for a while. There's no food in the refrigerator. No newspapers. Nothing out of place."

O'Clair went through the house and had to agree with him until they looked in the garage and found a five-inch piece of rebar barely visible in the jaws of a vise on the worktable. There were metal shavings on the hacksaw blade that hung from a pegboard on the wall, and more shavings on the concrete floor, like Walter had brushed them off when cleaning up.

Holland said, "About the rebar, either he left it on purpose or he was in a hurry and forgot about it."

"This guy doesn't forget, doesn't make mistakes." O'Clair thought about Gloria McMillen, picturing her the morning he found her on the beach, and now thought he understood what Walter was doing. "He rents a different house for each girl. Doesn't stay in them, he does his business and moves on. How many properties on his original list are accounted for?"

"Eleven. Three owners we haven't been able to reach, one said he wouldn't give out that information, protecting the privacy of the guests."

"You tell him two girls had been murdered, and a third had been kidnapped?"

"He said, 'Get a warrant.' Which I'm in the process of doing."

"You don't get it quick, I'm gonna talk to the guy."

Holland looked at him but didn't say anything, used a handkerchief to loosen the vise, pulled out the piece of rebar and put it in an evidence bag.

"I'll drop you off, get the team over, and we'll meet this afternoon. Hang in there, we're gonna find her."

When Holland stopped by the motel two hours later O'Clair was on the computer, studying two blurry photographs Walter had e-mailed with a note that said: *Looks like you can use some help.*

Holland sat in a chair next to the desk, staring at the screen. "What're we looking at?"

"I think they're roads, but I can't see enough detail to tell you where they are or what they mean. Walter must've stuck his phone out the window and snapped the shots."

"I'll send them to Borowski at the lab, ask him to blow 'em up, try to enhance the images, see what we've got."

It was now three thirty, and O'Clair was feeling the stress. He had less than eight hours to find Virginia.

"Regarding the asshole who wouldn't give me the name of his tenant, I obtained a warrant and served it, got the name and it's not Walter. It's an elderly couple from Wisconsin and their grandchildren." Holland paused. "And the hairs we found at the Bay Colony house were from Jady Martinez."

"Get anything on the rope?"

"There was a latent and you're not going to believe whose it is." Holland waited a beat and said, "Henry Cooper."

O'Clair wasn't expecting that. Jesus. Henry was dead. He'd seen the body.

"Walter rented the place from December 15 through the end of January but didn't get the key till after Christmas. The owner hired a real estate company to handle the rental, which is fairly typical." Holland wrote the name of the company and the office manager on a piece of spiral notepaper, ripped it off the pad, and gave it to O'Clair. "Here you go."

"Jady was killed on January 4; her body was found the next morning. Henry was murdered in Atlanta four days later." O'Clair paused. "How about the rebar?"

"It matches the piece we took out of Gloria McMillen, but no prints."

"I think we should check airline manifests, see if Walter or Henry's name appears on any flights from Lauderdale or West Palm to Atlanta and back."

Sunrise Reality was on Atlantic Boulevard in downtown Pompano. O'Clair walked from the motel, it was about six blocks. He told the receptionist he was there to see Kathy Ferris. He'd called ahead and told her he was a retired detective helping the sheriff's department with a case. He didn't mention Detroit or say the word *homicide*.

Kathy came out and introduced herself, then escorted him to her office. She was petite and energetic, with short dark hair and a small nose.

"Do you remember Mr. Kindred coming to pick up the key to the 5th Street house?"

"I do. Mr. Kindred had rented the place for six weeks, starting the last two weeks in December through the whole month of January, but he came ten days late."

"Is that unusual?"

"Quite."

"Did you ask him why?"

"He said he'd been busy."

"Did you ask to see his ID?"

"He had paid in full, plus a security deposit. There was no reason to think he was anyone but Walter Kindred."

"Do you remember what he looked like?"

"I'm sure I could pick him out of a lineup, if that's what

you're asking." She wore heavy lipstick and had flecks of red on her front teeth.

O'Clair unfolded the Xerox page Holland had given him. "Is this the man who picked up the key?"

Kathy Ferris studied the license for a few seconds and looked at him. "I'm not going to swear on a stack of bibles, but I think so."

Now O'Clair took a black-and-white photo of Henry out of his pocket and held it up. "Or is this the man?"

"It's the same person, isn't it? If not, they sure look alike. The man who picked up the key, I remember him 'cause his eyes were two different colors."

*

O'Clair was thinking about the photographs of Walter he'd seen when he talked to Mrs. Kindred. Most of the early shots when he was a young kid were black and white, but even the later color photographs didn't reveal enough detail to suggest his eyes were different colors.

O'Clair called Mrs. Kindred. He had her number saved in his phone. It rang and a black woman said, "Kindred residence."

"This is Detective O'Clair. Is Mrs. Kindred home?"

"She takin' her nap presently."

"This is important," O'Clair said.

"Been told never wake the lady of the house 'less it an emergency."

"Somebody could die if I don't talk to her. Is that enough of an emergency?"

The maid hesitated, he could hear her exhale a couple times before she said, "Sir, please stay there, I go *up*-stairs, see I can wake Mrs. Kindred."

O'Clair waited and went outside, looking out at the pool and the lounge chairs lined up perfect as they had been since everybody walked. He waited, looking out at the ocean, saw a freighter creeping on the horizon. He went back inside and opened a beer, still holding the cell phone like it was glued to his ear, and he heard a tired voice say, "What is this about, Detective?"

"What color are Walter's eyes?"

"That's your emergency?"

"I don't have time to explain everything. Just tell me."

"One is blue with an orange iris. The other one is green with a brown section."

O'Clair said, "Thanks," and hung up. He called DeAndre.

"Lieutenant Jones."

"When I was at the morgue in Atlanta, the ME investigator showed Mrs. Cooper a close-up shot of his face and said, 'Is this your husband?' She said, 'Yes, that's Henry.' He said, 'Are you positive?' She said, 'Look at his eyes. One's blue and the other one's green.' That's why I believed her. I just found out Walter has the same thing. It's called heterochromia."

"So what're you saying?"

"Henry's body is going to be shipped to the Webster Funeral Home on East Grand Boulevard. I don't know if he's there yet, but he's scheduled to be cremated. You must have friends on the bench. Get a court order, stop it. Henry's in the system. Print the man at the funeral home, we'll know for sure if it's Henry or not."

"I know a judge I think I can sell it to."

"There's one more thing. Can you get Walter's bank statements? See who he's been writing checks to. Maybe we'll get lucky and find the owner of the third rental property. See too if there've been any cash withdrawals. Go to his townhouse in Birmingham, what you're looking for is probably on the floor in the foyer with the rest of the mail."

"And what if he's there?"

"We're looking for the wrong guy."

*

Holland stopped by with enhanced, blown-up prints of the photos Walter had e-mailed. Now O'Clair could see detail.

"The first one's a shot of the bridge at Hillsboro. He's heading north, put his phone out the window and took a picture."

It was still blurry, but O'Clair could see the bridge was open and big boats were passing through.

Holland showed him the second shot, which was an intersection. O'Clair could see the faint shapes of high-rise condos in the distance.

"He's on A1A heading south, passing SE 10th Street."

"Is he trying to tell us he's somewhere in between?"

"Not just somewhere, Hillsboro Mile. It's also called Millionaire Mile. It's where the serious high rollers live at. I've seen estates advertised for twenty-five million. They've got ocean on one side and Intracoastal on the other. Most of them you can't even see from the road. They're set behind gated walls and sculpted shrubs."

O'Clair went to the vacation rental site and pulled up the last house on Walter's list. Not that there was any guarantee Virginia was there, but this was all he had. According to the calendar, it was rented straight through March. Holland had phoned and e-mailed the caretaker, J. Alvarez, a number of times without success. "The website says it's on Hillsboro Mile." O'Clair stared at a photo of the house. It was all white, two floors, surrounded by a wall of trees, the blue-green Atlantic in the background. "Let's go find it."

THIRTY-FIVE

"The death certificate says Henry Cooper," Mr. Webster, the funeral director, said. He was a big black man in a black suit. "Mrs. Cooper identified him. Let the dead rest in peace, Lieutenant."

"He looks like he's resting fine to me," DeAndre said.

"Are you mocking me, sir?"

This dude was serious. DeAndre guessed he would be too, looking at dead bodies all day. "Why don't you go relax. Let us do our job."

"I resent your tone, Lieutenant."

"You can resent it all you want—just stay out of our way."

DeAndre brought Harold Lavender, his fingerprint man, along. Harold was tall and quiet, with dark, close-cropped receding hair, and a lot of baggage under his eyes.

They were in the preparation room at the funeral home, standing next to the body that was on a stainless steel table covered by a white sheet, two banks of fluorescent lights overhead, the smell of disinfectant in the air.

"Mr. Cooper's scheduled to be cremated this afternoon."

"He's not going anywhere till we verify his identity," DeAndre's tone telling Mr. Webster who was in charge.

"Mrs. Cooper wants to put this terrible tragedy behind her."

"She has a problem, tell Mrs. Cooper to give me a call." DeAndre took a card out of his sport jacket pocket and handed it to him. No reason to pursue her until he found out the body wasn't Henry. The funeral director didn't like it but there was nothing he could do.

"Let me see him." DeAndre had met Henry Cooper six years earlier when he and O'Clair had questioned the man, and of course he'd seen the Atlanta crime scene photos, including shots of his different color eyes. There was no way to fake that.

The funeral director pulled the sheet back, DeAndre staring at a pale, bluish face with dark hair and a forty caliber entrance wound in the center of his forehead that looked like a third eye. He couldn't be sure it was Henry, just as O'Clair couldn't. DeAndre nodded and Mr. Webster replaced the sheet.

"OK, Harold, let's do it and get out of here."

Lavender unzipped his equipment bag on a stainless steel counter next to the body, and brought out the fingerprint kit. Harold stood on the right side of the deceased, lifted the sheet, picked up the right hand, and inked his thumb and fingers, rolling them onto a blotter. Walked around the table and did the same to the other hand, and when he was finished he showed the prints to DeAndre.

"Good detail," Harold said in his flat, straightforward way. "Should be a slam dunk."

"Keep him on ice till you hear from me," DeAndre said to Mr. Webster, who gave him a hard look.

He took Grand Boulevard to the freeway and headed north, made it to Birmingham in twenty-five minutes. Quaint little town full of restaurants and coffee shops, and nice-looking, well-dressed white people. He checked the map, found Merrill Street and Walter Kindred's address. Parked in front and sat looking at the townhouse, an end unit, six more just like it stretching all the way down the block. He had the search warrant folded in his sport jacket, recalling Judge Leshore's reaction when DeAndre told him the suspect in a double murder was a rich white suburbanite. The judge, known for his racist point of view, signed the warrant, and gave DeAndre a look that said, "What you waitin' for, Lieutenant? Go arrest the man."

He looked in the side mirror, let a car pass, opened the door, got out, and walked up to the front porch. He rang the bell and looked at his watch. Crouched and opened the mail slot and looked in, but couldn't see much. O'Clair had said there was a pile of mail on the floor, but it wasn't there now.

DeAndre wandered back to his car and waited. The locksmith arrived first and parked his van on the street in front of him. The Birmingham police car pulled up a few minutes later. DeAndre got out and introduced himself. The locksmith's name was Ron, he carried a tool box. DeAndre checked out the tat on the front of his neck that said: *Game Over*, two Super Mario dudes on each side of the words, DeAndre thinking it must've hurt something awful to have that inked.

The Birmingham cop's name was Lynch. He was big and looked pale in the dark blue winter jacket and uniform. "Got the warrant, Lieutenant? I'm supposed to take a look at it."

Like this meathead knew anything about warrants. DeAndre grinned, took it out of his sport coat, and handed it to him.

"What's he accused of?"

"Double murder."

Patrolman Lynch whistled and handed it back. "Who'd he kill?"

"Two girls."

"How'd he do it?"

DeAndre ignored him now. The locksmith with the neck tat knelt at the door, examining the lock. He opened his toolbox, took out a leather case he unwrapped, exposing a full set of picks. He selected a couple and went to work, moving the picks back and forth in the lock until the door opened. O'Clair would've done it in half the time.

The patrolman said, "What're you looking for?"

DeAndre said to himself, *Cut this fool off.* "I can't discuss the case."

"I understand."

DeAndre hoped so.

An hour later he was in his car heading back to homicide, wondering what had happened to Walter Kindred's mail, his laptop computer, and the bank and brokerage statements O'Clair had said were in the desk in the man's study.

DeAndre heard the Kirko Bangz ring tone, a gift from his daughters, and took the phone out of his shirt pocket and looked at the number. It was Harold. "What do you know?"

"Ain't him. Ain't Henry Cooper," Harold said. "Whoever the man is, never been arrested."

"Thanks, Harold." DeAndre disconnected. He was going to call O'Clair but decided to wait till later, till he had the whole story.

*

Amanda Cooper took the top off the trash bin, lifted the plastic bag that felt like it weighed fifty pounds, dropped it in, and fit the top back on. She looked past the Chrysler, through the open garage door, and saw someone walking up the driveway. As he got closer she recognized the well-dressed black detective who had come by with O'Clair.

He stood just outside the garage and said, "Mrs. Cooper, DeAndre Jones, Detroit Police Homicide, how're you doing today?"

"I know who you are." She paused, waiting for him to

come closer. "Let me guess. You were driving by, decided to stop and say hello?"

"I need to talk to you."

That didn't sound good. "What do you want to talk about?"

"Your husband."

"In case you forgot, Henry's dead."

He was in the garage, now moving toward her. "I understand Mr. Cooper's body arrived at the Webster Funeral Home."

Amanda glanced at her watch. "He's probably ashes by now."

He came closer, right up next to her. "I don't think so."

"How would you know that?"

"I told Mr. Webster not to cremate him until we verified his identity."

She felt a rush of nerves, and tried to stay calm. Amanda smiled and said, "You're joking, right?" She pressed a button on the wall and the garage door started to go down. She opened the door to the house. "Let's go in. It's too cold out here."

He went first, walking into the kitchen. She followed him and closed the door, saw him looking at the suitcase standing upright across the room.

The black detective said, "Do you want to go sit?"

"This's fine right here, if it's OK with you?" Amanda walked over and leaned against the counter. She reached in her purse, moved her hand over the .380 Cheetah, grabbed her cigarettes and lighter. She tapped one out of the pack and lit it. "Now what's this all about, Lieutenant?" Her voice was friendly and casual.

"Why don't *you* tell *me*?"

"I identified Henry's body. Don't you think I know my

own husband?" She took an ashtray out of a drawer and rolled the end of the cigarette in it, trimming the ash.

The black detective looked at her, but didn't say anything.

"I've got his wallet, want to take a look at his driver's license and tell me he isn't Henry? This is crazy."

"It's Walter, isn't it?"

"Who's Walter?"

"That the way you're gonna play it?"

Amanda drew on the cigarette and stubbed it out in the ashtray. She picked up the pack and lighter and put them in the purse, gripped the .380, brought it out, and aimed it at him.

He said, "I guess there's a little more to it, huh?"

He was cool, a gun pointed at him, he didn't flinch. "I don't have time to explain everything; I have a plane to catch. You were right, the body in the funeral home is Walter."

"Where's Henry?"

She didn't answer, wondering now if he'd told anyone he was coming here.

"Why'd Henry kill the girls?"

"You'd have to ask him. Henry's got issues."

"You don't care that he murdered four women?"

"Six, if you count his mother and the escort in Atlanta, and there are probably a few I don't know about."

The black detective shook his head. "How you kill your own momma?"

"I asked him that. He said, 'Put your hands on her neck and squeeze till she stops breathing.'"

"You're the one covered up the murders of the two hookers, aren't you, framed poor Alvin?"

"Yeah, there's a real loss to society." She paused. "The evidence was there and it was all pointing at Henry. He was the dead girls' landlord. He paid for their services. And he had their eyes in a jar in the basement. I thought it was just a matter of time till you figured it out. The day you came by, I thought you were going to arrest him."

"What about the murder weapon? Who'd he get it from, Peggy?"

"I don't know. Henry had a number of guns."

"You knew all this. Why didn't you come talk to us?"

"You think I wanted to be known as the wife of a serial killer? People would assume there was something wrong with me too. I married him after all. And they'd think I knew about it and didn't do anything."

"You didn't."

He started to say something else and she shot him just left of his designer tie, he went down on the black-and-white tile floor, blood starting to blot his light blue shirt. Amanda walked out of the kitchen.

*

DeAndre opened his eyes, not sure how long he'd been unconscious, or even if he had been. His shirt was soaked, heavy with blood. He could hear the hissing sound coming from his chest. He'd been shot through the right lung, a sucking chest wound. He was on his side on his gun. He rolled on his back, head against the bottom of a cabinet, felt a bolt of pain shoot through him, and laid there for several minutes till it passed.

DeAndre unhooked the holster strap, gripped the Smith & Wesson .40, pulled the slide, and thought about his wife and daughters, telling himself he had to get through this. They were counting on him. He had to be there to see those girls grow up, and protect them from the wild dogs.

He took out his cell and texted Harold: *been shot, 918 boston blvd, call ems.* He turned off the phone and waited.

*

"Lieu, hang in there, man. EMS on its way."

DeAndre opened his eyes and Harold Lavender was crouching next to him. There were two detectives standing behind Harold, and a couple uniforms across the room. "You get Mrs. Cooper?"

"Lieu, ain't nobody else here."

"Call O'Clair, tell him the man in the funeral home isn't Henry Cooper. You got that?"

"O'Clair? Lieu, he don't work with us no more." Harold frowned, looked at him like he was crazy. "You sure about this?"

THIRTY-SIX

It was a little after five when they got in Holland's Malibu and drove north to Hillsboro Inlet where the ocean and Intracoastal met, crossed the bridge in Walter's photograph. Now they were cruising past multimillion-dollar properties on one side and big boats moored at private Intracoastal docks on the other. Holland was right, you couldn't see the houses that were set back behind walls of brick and stucco, and trimmed and sculptured shrubs.

"I think we should rent a boat," O'Clair said. "It's the only way we're gonna be able to find the place."

"First, let's cruise to SE 10th Street and come back, maybe we'll get lucky."

They didn't, and O'Clair was getting more frustrated by the minute, calculating the time he had left to find Virginia. Holland drove them back across the bridge to the Pompano side and parked. He grabbed binoculars out of the trunk and O'Clair went ahead and rented a twenty-foot Chris Craft Lancer.

It would be dark in less than an hour. Traffic was heavy on the waterway, fishing boats and pleasure craft passing them, coming in from the ocean as they went out. Holland drove, engine rumbling in low gear, moving through the *No Wake* zone, and then they were in deep blue water, cruising by the same estates they'd driven past twice. Now O'Clair could see the houses set back off the beach, and realized that Walter, if he was looking out, could also see them.

The beach was deserted, sun starting to fade. It was windy and white caps were rolling in, hitting the boat, O'Clair bouncing around in the bucket seat, trying to hold the binoculars steady. A few minutes later he saw the modern white house from the vacation rentals site. "There," he said to Holland, pointing and yelling over the sound of the wind. "Get in closer to shore, will you?" They passed the house and Holland eased up on the throttle, slowing the boat, waves hitting it hard, banging into the side.

"What're you gonna do?"

They hadn't discussed that. "I'm gonna go check it out."

"You're gonna get yourself arrested, and get me canned."

"What do you think we're doing out here, sightseeing?"

"Let's wait till dark, go in from the road, do it right. We're too obvious. He'll see you coming if he hasn't already."

O'Clair was pumped. He wanted to dive in, swim to shore, and go in the house, but he knew Roger was right. Holland went past it, turned the wheel, made a wide-sweeping U-turn, the boat getting thrown around in the rough sea, and went back the way they'd come. As they passed the house a second time, O'Clair zoomed in with the binoculars. There were lights on inside but he didn't see anyone.

"Count how many lots it is from the inlet."

"I already did."

*

It was dark when they pulled up in front of the house and parked on the side of the road, less than a foot from the wall. O'Clair got out, climbed on the roof of the Malibu, and jumped to the top of the wall that was brick and matched the house. He went over the wall and dropped on the other side. The house was lit up thirty yards away. He heard Holland land hard in the garden behind him and helped him up. There was a Mercedes and a BMW parked next to the garage. They went the other way, crouching through trees and shrubs to the side of the house. O'Clair heard music, looked through a window at the kitchen. There was a wooden salad bowl on the granite counter and dirty pans on the stovetop. Something wasn't right, and O'Clair saw why, looking in the next window at eight people in the dining room, having dinner. Walter Kindred was not among them.

On the way back to the Pirate's Cove, O'Clair said, "What're we missing? Walter told us where he is, the general area. I think the house we're looking for is on his original list. Maybe we can't find him 'cause the house was rented . . .."

Holland glanced at him, waiting for further explanation as they passed oceanfront motels lit up in multi-colored neon.

"Let's see if anyone with the last name Meldrum rented a house on Hillsboro Mile. Walter's birth name is Gary Meldrum."

"The name sounds familiar, but it wasn't Gary."

"How about Francis?"

THIRTY-SEVEN

Virginia was thinking about something he'd said. 'I know what you've been doing in there.' It sounded like he'd been watching her. Maybe there was a peephole in the door. She got up and ran her hands over the wood from top to bottom, but didn't feel a brass fitting with a circle of glass in it.

When she had pushed the towel out from under the door she'd noticed a can light in the ceiling, and saw the built-in shelves on one side of the room. What else did she see? Remembering something small and dark mounted high on the far wall, she saw it again when he'd pushed her back in the room after trying to escape. Virginia moved to the shelves, pulled on the frame that felt strong and well made, testing the wood, seeing if it would support her weight. She checked the depth, measuring with her hand and arm.

*

Frank watched her moving around the dressing room on the laptop screen. She was standing under the camera looking up at it now. Virginia reached and tried to touch the lens but it was too high. Then she was out of view. She must've pressed her body against the wall, under the camera's blind spot. He was looking at the room, mattress on the floor, shelves on one side, bare wall on the other, door straight ahead. Now the room started to shake, the lens was out of focus, and the screen went black.

*

Virginia couldn't see anything and had to do it all by feel. She put her foot on the lowest shelf, stepped up, and it held her. She climbed up, holding on with her right hand and reached out with her left sweeping across the wall, feeling for the camera. It was small and cylindrical, mounted on a bracket. She gripped the plastic housing, shook it up and down, pulled the camera off the bracket and ripped out the wires. She knew he'd be mad, but didn't care. *What're you gonna do about it?*

Virginia climbed to the top of the shelves and touched the ceiling. She reached out, moved her hand around and felt the light fixture, spread her fingers around the curve of the light bulb and unscrewed it. Now she had a weapon, and if she could get close enough to him she could do some damage.

*

When the Stouffer's macaroni and cheese was ready he took it out of the oven, and sprinkled white pill dust into the cheesy mixture. Frank wasn't taking any chances. He'd wait till she passed out. He took the tray into the bedroom, crouched, put it on the floor and knocked on the dressing room door. "Hey in there, you hungry? I brought your dinner." The last supper, Frank was thinking. She didn't answer and he wondered if she was asleep. He pounded harder this time. "Hey . . ."

"What do you want?"

"I've got your dinner. I know you're hungry. You have to be."

She didn't respond.

"I'm going to open the door. Get back against the wall." He knew she didn't have anything this time, there was nothing in the room. He'd taken the bedpan after she hit him with it. "I have a gun. If you make a move I will shoot you." He unlocked and opened the door a crack. There was enough daylight to see her at the far end of the room.

"I need to use the bathroom."

He slid the tray in with his foot, closed and locked the door. Give her time to eat and fall asleep. It was almost over. He had a jar filled and waiting.

Frank went out to the pool, laid back on a lounge chair. The sun was down but it was still hot. He sipped his wine, thinking about Walter coming to his suite at the Ritz-Carlton in Atlanta.

*

They were sitting in the living room, drinking single malt. Frank picked up the bottle of Macallan's and tilted it toward Walter, who nodded. Frank leaned forward and poured a couple inches of whisky into the glass.

Walter said, "Ever been to her grave?"

"Who're you talking about?"

"Donna Meldrum, our mother, who do you think?"

"I don't know where her grave is."

"Come on. That's bullshit and you know it." Walter sipped his drink. "Remember the article in the *Free Press*? It said something like: '*The body of Donna Meldrum, a known prostitute, was discovered in her apartment on Milwaukee Street. Police are investigating.*' Her sad life summed up in nineteen words."

"I don't think I saw it. We weren't mentioned as her loving kids, were we?"

Walter ignored him. "I called my parents' attorney, asked

if he could get a copy of the police report. I wanted to find out what had happened to her. A few days later the attorney's secretary called and set up a time to come to his office."

"This is starting to sound familiar."

"The attorney, Mr. Remington, handed me a folder. I opened it, read the police report, and looked at the morgue photographs."

"How was she killed?" Frank said.

Walter frowned. "You know better than anyone."

"What does that mean?"

"She had been strangled and you could see the murderer's fingerprints on her neck. The next shot showed her empty eye sockets. Her eyes had been cut out and there was no blood."

Walter drained his glass and placed it on the coffee table. Frank leaned over with the bottle and poured him more whisky without asking.

"I called you right after, drove over to your parents' house."

"Yeah, I remember."

"I knew you did it when I saw the deer head in your basement. The eyes were missing."

"I didn't do it, Frank did."

"Who's Frank?"

"Frank Meldrum."

"Is that how it works, you turn into Frank when the urge takes over?" Walter sipped his whiskey. "Why'd you take out her eyes?"

He got up, went into the bedroom, reached in the open suitcase, and took out the jar. He went back in the living room. His brother seemed frozen, unable to move. Walter glanced at his glass on the coffee table but made no attempt to pick it up. Walter looked at him, blinked, and yawned.

Frank sat, leaned forward, and placed the jar on the coffee table.

Walter stared at it. "What the hell's that?" He squinted and frowned, and now seemed to understand what he was looking at: two eyeballs floating in clear liquid. "Walter, it's me, Mom. How are you, Son?" Frank trying to make his voice sound like a woman's.

"You need help." Walter yawned again and his head started to bob, too tired to understand what was happening, and then he closed his eyes and fell asleep. Frank had crushed two Ambien in his first glass of single malt and was amazed how quickly the pills had worked. Walter would be out for a long time.

*

By now Walter's body had been cremated, and he had become Walter Kindred. He had Walter's driver's license, and Walter's BMW. He had access to Walter's money: six and a half million dollars, and Walter's computer. He had been communicating with Walter's broker at Merrill Lynch via e-mail, selling stocks and transferring funds to an account at SunTrust Bank that he had set up in Walter's name. Needless to say, the broker was concerned and wanted to fly down and talk to him.

*

Virginia was starving. She hadn't eaten anything since dinner the previous evening. Whatever it was, it smelled good. She ran her hands over the tray, felt a plastic spoon, a sealed carton of milk, and a soggy paper plate full of mac and cheese. She stuck her finger in it and licked the sauce off. It tasted good, but . . .

She picked up the carton, found the seam, unfolded the

spout, and took a whiff. It smelled OK. She took a drink and then started to guzzle it, milk spilling down her chin, until it was gone.

Virginia left the tray where it was and climbed up the ladder of shelves to the top, stretched out on her side and waited, wondering how much time she had before he came back. Virginia was sure of one thing: she wasn't going to go without a fight.

THIRTY-EIGHT

O'Clair was waiting for a call from Holland when his phone rang. It was a Detroit number. He said, "Hello."

"This O'Clair?"

"Yeah. Who's this?"

"Harold Lavender."

"Prints, how you doing?" Harold had always smiled when O'Clair called him that. He thought it was a good name for a fingerprint man. "What can I do for you?"

"Lieu's been shot. He in the hospital."

"He going to be all right?"

"Doctor says he in critical but stable condition. Took one through his lung. But say he gonna be okay."

"Tell me what happened."

"Was Mrs. Cooper done it. Shot the Lieu in the kitchen, left him for dead. DeAndre wanted me to call, tell you the man in the funeral home's not Henry Cooper. Also wanted me to tell you Mrs. Cooper had her bag packed. She was plannin' to go somewhere before the Lieu got there. Course she long gone by the time we arrived."

She was a fine little actress, in on it the whole time was O'Clair's guess. "Do you know where she went?"

"No sir."

"What time did you find DeAndre?"

"He text me at four fifteen, but I don't know how long he been lying there on the floor."

"All right, Prints, thanks. Keep me posted." O'Clair hung up. He was thinking about the conversation he'd had with Amanda Cooper on the plane coming back from Atlanta, Amanda saying she was going to move somewhere warm like Florida, and had a feeling she was coming down to see Henry.

O'Clair went online, checking flights. There was one on American Airlines that left Detroit at eight-ten, arriving in West Palm at eleven-seventeen. There was a Delta flight that left Detroit at five-forty-two, arriving in Fort Lauderdale at eight-forty-nine. West Palm was thirty-six miles from Pompano. Fort Lauderdale airport was only sixteen miles. So if Amanda Cooper was meeting Henry in Florida that seemed like the logical choice, based on what Harold had said.

He called Delta reservations, told the sales agent he was a homicide detective and what he wanted. She transferred him to a supervisor, who transferred him to customer relations, who asked him his badge number and what police department he was calling from, his badge number and the name of his superior. O'Clair hung up and called Holland's cell.

"Detective Holland."

"Any luck?"

"One of the houses was rented by Francis Meldrum. I've got a call into the owner. I'll stay on it."

"I need you to find out if Amanda Cooper is on flight 2170 Detroit to Fort Lauderdale."

"When?"

"Lands in twenty-seven minutes."

"I'll see what I can do."

"Do better than that. This might be the only chance we've got. Call me when you have something."

*

Frank dropped the duct tape on the carpet, turned on the flashlight, opened the door, and swept the beam across the floor and walls. The food tray had been pushed into a far corner. The mac and cheese didn't look like it had been touched. He expected Virginia to be passed out and she wasn't there. It was like she had vanished into thin air. The door was locked. What was going on? He stepped into the dressing room, shined the light on the wall of shelves, felt something hit his head, glass shattering, glass on his shirt and in his face. He looked up and she came flying off the top shelf, knocked him back into the wall and he went down. She did too. He saw her get up and move past him. Frank reached out, grabbed her leg, and brought her down. He held on and managed to get on top of her. She tried to scratch his face, went for his eyes and he hit her and felt her nose break. Now she was woozy, mouth open, eyes rolling back, blood seeping from her nostrils.

Frank went out and got the duct tape, pulled off a strip and wrapped it around her wrists, and did the same to her ankles when he heard the buzzer. Someone was at the front gate.

*

The airport was crowded, cars double parked, police trying to direct traffic, keep everyone moving. O'Clair watched people come out of the terminal, rolling suitcases. He crept along looking for a place to pull over, inched his way to the end of the building, and parked in a *No Parking* zone as a car was leaving.

It was eight forty-seven. He figured it would take her ten to fifteen minutes to walk to baggage claim from the gate.

But what if she didn't check a bag? What if the plane wasn't on time? What if she wasn't on the plane?

O'Clair got out of the Seville and went inside, found the baggage carousel for the Delta flight from Detroit. No one was there yet. It was eight fifty-four. He waited. At nine the carousel was lined with passengers claiming their bags. So the flight had been on time or even a few minutes early. He didn't see Amanda Cooper.

O'Clair walked toward the escalators, saw a sign that said: *Ground Transportation*, followed the arrow to the far end of the terminal, and went outside. There was a taxi queue, cabs lined up but nobody was in line. He walked back to the baggage carousel. Still no sign of her.

At ten after nine his phone rang. Holland said, "She's on the plane and it just landed."

He started to say something else and O'Clair disconnected and ran outside the terminal, looked to his right and saw a tow truck lifting the front end of his Seville. It was time to get a new one anyway. They could have it. He looked the other way and saw a blonde rolling a suitcase toward the taxis. He went after her, saw Amanda Cooper get into a cab.

THIRTY-NINE

Amanda glanced out the window at Fort Lauderdale all lit up as the plane began its decent. She was excited, thinking about her new life without Henry. They were splitting Walter's money fifty-fifty, at least that's what Henry thought. She had a different idea.

The plane landed and taxied to the gate. She rolled her bag through the terminal, went outside and felt the warm, humid Florida air, and stood there looking for him. She watched a man get out of the passenger side of a pickup truck and approach her. He had a paper bag under his arm.

"You Amanda? Melbert Durr, at your service. I've got your merchandise."

Mel smelled like dead fish.

"It's the 84FS Cheetah like we discussed, chambered in .380, 90-grain Hydra-Shok hollow points."

She was thinking *TMI* as he handed her the wrinkled bag that was wet with his sweat. She handed him an envelope with seven hundred-dollar bills in it.

"Nice doin' business with you. Need anything else, you know where I'm at."

Amanda had met Melbert on the internet after she agreed to meet Henry in Florida, and decided she needed a gun. She found an online web site, saw the Beretta for sale and contacted the seller. On the phone Mel asked if she had ever been convicted of a crime, or diagnosed with a mental illness. She said no. And he said, 'well you sound like a nice person, let's forget the background check and get right to business.' She offered him an extra two hundred to meet her at Fort Lauderdale airport. 'Two hundred would work,' he said. 'I'm coming from Belle Glade.'

Wherever that was.

Amanda unzipped her suitcase part way and squeezed the paper bag in. Then she got in a taxi and took it to Hillsboro, the address Henry had given her. She paid the driver, got out with her suitcase, and tried the gate. It was supposed to be unlocked. She rang the bell and waited, and then heard Henry's goofy voice on the intercom, trying to be funny.

"Who is it?"

"Your fairy godmother. Now will you open the fucking gate?"

*

They got off at the Hillsboro Boulevard exit, followed Amanda Cooper to the beach road and over the bridge at Hillsboro Inlet, to Hillsboro Mile, passing the same gated estates O'Clair had passed earlier that evening.

When Amanda's taxi slowed down and pulled over, O'Clair said, "Keep going." The driver went down the road a few hundred yards or so and O'Clair said, "Okay, go back, will you?"

"Is there a destination in our future?" The driver said, glancing at him in the rearview mirror.

"I'll let you know."

When they drove by again, he saw Amanda inside the property, rolling her suitcase on the driveway toward the house. "This is good right here."

The taxi stopped. O'Clair paid the man and got out.

*

Virginia was having trouble breathing, afraid she was going to suffocate. He'd put a piece of tape over her mouth, and her nasal passages were almost closed. She snorted and inhaled, trying to force air into her lungs. He had also taped her wrists and ankles together and wrapped her in plastic. Virginia was weak but she wasn't going give up. She brought her hands up, felt for the seam, dug a fingernail in and unwrapped the tape that was over her mouth and around her head, going slow, pulling out hair.

*

Henry met her at the front door. "Welcome to Florida. How was your flight?"

"Like being on a slave ship."

"Let me take that." Henry picked up her suitcase. "Jesus, what do you have in here? I could get a hernia." He carried it in the house and set it down in the foyer. "First question, do you want to stay up, or down?"

"Down."

"Second question. What can I get you to drink?"

"Vodka on the rocks with a slice of lime. Make it a double."

Amanda followed him into the kitchen. He took two glasses out of the cupboard, his back to her, filled them with ice, poured Stoli in hers and whisky in his, cut a slice of lime, turned, and handed her the drink. The side of Henry's face was swollen and bleeding. "What happened to you?"

"I tripped out by the pool."

"Come on. Who do you think you're talking to?"

"Well, you know everything, and you're never wrong. So why don't *you* tell *me*."

She frowned, sipped her drink and stared at him. "Vir-

ginia did that to you, didn't she? She's probably scared out
of her mind."

"Tell me what happened in Detroit."

"Lieutenant DeAndre Jones stopped by the house as I was
getting ready to leave. He told me the body I shipped back
from Atlanta, the body at the funeral home, wasn't you. I
thought Walter had already been cremated."

"What'd you do?"

"I had the Beretta in my purse."

"Did he know the body was Walter's?"

"He suspected and I confirmed it." Amanda moved to the
counter, put her drink down and ripped a piece of paper
towel off the roll, turned on the cold water, and got it wet.
"Come here."

"What're you going to do?"

"Clean you up. You're not presentable. You look like you
were in a car accident."

"Always worried about appearances, aren't you? It
doesn't matter. Don't worry about it. I'm fine." He paused.
"So how do you like the place?"

She dropped the wet towel in the sink. "It's amazing. You
always did have good taste. How much is it?"

"You mean to rent or buy? It's thirty-two grand a month
in high season. And it's on the market, currently listed for
seven and a half million. It has six bedrooms, eight baths,
fifty-six hundred square feet, two hundred feet of frontage,
and it even has a place to dock your mega yacht on the
Intracoastal."

Henry loved the good life but could never quite afford it,
and this place, even with all of Walter's money, was out of
his league.

"How long are you planning to stay?"

"I'm leaving in the morning. What about you, where're
you going?"

"St. Bart's, and after that I'll see. You did transfer the money, I hope." She'd given him her offshore account information. The money wasn't there the last time she had checked, an hour earlier.

"I haven't gotten around to it yet. I started thinking, why give you half?"

"Let me think. How about for covering up for you in Atlanta? We can go back further if you want. Remember the two hookers in Detroit; that time I kept you out of prison or a psycho ward? What do you think that's worth?"

"You're holding in a lot of anger, aren't you?"

He had no idea.

"Relax. The money should be there tomorrow. Everything's fine."

Amanda didn't know if he was being straight with her or not, but wanted to believe him. She would contact her bank in the morning. She decided to change the subject. "Where's Virginia?"

"In one of the downstairs bedrooms." He looked at his watch. "She's got thirteen minutes. Can you wait? I told O'Clair 11:03. You can watch if you want."

The idea of seeing someone strangled intrigued her. "Let me freshen up first. And I'm going to need my suitcase."

Henry led her to the bedroom that had an ocean view, lifted her suitcase, and put it on the bed.

"When you're finished, walk down the hall," he pointed. "And meet me in the garage."

"Don't start without me." Amanda went in the bathroom and closed the door. She stared at herself in the mirror. She looked tired, or was it stress? Shooting the black detective had really shaken her up. Not that she had a choice. What was done was done, there was no going back.

She washed her face then went in the bedroom, unzipped and opened the suitcase, took out the paper bag, reached in and gripped the Beretta, released the safety, pulled the slide, and chambered a hollow point. She zipped the suitcase closed, slid the gun in a back pocket of her designer jeans, blouse hanging past her waist, and walked toward the garage.

FORTY

It was ten thirty. O'Clair had the phone in his hand, ready to call Holland and give him the address, but decided against it. Holland might overreact and do something stupid. O'Clair hoisted himself over the entrance gate and moved to the north side of the property, behind the four-car garage. There was a brick walkway between the garage and the outer wall of the property that led to the back of the house.

O'Clair crept along the side wall, looking in windows at dark rooms. He hid behind a stand of palm trees at the edge of the patio. He could see the ocean and smell the salty air. He scanned the pool enclosure. The pool lights were on and the water was dark and murky. The back of the house was glass, floor-to-ceiling windows and sliding doors. Above the windows were bedrooms and a balcony that wrapped around the second floor.

He moved along the wall of windows, looked in a big room with a lot of furniture, and no one in it. There were lamps on and a giant flat-screen TV showing *Wheel of Fortune*. He watched the carnival wheel spin and Vanna White walk to the board and reveal a letter.

Crouching at the sliding door, O'Clair pulled the handle, it was locked. He kept moving and saw lights on in the kitchen. There were two lowball cocktail glasses on the island counter, but no one was there either. He pressed the button on his phone and the face lit up. It was ten fifty-three. He had ten minutes to find Virginia.

O'Clair went around the house to the front door and took out his set of picks, selected one, inserted it in the lock, and maneuvered till the door opened. He listened and heard voices he was sure were coming from the TV. He stepped in and closed the door. There was a staircase straight ahead that went up and split at the second floor.

*

Virginia laid in the dark. She heard a key slide in the lock and the bolt turn, heart pounding, scared out of her mind, believing her time was up. She was standing when the door opened and she saw him pointing a gun at her.

"Turn around, put your hands behind your back."

She did and heard the handcuffs click, felt the metal rings clamp down on the bones of her wrists. He was hurting her, paying her back for trying to escape. He walked Virginia out of the dressing room and down a hallway, past a laundry room, to the garage. The first two spaces were empty. She saw the gunmetal BMW Oak had told her to watch out for in the third space, and next to it was the Honda sedan he'd brought her to the house in.

He led her to a metal work table, picked Virginia up, and laid her down on her back. He tied her ankles together with nylon rope and wrapped another piece of rope around the table, holding her legs in place. Then unlocked the cuffs and tied her wrists together in front, and brought a third length or rope around the table, pinning her arms against her body.

"Where's O'Clair?" Looking down at her with those crazy eyes. "He was supposed to save you."

"He'll be here," Virginia said, hoping she was right, but knowing she wasn't.

*

Henry had the girl tied down flat on her back on a metal table, Amanda wondering how she would react in a similar situation, knowing she was going to die.

Henry glanced at her, blank-faced, and said, "Come on. What'd you do, go to the beauty parlor? What the hell took so long? It's two minutes after eleven."

"I'm sorry, Mr. Impatient. I had to freshen up." Amanda walked up and handed him a drink, holding hers, looking at the girl's swollen face and wild eyes. Even so, she was hot-looking.

"Virginia, this is my wife, Amanda. Amanda, Virginia Delaney."

"I've heard a lot about you."

Virginia stared at her, eyes pleading.

Henry said, "Got any last words?" He glanced at Amanda. "I read an article on the things death row inmates said before being executed. One prisoner goes, 'The state of Ohio should not be in the business of killing its citizens. May God bless us all that fall short.' Another one goes, 'Time to get this party started.' It's got to be a relief finally accepting the inevitable. Virginia, that how you feel about it?"

Henry sipped his drink and placed it on a card table that had folded towels and an X-Acto knife on it. There was also a jar filled with clear liquid, and a coiled length of green nylon rope. Henry picked up the rope and unwound it.

"I've done it a few different ways. First time I used my hands and seemed like it took forever. I think this is the easiest, most effective method. Don't do anything a machine can do, if you know what I mean."

Henry tightened the rope around Virginia's neck till it was taut and tied a knot. Virginia started to squirm and yell, pulling on the ropes, and sliding her body on the stainless steel tabletop as far as she could till the ropes stopped her.

He twisted a plastic ballpoint pen inside the rope and rotated the pen until the rope was tight on her throat, cutting into her skin, about to cut off her circulation, and now she went crazy, bucking and twisting. Henry gave the pen another half turn and her face was flush, eyes bulging, head moving from side to side, giving it everything she had.

*

O'Clair entered the fourth bedroom, two hands on the Glock. It was dark but the outside lights provided enough illumination to see someone was staying there. The bed wasn't made and there were clothes thrown on a chair. He opened the sliding door to the balcony, walked out and looked down at the pool.

He went in the bathroom. There were toiletries on a counter, towels on the tile floor. He checked the bedroom closet. There were hats and shoes, clothes on hangers, and above the clothes there were small pint-size canning jars lined across the shelf, two deep. There had to be thirty at least. He turned on the closet light, looked again, and was startled by what he saw. Each jar had two eyes floating in clear liquid. Amanda Cooper had said Henry traveled a lot, and now O'Clair understood why. He checked his phone. It was ten fifty-two. He had eleven minutes to find Virginia.

O'Clair went back downstairs, moved through the foyer into the dining room and stood in the dark, looking through the doorway into the kitchen. The cocktail glasses he'd seen earlier were gone. The TV was still on, now showing a movie. He moved through the kitchen into the family room, looked outside. No one was there.

The hallway off the TV room led to a small paneled study with an ocean view. He took a quick look and kept moving.

In the next room there was a big suitcase on the bed. O'Clair unzipped the top and looked in. It was filled with women's clothes.

There was another bedroom down the hall that didn't look like it was being used until he opened the dressing room door and saw the air mattress on the floor, and a food tray in the corner. He turned on his phone. It was two minutes after eleven. They weren't in the house. Okay, so where'd they take Virginia? And then he heard a scream.

*

Virginia was moving, kicking, fighting for her life. He lost his grip on the pen and the rope spooled free; she sucked in gulps of air. "Jesus, hold her down," he yelled at Amanda, going from calm to crazy in a split second. Virginia had seen that look on his face before.

Amanda stepped away from him, still holding her cocktail, still relaxed. "You want to kill her, be my guest, but I'm not going to help you."

He came at Virginia, grabbed the rope around her neck and twisted it with his fist, holding her upper body down with his other hand. She fought him until she couldn't feel anything, and started to fade. Virginia thought she heard Oak's voice. Was this really happening? He let go of the rope and stepped away from her. Virginia sucked air in rapid breaths, wondering what was going on. Watched him pull a gun from under his shirt, backpedaling, moving away from the table toward the cars.

*

O'Clair pushed the door open and saw what was happening. Amanda Cooper, closest to him, dropped her glass. It hit the concrete floor and shattered. He aimed the Glock at Henry and said, "Get away from her and put your hands where I can see them."

Henry raised his hands. O'Clair saw Amanda pull a small black semiautomatic from behind her back, and shot her in the chest, thinking, *That's for DeAndre*, and she went down and didn't move.

Henry was running toward the BMW when O'Clair fired and blew out the rear passenger window. Henry went around the back of the car and ducked down on the other side. O'Clair moved to the work table, keeping his body in front of Virginia, gun aimed at the BMW, while he cut the ropes with Henry's X-Acto blade.

Virginia sat up and he put his arm around her. "You're gonna be all right." He heard a car door close and an engine start. "Go inside. I'll be back as soon as I can."

O'Clair ran to the BMW, leaned over the hood, and trained his sight on the blacked-out driver's side window of the Honda. The garage door was going up. O'Clair fired and blew out the window, fired and blew out the left rear tire as the car was accelerating out of the garage. O'Clair ran after it, fired, and blew out the rear window, and now the Honda, heading for the gate, veered off the driveway and crashed into the wall, one of the headlights reflecting off white stucco.

Henry got out, left arm bloody and hanging at his side, looked in O'Clair's direction, fired twice as he went around the car, and disappeared into the garden. The shots were wild. O'Clair took cover behind a palm tree. Henry was wounded and trapped in the corner of the garden where the walls met. He had nowhere to go, nothing to lose, and that made him more dangerous.

*

He had been shot, the round passed through his left forearm

and was pouring blood. He sat in the dirt with his back against the wall, smelling manure. He balanced the semiautomatic on his knee, and aligned the sight with his right eye. He was shooting with his right hand and he was a lefty. He rested the gun in his lap, and pulled at a shirt sleeve with his good hand, tearing off a long piece. He clamped the fabric between his teeth and ripped off strips that he tied together and used as a tourniquet to stop the bleeding.

*

O'Clair moved across the grass, crouching twenty feet from where he thought Henry was, looking for anything that moved. Most gunfights, in his experience, happened from about this distance and lasted less than a minute. "Henry, you've got two choices: you can leave here in a body bag or a pair of hand cuffs, it's up to you. Throw out your weapon."

O'Clair gave him time to consider his options and then rose up in a modified Weaver stance: legs bent, arms extended, two hands on the Glock, finger on the trigger, but Henry wasn't there.

*

He knew he had to keep moving, get to the house and take care of his arm or it was all over. He took a breath, steadied himself and moved, crouching along the wall through the garden, behind trees and shrubs, light-headed from the gunshot. He had to stop and rest a couple times, but made it thirty yards to the edge of the boxwoods that ran along the wall behind the garage, and now thought he might have a chance.

*

O'Clair followed the garden to the boxwoods, the only way

Henry could've gotten past him. He looked down the walk-way behind the garage toward the house. Henry was wounded, so his choices were limited. O'Clair couldn't see him going to a neighbor's, breaking in, and stealing a car. It would take too long and expend too much energy. He was convinced Henry was still on the property.

O'Clair went through the garage, into the house, and stood in the back hall, arms bent, holding the Glock, barrel pointed at the ceiling. He listened, heard the TV, and saw something move out of the corner of his eye, turned and pointed the Glock at Virginia coming out of the laundry room. She was holding Amanda's pistol at arm's length down her leg. O'Clair put his arms around her and held her tight, looking down the hall, and felt vulnerable standing in the open. He moved Virginia back in the laundry room, put his gun on the washing machine and held her damaged face in his hands, and she let go, tears rolling down her cheeks. He whispered, "You okay?"

Virginia looked at him and nodded.

He knew she wasn't. "You're the toughest girl I know."

"Who is he?"

"Henry Cooper. He's still out there, but he's wounded. I'm gonna find him and end it. Stay here and wait for me." O'Clair handed her the Glock. "Take this. You see him, don't hesitate."

FORTY-ONE

O'Clair walked down to the end of the hall with Amanda's
Beretta. He looked across the family room, thinking maybe
he was wrong, maybe Henry did take off. He moved
through the room, glanced at the TV, opened the sliding
door, and went outside. He checked the garden, crouched
and watched and listened, heard the wind blowing and
waves crashing on the beach.

Now he walked around the pool and stood on the patio,
looking out at the rough sea. Where the hell was he?

O'Clair went back to the house and walked in, pointing
the Beretta, crouched next to a chair in the family room,
looking at the TV showing a McDonald's commercial. He
moved into the kitchen, glanced toward the hallway where
Virginia was, and felt a gun barrel pressed against the base
of his skull.

*

"Put your pistol on the counter," Henry said.

He must've been hiding in the pantry. O'Clair reached
out and laid the Beretta down next to a bottle of aspirin that
was spilled on the island countertop.

"Where's Virginia?"

"I don't know."

"When I'm through here, I'll find her and finish the job."

Henry groaned and took a breath, sounded like he was in pain.

"How many girls have there been?"

"What difference does it make? They were hookers mostly, like dear old mom. I was doing my civic duty, getting rid of the trash."

"Was Amanda involved?"

"God, no."

"But she knew what you were doing."

"She knew about a couple of them, but didn't want to know more."

"Why didn't she turn you in?"

"It would've made her look bad, and Amanda was all about appearances. I never worried about getting caught and going to prison, I was married to her for fifteen years."

"Why do you take their eyes?"

"That's how I remember them."

*

Virginia heard them talking in the kitchen. She could see O'Clair on the other side of the island counter, part of Henry's body visible behind his wide bulk. She moved down the hall to the front of the house, went through the foyer into the dining room, heart pounding, hands shaking, holding the Glock. O'Clair was right there, three feet away, Henry holding a gun to the back of his head, Henry talking.

"You were so full of yourself during the trial, and after at the bar. You screwed up royally, arrested the wrong guy, and you were showing off, telling everybody how good you were. I couldn't believe it. I'd been thinking about you for awhile, drove by your house last fall and saw the *For Sale* sign. I talked to the real estate agent who said you moved to Pompano Beach, bought a motel. So I thought I'd give you another chance, and you screwed up again. It's been fun though, I'll tell you."

O'Clair looked to his left and saw Virginia in the dining room, just inside the doorway. Behind him he heard Henry thumb the hammer back. O'Clair spun to his right and drove his fist into the side of Henry's face. Henry went sideways, off balance, into the Sub-Zero, still holding the gun, firing into the floor. And now Virginia came through the doorway, two hands on the Glock, the way he'd taught her, arms extended, and shot Henry three times, the gun jumping, Henry's body jerking as the rounds punched him in the chest. Henry went down on his back, eyes open, looking up at them. O'Clair crouched, took the gun out of his hand and touched his neck, feeling for a pulse, but there wasn't one.

He put his arm around Virginia and brought her into the family room, sat her in a chair, and turned off the TV. O'Clair went and got aspirin and a plastic bag filled with ice cubes.

Virginia held the ice pack on the side of her face, and took a breath. "What about the cop who was shot? I feel terrible about that."

"Holland says he's going to be all right. The man's blessed. A forty caliber round went through him and missed his vitals."

"Thank God." She paused. "What about our guests, is anyone left?"

"We're gonna have to start over or sell the place."

"Do I get a vote?"

O'Clair's eyes held on her.

"What're you thinking?"

"Even with a broken nose and two black eyes you're the best-looking girl I've ever seen." He could see it hurt her to smile. "I'll tell you one thing: I'm not going to let you out of my sight."

"You promise?"

He phoned Holland, gave him the address and told him to come alone. Then he went in the garage and picked up the shell casing he'd fired earlier, and put it in his pocket. He wiped his and Virginia's prints off the Glock with a towel on Henry's card table, and placed the gun in Amanda Cooper's right hand. Now, as far as anyone knew, Amanda shot Henry.

He was standing on the driveway when Holland drove in twenty minutes later and got out of the car, Roger staring at the Honda with the blown out rear window that had crashed into the wall. Holland walked over, looked at the car, reached in, turned off the engine and lights, and came back to where O'Clair was standing.

"Who's blood is that all over the interior?"

O'Clair told him.

"Where is he?"

O'Clair led him into the garage. Holland looked at the BMW, and then saw Amanda Cooper sprawled on the sealed concrete floor. Streams of blood had leaked from her body, moving with the level of the floor all the way to the back wall on one side and the garage door on the other.

Holland glanced at O'Clair. "Who's that?"

"Henry's wife. She shot Lieutenant DeAndre Jones before she left Detroit."

"Who shot her?"

O'Clair didn't say anything. He went inside and Holland followed him through the house into the kitchen. Holland stared at Henry on the floor, blood pooling under him, and shook his head.

"I was never here, and I don't want Virginia involved."

"But she was involved."

"Not anymore."

"Jesus, how am I gonna explain *this*?"

O'Clair looked at him and said, "Wait till you see what's upstairs."

DISCARD